D0770283

Growing Up
WALLA WALLA

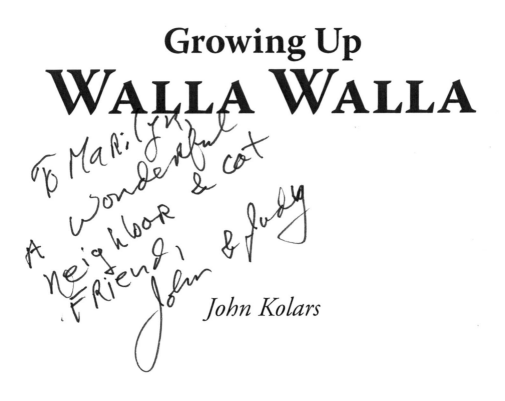

John Kolars

Bloomington, IN Milton Keynes, UK

authorHOUSE™

AuthorHouse™
1663 Liberty Drive, Suite 200
Bloomington, IN 47403
www.authorhouse.com
Phone: 1-800-839-8640

AuthorHouse™ UK Ltd.
500 Avebury Boulevard
Central Milton Keynes, MK9 2BE
www.authorhouse.co.uk
Phone: 08001974150

First published by AuthorHouse   5/12/2006

ISBN: 1-4259-3413-7 (e)
ISBN: 1-4259-3423-4 (sc)

Library of Congress Control Number: 2006903695

Printed in the United States of America
Bloomington, Indiana

This book is printed on acid-free paper.

FORWARD

This book is both a memoir and an historical review. In it I have attempted to capture the sense, the ambience, of Walla Walla in the Thirties and Forties through the eyes of a small boy and then a youth. It is about growing up. Though this story sometimes takes the reader to other towns and cities it always leads back to Walla Walla.

In order to free myself from any constraints, I have invented an alternate ego, Oliver, who has told this all to me, his amanuensis. I have made no attempt to research those decades in a scholarly manner. I suspect that readers will find many errors of fact, for example, store names, street intersections, the timing of some events, a *Rashoman*-like skewing of perceptions.

I learned a lot about myself in the course of writing this, and little by little became aware of my bright and dark sides, just as little by little I discovered Walla Walla's two personalities. Walla Walla, back then, was a rough frontier town as well as a cultural oasis.

I remember the disillusion I felt as a youth, and again as I wrote the first drafts of this book, when the scope of our town's rough side became clear to me. But as I reworked the manuscript, my mood mellowed and I have come to accept both Wallla Wallas and my Walla Walla self. We have grown up, first together and then apart.

I have altered names and places wherever I felt the protagonists might not wish to be identified. In some cases just a name has been changed, in others localities as well. Some names have been left unchanged.

This book is dedicated, in loving memory,

to

AGNES VERNE LITTLE

ACKNOWLEDGMENTS

I wish to thank my early readers Lisa and Rick Frey and Richard and Kathleen Ossey, who kept asking me for more chapters, and special recognition to Gordon Jaynes, who having shared Walla Walla with me back then, has encouraged me, half a century later, to see my efforts into print.

Most special thanks to Judy, my wife, my computer guru, my goad, who has seen the merit of it all, even of both my personal Walla Wallas.

CONTENTS

GROWING UP WALLA WALLA

PROLOGUE

Three AM. The last star of Orion, the hunter, his right hand raised, is all that remains above Walla Walla. Oliver is sitting there watching it.

There was this movie, *Son of Kong*. Oliver didn't see the first one, *King Kong*, but as a kid, he saw *Son of Kong* at the Roxy Theater.   *Son of Kong* was special, a great, enormous gorilla, a dish water blond gorilla. Everybody was terrified of him, but he was a gentle, kind, misunderstood gorilla. Misunderstood except for the beautiful lady who was frightened at first but then came to love him. The secret island he lived on was sinking, Son of Kong's foot was caught, wedged in the rock. The pale, peroxided lady – a starlet, Fay Wray -- is going to drown, but Son of Kong picks her up and puts her on his finger, the very tip of it, and she sits there, and as the water rises higher and higher, right over his head, Son of Kong holds his breath, with just the tip of his finger sticking out of the water, until a ship comes and rescues her, and then he drowns.

What does Orion the Hunter, his finger there above the Blue Mountains, have to do with Oliver? Just who is Oliver?

I am I, was Oliver long ago. A kid in Walla Walla. Someone else, someplace else. Grew up there. Grew up Walla Walla.

1

Now, as I write this, I am sitting on the tip of Orion's finger sixty years later, waiting for an imaginary ship, time rising around me.

The ship isn't coming.

So this is a good time to put it all down; the way it was, those early years in Walla Walla, Oliver's years.

CHAPTER ONE
THE BIG FROM WHENCE?

I

Do you remember when the lid slid back on consciousness, your first memories? What are Oliver's? Is he frightened that he came from nothing, remembers nothing before the big From Whence? Or is he into reincarnation? No, but he wonders at times about the time before memory. Before him, before you. Do you?

To understand Oliver you have to go back to the maternity ward at St. Mary's Catholic hospital in Walla Walla, *the town they liked so much they named it twice.*

Or maybe twice to fit the two Wallas that occupied the same place; schizophrenic Walla Walla with its tree shaded streets, its big houses New England prim, music drifting from Whitman Conservatory. The first Walla at tea. "We are so fortunate. Walla Walla has no slums, none at all." And then the other Walla, the back room card games, lower Main Street Walla with its second floor hotels, farmers and field hands into town on Saturday night, fun if you knew where to find it. Lutcher's Saloon. And no slums, just the really poor kids living across the street from Oliver when he moved to town, poverty patches sewed on middle class comfort.

But Saint Mary's is not where Oliver really began. You have to go further back, further back. Oliver was told the town's name belonged

3

to the Nez Pierce Indians. Excuse me, the Nez Pierce Native Americans
-- PC and all that. But Nez Pierce is French. What did the Nez Pierce
call themselves? Oliver hadn't a clue.

When he was older, living in the Southwest, he learned that The
Navajo call themselves the *Dineh*, the People. All the rest aren't people.
Just like all those people who aren't Anglo-Saxon aren't really people, or
who aren't Japanese aren't people, or who aren't Irish aren't people. That's
his grandmother, Irish, for whom the Italians across the field weren't really
people. Maybe that's what the Nez Pierce felt about themselves. But if
they did, the French fur traders didn't. The Indians they met were simply
the Pierced Noses, or they weren't. Look at an Indian's nose and right
away you'd know if he was or wasn't. The early white settlers knew the
tribes weren't really people. That made it easier.

All the time Oliver lived in Walla Walla he never knew a single
Nez Pierce, never saw a single pierced nose. Not one of them was there
to tell him who they really were. They just went down in his personal
history with someone else's name. And what about the Cayuse and the
Wallawalla tribes that were never mentioned? Oliver never heard about
them until years later, just about the Nez Pierce, and actually they lived
farther east. All he knew was that the place where he was born was
called Walla Walla, Nez Pierce for *Many Waters*.

And before the Nez Pierce, there was the dust falling like snow,
blown from the western scablands, mantling the hills. The loess of the
Palouse Hills. The richest soil on earth. Six feet, ten feet, twenty feet
of pure topsoil covering the black basalt underneath.

That's what Oliver remembers, running like crazy down dark brown
slopes smooth as a breast. Unable to stop. Falling, rolling, always
unhurt in that deep, dark dust.

But Oliver fell down later than the first Indians, later than the
Whitman Massacre, fell down after Chief Joseph almost escaped to
Canada, after the Idaho gold rush fizzled out, after the dirt farmers
came. Fell down in the time of the wheat: breast bare fallow brown
loess, green fire covered spring slopes, bread crust gold harvest hills,
and in the east, Blue Mountain blue.

Sometimes the mountains weren't blue, just mountain colored. And when it was winter, everything white as his father's hospital sheets, Oliver would go to bed at night thinking about having to get up in the dark, pushing his bike through the snow, think about delivering the Sunday paper, the *Walla Walla Union Bulletin*, and then he'd hear the mountain clearing its low, subsonic throat. He'd wait then for the house to shake as the Chinook, that mysterious katabatic wind, swept down from the mountains, compressing, heating up like the tire on his bike when he filled it at the service station on the corner of Roosevelt and East Alder streets, all those compressed molecules battering around inside. And in the morning the snow would be gone, taken off by the Chinook and the frozen soil would be thawed, and the mountains would be blue, bluer, bluest! And for a while it wouldn't be winter.

Not far enough back. It all began before the great gathering of tribes, before the Great Council, the Treaty of Walla Walla, ignored, never mentioned in school.

Look at it this way, Oliver's zygote was tiny as a mote, weighed less than weight. And later he was an eighty pound runt, but what a runt! And later still, one hundred fifty pounds. Of what? Where did all that stuff, bones and flesh, and GLANDS, come from?

He ate the Palouse, those loessic hills, those blades of wheat, those Indians dead and buried. Ate the Sager children who sheltered with the Whitmans, John Sager who didn't hide under the floor of the cabin, and died. Ate Marcus Whitman, too. All turned to dust. Dust to Wheat. Wheat to Oliver.

Grew up there. Learned what he was told, saw through a kid's eyes. Grew up Walla Walla.

II

What's the first thing Oliver remembers? Is it some of the cute lies his mother told him? But nobody told him about lying on his back, spit on his tongue. Pushing the spit against his lips. Opening his mouth, a thin spit membrane there for an instant.

"Mmmwaw," the membrane breaks. Is that the first memory?

Or is it being taken to the Veterans' Hospital west of town? The place nobody talked about. TB was like cancer. Maybe if we ignore it, them, they will go away. The hospital doesn't fit the New England image that the town fathers were so proud of, not the tuberculosis sanitarium where Oliver's father lay dying, his knees raised under the white sheet. Oliver's being lifted up, sliding down that white hill, white as snow, white as death. No Chinook to melt those snowy sheets.

He remembers a funeral, not his father's funeral. One of his father's friends from the ward. He remembers the graves in neat, white rows alongside the mausoleum out on the west side of the cemetery. The honor guard, the rifles going crack in ragged beggar unison.

Meanwhile, his father begging to die. Of course, his father didn't beg Oliver. Even though his WW I veteran's throat was being eaten away. Tonsils taken out while on ship board duty, on the battleship Wyoming, crisscrossing to Europe. "Lafayette, my tonsils are here!" No time off to recuperate; the wounds never healed. Then the TB. Later he couldn't drink or eat. Even if all he wanted before he died was a glass of water. That's the kind of thing grownups, even dying ones, don't share with kids. Just those snowy knees; Oliver's early memory.

One of those two memories is the first. Don't ask Our Hero which.

CHAPTER TWO
CHICKEN RANCH

I

So now what? Go back to the house in the middle of the wheat field. Dust piled like curry. Why curry? That's Oliver mixing his memories. That aroma came later, after he learned about curry. On his way to Fort Bragg. Another story, another person. The rain coming down on the red hills, smelling like curry. Leave it!

The dust kept coming in. It was really bad when the wheat fields that surrounded the farm house were plowed and left fallow. His grandmother dusting, wiping and wiping, but always the thin film appeared like the breath of a ghost, earth's ectoplasm haunting her. She fought it, exorcised it, hated it as much as she hated the British whom she had never seen. An Irish woman listening to three generations of women sprung from County Sligo. Never letting go of their hate. That's a story to come. Be patient.

Dust and locust trees. When Oliver's father moved west with Oliver's mother, there had been hope. The dry air lured generations of TB patients who came west, following the sun, coughing up their lungs. Well, his father had coughed his throat and his hope away. Later in school, Oliver learned a tune, the kids sang to the melody of My Bonny Lies Over the Ocean::

My Bonny has tuberculosis.
My Bonny has only one lung,
She coughs up the big yellow oysters,
And rolls them around on her tongue.

But hope ran out, like luck from a horse shoe nailed the wrong way, open end down, over a door. It was years before he connected the song and his father, and by then it didn't matter. The song was disgusting. No polite person would sing it. His father was dead, death was disgusting and no polite person would discuss the dead, unless they had died charging a German machine gun, like Uncle Joe did at Saint Michael, not getting thinner and thinner and just coughing himself away.

On the other hand, everyone said his father was a saint. The way he died, not complaining. It's very important not to complain if you're dying. It took Oliver a long time to figure out that his father was just another human being. He and Oliver wouldn't have gotten along. Father came from a strict Catholic family in Minnesota ruled over by a patrician who was the little Minnesota town's most important lawyer. Spoke fluent Czech and eloquent English. The emigrant farmers would come into town babbling half Czech, half English, "Charlie K-------, Charlie K-------, I got problem. Help me!" And he did. A fine, principled man, Charlie K, who kept himself broke running a Democratic newspaper in an uptight Republican farm community. Oliver's paternal grandmother came from Czechoslovakia, had five children and died of cancer at the age of forty. Oliver's grandfather remarried the children's Irish school teacher. Oliver always thought of her as his Czech grandmother.

The five children found the remarriage difficult. Joe, the oldest, one day bad-mouthed his stepmother at the dinner table. Grandfather stood, stern and principled, and said, "Apologize immediately to your mother or leave this house!"

Joe refused, left the table and the house, enlisted in the army and went to France with the AEF and died a heroic anonymous hero's death, which no one was allowed to forget.

Oliver's father, they said, took after his father. It turned out that Oliver was something of a handful. It's unlikely he and his father would have understood each other. Anyway, when Oliver figured all this out he wrote a poem:

> My father died.
> The myth created
> By my mother
> Grew by my side
> As her facts were stated;
> Brother and brother,
> Two children grew
> In the house of flesh
> That was the son,
> But neither knew
> Of the other one.

That helped some.

But way back, when there was hope, Oliver's father thought he would earn a living raising chickens. So he took his savings and with help from his parents bought a mortgage on a piece of land in the middle of a wheat field south of Walla Walla not too far from the Vet's hospital, just to be on the safe side. They built a house and chicken runs, and brooder houses, and a feed bin, and called it a ranch, because every farm out there was called a ranch. There were wheat ranches, and cattle ranches, so why not a chicken ranch? They surrounded it with locust trees which grew fast and offered shade. That's another thing Oliver remembers, the locust trees.

His Irish grandmother told him how the prophets went into the desert and ate locusts, so Oliver went out into the yard at the farm house and tried to eat the little white flowers which tasted sweet but he thought could never have kept a prophet alive. Then Oliver tried the little seeds that came in pods which fell off the trees, but they were bitter, and probably poison.

That was something Oliver's grandmother reminded him about every day, that things were poisonous. Home canned green beans led her list, potato salad that killed picnickers every year with horrible stomach aches came next, followed by practically any food left "out" overnight. Then there were infections you got if you pulled a hair out of your nose. That was called catarrh, and her aunt had pulled a hair out of her nose and got catarrh, and her nose rotted and she died, and rabid dogs and hydrophobia skunks, and spiders, and the poison the English had put on the potato fields so that the potatoes would rot and the Irish would starve, but instead some of them came to America like her family did.

He knew that little children had to be especially careful of poisonous things which probably included locust seeds, so Oliver spit out the bitter paste in his mouth and thought he was dying until the taste went away. And GYPSIES! They weren't exactly poison but stole small children who were never ever seen again.

After a while Oliver's father died, and his mother had to find a job. So that's why her mother and father moved out west from Michigan to take care of Oliver and his big sister. Grandpa Percy simply transferred to the west end of the NP, which is the Northern Pacific Railroad if you didn't know. Took a job in Auburn on the other side of the Cascades. As soon as Oliver's grandmother got Percy settled, she packed her suitcase and came to Walla Walla. That's how she got to the house in the middle of the wheat field, where she took care of Oliver and wiped up the dust.

II

Oliver's older now. He comes and goes outside. His mother's away at school, getting a teaching certificate. At College Place. It's somewhere over there beyond the hill, beyond the poor farm that his grandmother despises. She despises the poor almost as much as she despises the English and the Marconis, the Italian family that live a mile away across the wheat field. When the wind is right she is sick from the smell of the garlic she is certain they are eating.

Oliver is never lonely. He misses his mother, but lonely in the sense of no playmates never occurred to him. To miss playmates, you have to know about playmates, and he had never had playmates. He had all the images that lived in his mind.

He wasn't very old when he learned about dinosaurs and could say "brontosaurus" and "Tyrannosaurus Rex." That must have been because of his grandmother, who being Irish and having taught school back in Michigan, loved words and read to him and rolled the words around her tongue until he rolled them around on his tongue just as easily as she did. Oliver roamed the fields saying all those words to himself and to his dog and hoping that someday he would find dinosaur bones and maybe dinosaur eggs just as Roy Chapman Andrews did in the article his grandmother read to him from the Sunday Supplement of the *Spokesman Review.*

And then there were words that didn't have images, like *propinquity*. That was a favorite word of his grandmother's. Propinquity. People never fell in love; it was just propinquity that made them get married. Oliver liked the word, even though he didn't understand it. If something went unaccountably wrong, beyond his ability to understand, it was propinquity that made it happen. At least that was the feeling he got when his grandmother discussed people getting married; something bad had happened to make them do it. Sometimes when he was feeling sad out in the wheat field he would say to Boots. "It's propinquity, just old propinquity."

One odd thing about those early days. Oliver cannot remember anything about his sister during that time. To this day, he has no idea where she was. Probably by the time he was old enough to remember, she was away every week day at the Catholic school in town. Later, in grade school, Oliver found out that the girls in Catholic schools weren't allowed to wear patent leather pumps because the boys could see the girls' nether parts reflected on the shiny leather. That was still at a time in his life when his grandmother called girls' special places where they peed their nether parts, unlike Oliver's which were, he learned, his privates, or just plain "yourself," as in the phrase, "Stop pulling at yourself" which his mother and grandmother whispered fiercely at him when they went to town.

But where was his sister on the weekends?

Oliver remembers his whole life at the beginning like it was a jigsaw puzzle with pieces missing. One special memory: it's dark, being carried in from the Chevy to the farm house, all asleep and half waked up. He remembers only parts of the farmhouse. There was a kitchen with a hand pump for water before the electricity came, and a front sitting room nobody ever sat in, and a long dark hall that led to his mother's bedroom on the left and to his grandmother's bedroom on the right. At the end of the hall there was a ladder to a small attic. That's where Oliver found the chunk of rock crystal all shiny and magic. He still has it, his oldest possession. Possession? No companion, lode star. There was no room for Percy. Remember, Percy was in Auburn across the state, drinking himself into a snowdrift where they'll find him later on.

III

Oliver's mother was away most of the time, going to school or hunting for work. Oliver tried to get her attention, which wasn't easy. Early in the morning, in Doctor Denton's, muddy feet, dew wet to the knees, and probably piss wet down to the dew-wet, bringing in asparagus that grew untended out behind the gooseberry bushes. He couldn't recall that they ever ate it. Maybe. Once it was a fistful of dandelions. "Oh, those are weeds," his mother said, and out they went.

Every day his mother gets in the old Chevy with the running boards and the flat windshield and drives to College Place, mysterious end of the world inhabited by people who don't eat meat and go to church on the wrong day, but Oliver's mother can afford what it costs to go to college there and that is more important than their not being Catholic.

And every day Oliver's grandmother takes care of the house, of him. But she only goes outside to empty the wash tub or to kill a chicken for Sunday dinner. Oliver goes out into the fields with his dog, Boots. The dog's erect, plumy, black and white tail sticks above the wheat, wheat the color of Oliver's toe-head. The tail's a beacon for his grandmother. Follow the tail and you'll find Oliver.

IV

Oliver's memories are coming faster.

Oliver's chicken ranch, abandoned except for the house, sits in the middle of someone else's wheat field. Since his father died, his mother and grandmother do not want to raise chickens for a living. They still live in the house. The laying sheds, the brooder houses, the incubator shed, the feed bins are all empty. Oliver is afraid to go way back to the very end of the brooder house. He gets as far as the empty feed bins where he knows some mice live. He talks to them, since there is no one else to talk to.

Every morning before Oliver goes outside to play, his grandmother warns him. "Never go *over there*." Over there is off beyond the brooder houses. "There is an abandoned well over there," she says, "and you will fall into it and you will never be seen again and your mother will cry." So Oliver never goes *over there*. But the rest of the world is his as far as the long wheat field furrows lead him.

The farm's abandoned buildings are part of that world. The empty hen houses and brooder houses, the scratch pens, strange, ghostly places, still smelling of chicken ghosts and chicken shit, all left uncared for when his father went to the vets' hospital, and like *just in case* died there. And ringing the chicken ranch, the dusty, fallow fields, or the green fire, or the ripened stalks, and west beyond the fields the hill which hides the poor house, or away east, the blue of the Blue Mountains that are farther away than the poor house, farther even than College Place.

V

Oliver is out in the wheat field where he spends most of his time looking at all the very small things that only children see and know. Tiny snail and clam shells smaller than a match head. There once was a lake where the wheat field is now. The earth is very soft and deep and Boots and Oliver dig holes. They take turns. Boots is better at it than Oliver. The holes are very deep. Sometimes Oliver stands in them and only his head and shoulders stick out of the dirt. It's pretty clear that Oliver is already trying to build a home of his own.

And there was Cuddles the cat who lived to be nineteen and never wanted food, just company and recognition, and had kittens twice a year, most of which simply disappeared, eaten by weasels and hawks though Oliver's mother gave some away when she could.

Mother tells him that when his father was still raising chickens and hadn't gone to the hospital forever, when Oliver was a tiny baby, they took Cuddles to a feed elevator and store way on the other side of town because she had just too many kittens and she would be all right there because feed elevators always have lots of mice for cats to eat, and six months later she walked up to where Oliver's father was splitting wood out back of the house and she had come six miles all the way across town and everything and they decided she could stay because she was very tired and thin and she did.

One day, Cuddles brought Oliver a tiny mouse that wasn't hurt. He wanted to keep it as a pet and put it in a clay flower pot with a thimble full of water which he got from his grandmother, the thimble not the water, and he had to be sure and give it back to her when he was through with it and some wheat, but the mouse got out through that hole which is in the bottom of all red clay pots. When they moved into town they left Cuddles behind because "she wouldn't be happy in town." Oliver always wondered about that. The last time he saw her Oliver had come back from the army and went out to the farm which was by then totally abandoned and he called Cuddles!! and she came up. She was pretty old, but she knew him and he petted her and that is the last time he saw her. He and Cuddles were both nineteen.

VI

But Oliver still has a long ways to grow. He really doesn't like the farm house. It is full of tears and fears. He likes it better outside with the heads of wheat brushing against him. He can drop and hide and make burrows among the stalks. Oliver doesn't know that Boots gives his secret places away.

Sometimes Oliver sits under the yellow rose bush, to him big as a house, his special house, scribbling on a lined tablet with a thick pencil.

Round and round. He is drawing dinosaurs. Good dinosaur drawings full of curved lines and jagged teeth. They could bite people, make them listen to what he and Boots had found, like the pheasant's nest with eggs which Oliver didn't touch, not even once.

Other times he builds a house: two orange crates, the wooden kind with the divider in the middle so that when you turn them on end you have a shelf to put things on. Two orange crates on his red coaster wagon, covered with a blanket. Oliver small enough to crawl inside and be safe.

Sometimes Oliver pounds on a board with a hammer. Pounding and pounding, determined to make as much noise as the town, the sound of the town coming over the hill to the north on calm mornings. Oliver wants to be there, to be part of the town's noise. He throws himself on the ground, face down, spread eagled, convinced that by gripping the earth and digging in his toes and shrugging sideways he can move the earth, make the town pay attention, make people pay attention.

VII

Oliver learns his first song. His grandmother helps him learn it. They listen to it on the radio, the radio with the tall, spool legs, and the vertical dial in the center of the set, with numbers on it from 0 to 100. KUJ Walla Walla, and if the reception is good, KHQ Spokane.

The Lullaby of Broadway. "Come along and listen to ..... Goodnight ladies .... When Broadway babies say goodnight it's early in the morning." Oliver sang that song when his mother came home early one evening. He was trying to explain that he missed her when she came home after he was asleep. She didn't understand, but she helped him with the part about "Good night ladies" which she said he sang flat.

As time goes by Oliver becomes aware of the world at the end of the wheat field, beyond the rise to the east, over by the Locust Grove Service Station. It is what later on would be called a cheap motel, oil cloth and linoleum. Back then they were called CABINS. Once Oliver tries to go there to explore, but he and Boots are found at the far end of the wheat field and brought home.

VIII

Oliver started first grade at the Catholic school in town the year his mother lost the farm. Sitting in the lawyer's office, grandmother and mother crying and signing papers. Oliver really didn't know what was happening. He thought about how it would be if he went and got Tyrannosaurus Rex and Tyrannosaurus Rex bit the lawyer, and his mother and grandmother hugged him and they all went home happy. He thought a lot about the dinosaur biting the lawyer.

IX

Odd memories hard to fit in, somewhere before they lost the farm and moved to town. Visiting his grandfather in Auburn, a news boy late in the night, Will Rogers and Wiley Post dead in an airplane crash in Alaska. Oliver didn't know who they were. Falling out of the apple tree in their back yard, hitting the chopping block he'd dragged there to climb up in it, shattering his elbow. Oliver was five. The long trip in his mother's car to the hospital in Seattle. Pain. Being made to drink castor oil by an evil nurse. The body cast and exercising his arm in hot water so that it wouldn't be stiff when he grew up. More pain.

Driving in the Chevy on dusty roads to remote farms where overall-wearing members of local school boards talked to Oliver's mother about teaching jobs. Her coming back to the car and crying once they started driving away -- NO Catholics necessary -- only it was years later before that really impacted Oliver.

Back home, running out into the yard to see the autogiro fly over. A strange aircraft with stubby wings and a propeller and a horizontal rotor blade. Always running out in the yard when any kind of airplane flew over. Each one a rare and special event.

The man in the coupe with the aerial on top who roamed the countryside hunting for things that caused radio interference. The Watkins Products man selling bottles of vanilla extract to his grandmother who used a great deal of it. Cuddles the cat who only came home to have kittens. Super hunter, mice, a weasel, pheasants.

Meeting his mother once at the far end of the road across the wheat field and riding the running board until he fell off. The rear wheel of the Chevy passed over his legs, pressing them into the deep dust. He wasn't hurt. "Not one bit," he told his frantic mother, and he wasn't. But he never got to ride on the running board again.

And then there was being dragged to the outhouse by his grandmother. Oliver's left arm being pulled up straight by her five foot height. She carried a chunk of firewood in her other hand and would beat around under the seat of the commode. All the while telling him she was making sure that no black widow spider would bite his poor bottom and that he wouldn't die a terrible, painful death.

X

Along with childhood came the strange faith in words and their literal meanings that children have. Once, when Oliver and his mother and sister were visiting his grandfather and grandmother in Auburn, word came that their house in Walla Walla had been broken into. When Oliver's mother read the telegram aloud, Oliver heard it as their house had been broken "in two." All the way home on that hurried trip across the state he pictured the farm house tumbled on its side in two pieces. A local police detective "Pussyfoot" Nelson had sent the telegram. He had found some letters with Oliver's mother's name on them when he raided a suspicious group camping on the edge of town. "Pussyfoot" Nelson! Oliver could hardly wait to see that strange detective with cat's feet. And the house, it seems, had been entered by means of a skeleton key. Oliver's imagination was racing and he pictured this mysterious key shaped like a skeleton!

It was all an anti-climax for Oliver when they returned home. The house was upright and in one piece, "Pussyfoot" Nelson had feet just like any one else, and the key he showed Oliver's mother was almost like the one they used themselves, not at all in the shape of a skeleton.

And Big Little Books with pictures in the corner that moved when you flipped the pages. There was deception there, too. Oliver remembers Mickey Mouse's adventure inside the dirigible which had a whole big city inside the gas bag instead of gas. It was years before he realized that people were only inside the little cabin underneath. There were other odd things, like when Peg Leg Pete, who was a dog, tied up Mickey and ran off with Minney, who was a mouse. Strange miscegenation. All Mickey could say from under his gag was *mmmmmmrrrrmmmffffff!*, a good word signifying subdued frustration, which Oliver sometimes feels, even now.

Oliver was disappointed when he found out words can mean something besides what they seem.

--- --- ---

Well, enough of this. Let's get on to where memories begin to hang together, like wash on the line, or the line of telephone poles across the wheat field to the gravel road, the road to town.

CHAPTER THREE
OLIVER'S IRISH GRANDMOTHER

I

Before the trip to town we should take a look at Oliver's grandmother, the key to his life on the farm. Her maiden name was Cassidy, as Irish as you can be without a brogue or a shamrock. She was very important to Oliver for she took care of him when he was small. "When I first saw you," she told Oliver, "you were no bigger than a bar of soap after a big day's wash." She was Irish, the kind of Irish that loved songs and doggerel, and taught him the way words can role off your tongue.

> Muh hisses O'Fluh harety puh had a puh hig
> The puh hig was duh hubble juh hointed
> And whuh hen she truh hied to tuh heach it to juh hig
> Shuh hee was duh hisapuh hointed

Which means:

> Mrs. O'Flaharety had a pig
> The pig was double jointed
> And when she tried to teach it to jig
> She was disappointed.

And here's one she didn't teach him, that Oliver learned from an Irishman in the army and never dared to sing her. It goes to the tune of the Irish Washer Woman.

> Oh the breezes, the breezes
> That blow through the treezes,
> And blow the girls' dresses
> Above the girls' kneezes,
> And when the boys seez'es
> They does as they pleezes,
> And gets bad diseezes,
> Oh Jeezes, oh Jeezes.

Sometimes she simply taught him words, big words, like in this song sung to "Show Me the Way to Go Home."

> Direct me the route to my habitual abode,
> I'm fatigued and I wish to retire,
> 'I had a hot toddy about sixty minutes ago,
> And it went directly to my medulla oblongata;
> Wherever I may penetrate, PeRam bu late
> On terra firma or aqua,
> You can always perceive me chanting this refrain,
> Direct me the route to my habitual abode.

Or sometimes the words were mixed up.

> What is a double petunia?
> Well, a petunia is a flower like a begonia,
> A begonia is a meat like a sausage,
> Sausage and battery is a crime,
> Monkeys crime trees,
> Trees a crowd,
> A Rooster crowd in the morning and made a noise,

A noise is on your face like your eyes,
The eyes are the opposite of the nays,
A horse nays and has a colt,
You get a colt and wake up the next morning with double petunia.

II

She sang to him every night with a thin creaky voice that got very fierce when she sang songs like *Michigan* which she missed very much, because that was where she was born and raised and left to come take care of Oliver when his father died.

There on the dusty farm she washed clothes in a big, galvanized iron wash tub, sudsing the laundry up and down on a scrub board, one just like the one the man in the band at the local grange hall played with thimbles on his fingers. She scalded the chickens she killed which made it easier to pluck them. The little pin feathers half buried in the skin were the hardest to get off. She swept and dusted and mended and told Oliver stories.

Some of them were bits of lore about the troubles back in Ireland. There was the Irish meal her grandparents had told her about, "Potatoes and Point." When potatoes were abundant, but little else, the family would sit around the table for supper. Hanging on a string from the cottage ceiling was a single dried herring. As each person took a frugal bite of boiled potato, he or she would point at the fish and imagine how good it tasted.

And then there was "Pill Jerk Peter." During the plague that accompanied the famine, there was only enough money in the family to buy one medicine pill. But there were six people! Peter, the eldest son, solved the problem. He tied a string to the pill and had each person, in turn, swallow it. One by one they got well, but the pill got smaller and smaller, until when it came Peter's turn -— he was the last – there was nothing left, and he died. But he died a hero, having saved his family.

Here is another story she told Oliver, a true story.

III

"My great great grandmother," she began, "came from County Sligo in Ireland. She was the last of her family there who had all died of the plague, if not from starvation. The potatoes rotted before they could be dug and rotted in the bins if you managed to get them out of the ground. It was the British who poisoned them to make us leave our homes.

"This story has been passed down from daughter to daughter in our family. and now it is your turn to learn it and pass it along."

Oliver never learned why she chose to tell him instead of his sister. Although his knowing broke the endless chain of women, he hopes that his daughter will listen and learn it and tell it to her daughter or son and that they will pass it on to their daughter and so on and on, that the Irishry will live forever.

"My great, great, grandmother told her daughter, who told her daughter, who told her daughter, who was my grandmother, who told me. My great, great grandmother could remember the tumbrel coming in the night, the cart for the dead. Her family had all died, and had to be taken away. You see, it wasn't enough that the British poisoned the potatoes, they brought the plague on their ships. And the plague swells up the glands in your neck and you cough and cough and then you die."

"Well, when your grandmother died," Oliver's grandmother began leaving out all the 'greats" to save time, for Oliver was getting sleepier and sleepier. "Her uncle, who was a bachelor already living in America in Michigan, had a farm of his own near Benton Harbor which he had homesteaded, had cut down the forest and cleared the fields. Well, he found out that the poor girl, his niece, was all alone back in the old country, and had no one to care for her. So he sent for her, sent her enough money to buy steerage passage in the hold of a ship. She lived in county Sligo which is near the sea. There was a ship called the *Zarathustra*, so my grandmother told me, that sailed from Sligo right to New York City. Well, she got on that pickle boat, which is what they were called because the captain didn't give you food just barrels of water and a slop bucket and everyone brought their own food like pickles and dry bread and sausages, and set out for America and her uncle. He would be your great, great, great great, great grand uncle."

"It was not very nice down in the hold of that ship, but they finally came to New York City (which was long before Ellis Island and Travelers Aide, Oliver adds to himself years and years later) and every one was getting off the boat and her uncle didn't show up to meet her."

"We know he arrived in New York from Benton Harbor because he wrote a letter to some neighbors, but he must have been shanghaied and died at sea or murdered and dumped in the river that flows by New York City, because he never was seen again. Well, there she was standing on the dock, and she was sixteen years old and every one was leaving, and what was to become of her, when a young man who had been with the family next to her in the hold of the ship came up to her and said, 'Well lass, there's nothing for it, will you marry me?' She thought for about a minute and said 'Yes she would' and they found a passing priest on the dock who dispensed with the bans and they were married right there and he became your great, great, great, great grandfather."

"They went out to western Michigan and took over her uncle's farm and later when the Gold Rush in California was almost over he and a friend who was a neighbor left their families and went out west to win their fortunes, but he didn't. He never found gold, and there's a letter his friend wrote to your great grandmother that was written in Sacramento City telling her how her husband had died that morning of the bloody flux which I guess is diarrhea. Her husband, your great uncle, hadn't said any good byes to her or anyone in particular because just like his friend wrote in that letter, 'You don't think that you will die in a far countree.' Your mother has that letter now, and there is also a little gold dollar he gave his daughter before he left for California and your mother has that too. I will tell her to give it to you when the time comes, and you must give it to your daughter."

And she did, and Oliver's mother did, and now Oliver has given it to his daughter, so the chain has added another link.

23

IV

Things are a bit confused for Oliver when he tries to remember back. They lost the farm to the bad lawyer, and his mother found a job teaching in Walla Walla, and he was taken out of St. Patrick's, and they moved to a house on Newell Street. When that happened, he didn't talk to his grandmother as much. She turned smaller and smaller and went upstairs and stayed in her bedroom like a little gray spider. His mother would go up and talk to her and bring dinner, but Oliver didn't go upstairs. Maybe it was just that suddenly there was the world outside waiting for him.

She stayed upstairs for a whole year, and then one day a telegram came from Auburn. Oliver's grandfather had been found drunk in a snow drift almost frozen to death. Oliver's grandmother read the telegram and got out of bed and took the bus to Auburn to take care of him. He stopped drinking, and when the railroad wouldn't give back his job, she and Oliver's mother went right to the director of the western end of the NP Rail Road in Tacoma and marched past his secretary, who said no they couldn't see her boss, and demanded that Oliver's grandfather be given his job, and the director did. They told Oliver that the director was afraid of two fierce Irish women. Oliver's mother said that his grandmother never went to bed again until Oliver's grandfather died five years later of something that must have been cancer the way the women whispered about it and wouldn't say the word out loud when Oliver was around.

After Percy died Oliver's grandmother moved back to Walla Walla and lived in a little house near the Catholic church and went to mass. She liked living there because it was near the railroad tracks and at night she could hear the trains whistle as the boxcars were shunted about.

She found work in the laundry on that side of town, but she fainted from the heat and didn't work there again. She never gave up her hatred of the British, and the Italians, and the Jews, and just

24

about everybody else who wasn't Irish, though she made an exception for the Czechs, because Oliver was half Czech on his father's side. And yet somehow or other she still was a good person.

Oliver visited her sometimes in the little house just west of Saint Patrick's Church and one block over, and when he came back from the army they continued a tiny ritual that they had begun years before, back when he was just a little bit bigger "than a bar of soap." Oliver's grandmother would stand up straight and hold out her arm horizontally and Oliver would stand as tall as he could stretch under her arm and measure how high up he came on her side. As the years passed he grew nearer and nearer to touching her outstretched arm with the top of his head. And then one day, actually long before he went off to the army he no longer could fit under her arm. Now, a returned veteran he would hold out *his* arm and his grandmother would stand under it, her head not quite touching. They both thought that was a great joke.

On one of his visits to the little house Oliver and his grandmother had a truly good conversation. He was going off to work in a children's camp on the Long Beach Peninsula. It was just before she died, though on that sunny, late spring afternoon they didn't know or even consider that such a thing could happen. It makes Oliver very happy to think about how that one time it was like two grownups talking, sharing their thoughts. She told him that when she died she would go to heaven and have snowy wings and walk streets of gold and be surrounded by all her loved ones. That was just like the heaven the Deathless One made for Jurgen's grandmother, in the novel *Jurgen*, that Oliver read years later.

Later that summer while Oliver while was working at the camp his mother telephoned him and told him that Granny had died. He didn't go home for her funeral but he should have. When he did return to Walla Walla he found that his mother had sold the entire house full of his grandmother's furniture and his grandfather's tool chest, and the family bible with all the dates in it, and the antique wool winder that his great, great grandmother had used, and the candle molds, and his grandfather's personal little telegraph key, his "bug," and everything for $50.00 to some rascally antique dealer. His mother had held nothing back. Oliver had nothing, nothing with which to remember his grandparents except all their words and thoughts that they had put in his head. Maybe that's the best thing that can happen when your grandparents leave forever.

Oliver's grandmother was important to him, and then as he grew a bit older, she wasn't so important, but now really is. Here is what Oliver wrote many years later.

My enormous grandmother
Took my hand and led me
Distances to sleep. Times were:
She showed me day-filled fields
All weeds and wonders higher than my eye.

She was a giantess to me;
My shoulder ached from reaching
Up to her huge hand. Times came:
She stood beneath my arm,
And I, the cuckoo child grown large,

Went wandering; we never met again.
Yet in night's teeter totter drowse,
She calls me, comes, but this time,
Out from sleep to lead me in,
My man-height dwarfed by memory reaching up.

That's all. It's time now to go to town.

P.S.

I asked my mother
for fifty cents,
To see the elephant
jump the fence.
It jumped so high
it touched the sky,
and didn't come down
'til the Fourth of July.

That's what she told Oliver.

CHAPTER FOUR
OFF TO TOWN

I

Growing up is finding out that the world is different. When Oliver lived on the chicken ranch he had nothing for comparison. Everything there was exactly the way things are, or were to him. To him, all children played by themselves. All children explored empty brooder runs and dug holes for houses. All children had fathers who died at the vets' hospital. All children were told they were loved and at the same time wished their mothers would notice them more. It was in town Oliver learned things could be different. That was where he started growing up, growing up Walla Walla.

II

Bumping along the rutted track, across the fallow wheat field hub deep in harrow churned dust, the Chevy gained the county road, went up over the hill and there were the Blue Mountains off to the east, mysterious as Tibet, that is later on when Oliver learned about Tibet. Left turn onto the pavement. If you turned to the right the road went to Milton and Freewater and Oregon. Oregon, another country; where down south was Pendleton with its cowboys and the Roundup and the anonymous Catholic church and its anonymous priest where his mother and sister later on would go to anonymous confession. And on the way, Milton and Freewater where no one stopped. Once upon a time, Oliver's mother said, an electric trolley had gone all the way to those two villages. But not now, and since Oliver couldn't imagine a trolley or an electric one, it didn't matter.

No, much better to zoom along the smooth, smooth road, real fast, twenty-five miles an hour, past the Locust Grove Service Station with its two pumps like columns and the hand crank on each making them look like toys. The big FLYING RED HORSE out in front, and the linoleum and oilcloth cabins out back under the trees. And then another mile and another world. Off to the left, on the crest of a low hill was a mysterious place Oliver's mother called the Country Club. Oliver caught a glimpse of bright green patches of grass with small groups of men walking across them. The men were playing a game called golf that only rich people were allowed to play. And that was that. His mother seemed angry and would say nothing more about it.

And then on the edge of town, another change. The Triple XXX Root Beer Stand! A magic barrel shaped building on the corner where a second road led off towards College Place. Cars were parked in front of the barrel; the window on the driver's side of each car was rolled part way down and had a special tray attached to it, and on each tray big icy mugs of the best root beer in the whole world! That's how Oliver remembers it.

"Please can we stop!!"

"On the way back if we have the money." The money, that thing again. It was *the money* that made them later on lose the chicken ranch. Not money, but always, *the money* -- another way of saying you can't always have what you want.

Sometimes they drove only as far as Kidwell's Grocery on the right just past Payne Grade School. Kidwell's Grocery was a special place. In those days there were corner groceries scattered everywhere. People would go to them as though to a ship's chandler's. A corner grocer would break a five pound bag of sugar if you only needed a pound and didn't have the money for five. A corner grocer ran tabs for the people he knew and would wait until payday to collect. Of course there were a few big markets, like the Safeway store downtown, but you had to pay cash there, and there you bought things like five pounds of lard in a tin. Kidwell's Grocery was in-between. Because of its location on the edge of town, it was like a corner grocery store for all the farmers who lived out south of town. It was bigger than a real corner grocery and smaller than a Safeway. Mr. Kidwell carried bulk items for the farmers who came to town maybe once a week, but you could get small amounts of stuff, and Mr. Kidwell did have charge accounts, which in the Depression when all this happened were lifesavers to people short on money. The same money, that is, which if mother had it you could stop at the Triple XXX Root Beer Stand on the way home, which didn't always happen.

When his mother went shopping, she bought what they needed, like soap and flour. She bought meat, less often, usually cheap cuts like heart and tongue. They killed their own chickens, Granny -- but she didn't like being called that -- chasing them around the little yard the two women still kept after the idea of a Chicken Ranch failed. She caught them with a long, stiff wire with a hook on the end, snared their legs and put them on the chopping block and smack!! off went the head and you put the chicken under a bushel basket until it died or it would flap around and around the yard. Oliver got tired of chicken and grew up loving heart and tongue and liver. No one ate steak.

Oliver still feels uncomfortable when he thinks of what happened at Kidwell's. That was another place where Oliver grew up. You see, growing up isn't just getting taller or having more experiences. Growing up is not just finding out how things *are,* but finding out how things *aren't.* Kidwell's was a place where Oliver encountered one way things aren't.

They had come into town to shop at Kidwell's, Kidwell's with the big stalk of bananas hanging from a hook, shelves of canned goods, a walk-in refrigerator with cases of milk and butter, and a counter with open gunny bags of peanuts and beans in front of it.

Oliver couldn't resist. While his mother was selecting a can of tomatoes Oliver took one peanut and slid it into his mouth. There were a zillion peanuts in the bag. He couldn't even tell the place where he'd taken the one out. It hadn't been easy to crack the shell, so he had put the whole thing in his mouth and chewed it through. But his mother who had eyes in the back of her head had seen his crime, Peanut theft!

"Get your hand out of the peanuts!" She bent over him and held out her handkerchief. Her voice sounded all funny, "Spit it out, right now."

The half chewed peanut clogged his mouth. What had he done? Oliver spit the mess of fiber and nut into the handkerchief, but his trial wasn't over.

"Now tell Mr. Kidwell you're sorry."

She guided Oliver by the shoulder over to where Mr. Kidwell was standing at the end of the counter. He looked as ill at ease as Oliver felt. "Mr. Kidwell, Oliver ate a peanut without asking and wants to tell you he's sorry and won't do it again. Of course, I will pay for the peanut."

Mr. Kidwell looked even more pained as Oliver was propelled in front of him.

"Tell him, Oliver."

"I didn't really eat it. She made me spit it out. She's got it in a handkerchief in her purse."

"Oliver!"

"I'm sorry."

Mr. Kidwell spoke more to Oliver's mother than to Oliver. "It's all right; they're five cents a pound, how many peanuts in a pound? It's not even part of a penny's worth." He turned to Oliver. "It doesn't matter. I know it was a mistake, and you won't do it again. Will you Oliver?"

Oliver shook his head. Mr. Kidwell laid his hand on Oliver's head and rotated it slightly, ruffling Oliver's hair. Oliver never understood what that was meant to do, but it seemed to satisfy his mother. "Thank you Mr. Kidwell, it won't happen again."

It did matter. Oliver felt discovered and humiliated, and for a long time didn't like to go in the store, until the day he learned that when the clerk unpacked the bananas there was a great big spider, bigger than this! And Mr. Kidwell held out his hand, fingers spread, that ran around the room until Mr. Kidwell could kill it with a broom. Straight from Costa Rica. Oliver wanted to see that spider but they had thrown it out yesterday. But after that he looked forward to going to the store, hoping always to see a huge spider from Costa Rica, but he never did.

It was part of growing up.

III

Farther along Ninth Street beyond Kidwell's was the real town. You could turn on Alder Street and go past the Catholic church and Saint Patrick's, the Catholic school, all the way to the library on the east side of town, or you could go a block farther and go right up Main Street. Going that way, you passed the Court House on the right which was OK and imposing and you later on heard about the students from Whitman College who assembled a wagon on top of the dome as a prank, but that was a story Oliver heard when he was in High School. The problem was that opposite the Court House stood a row of elegant two story Victorian brick business buildings that long ago had been abandoned by commerce and now housed Lutcher's Saloon and pawn shops and on the second floors, those houses where the ladies waited. So Oliver's mother and grandmother drove straight past them to upper Main Street where the Book Nook which sold books and sundries was right across the street from the Bee Hive which sold just about everything from Ladies goods to toilet paper and boxes of Kotex wrapped in distinctively anonymous, unlabeled, dark green paper, and Jensen's Department Store which was too expensive and the Red Apple Restaurant which served Jell-O salad and was respectable.

On the north side of the street from the Bee Hive and the Book Nook was a bridge railing above a deep dry stream bed filled with water worn stones and a thread of water which emerged mysterious and dark from under the buildings on the other side of the street. Only years later did Oliver learn about the upper end of the tunnel near the YMCA, and just once went on an underground/under building exploration until he emerged opposite the Book Nook.

A block west on Main Street, the Baker Boyer Bank stood opposite Talman's Drug Store, and kitty-corner from the drugstore was another bank which closed and never reopened after that day in October when Oliver's mother deposited her veteran's widow's check while everyone else was withdrawing their money.

When Oliver's mother got back to the ranch, she told his grandmother what had happened. "I went to the manager. He's always been so nice. But he said bankers have to be practical. He said, they called it *a run on the bank,* that I should have known better, and that once my check was deposited there was nothing he could do about it." The women both began to cry. Oliver was very angry at the bank manager that his mother had trusted. That was another part of growing up, of finding out how things aren't. Nice bank managers can't be trusted.

IV

There were business side streets which were one block long on each side of Main Street and on lower Main there was China Town off to the left on the north side. Dark little shops with dirty windows where later on Oliver would go to buy escape from the boring dull present with ten cents worth of litchi nuts. And the wrinkled little old man with a real honest to goodness queue would smile at him and Oliver was scared but that was adventure. One time, George who was Oliver's mother's boy friend and a fireman told him how during a fire inspection he had found a special back room in China Town with cots, and how it was a real honest to goodness OPIUM DEN! It probably was. Oliver wasn't certain what an opium den was. There were bears' dens, but what was opium, and why did only those old Chinese men use it? Why did that make them bad, and why did George call the nice old man a Chink, which his mother said was not a nice word?

Opposite China Town on the other side of Main Street, and about two blocks off, was a feed store and a place where in the first years Oliver can remember coming to town he saw rows of shabby men slowly shuffling forward. His mother said that it was a Bread Line and that the place was a Soup Kitchen. The men had no jobs and were being given bread and soup so that they could stay alive. After eating they went back down to the rail yards where there was a Hoover Ville, which was a shanty town made out of old boxes and stuff, which Oliver thought was unfair to blame former President Hoover for that and call it by his name even though he hadn't actually built it, but people were desperate and angry and hungry.

Oliver can remember even out in the country on the chicken ranch men coming to the door and saying they would cut firewood for a meal. His mother and grandmother were alone and wouldn't let them stay but many other people gave them work and paid them with food. In the summer when Oliver lived with his grandparents in Selah, Washington -- which is still to come -- he used to see the shabby men standing in the doors of the empty box cars that the trains pulled. There was a Hoover Ville in Selah, too.

V

Two blocks down Second Street to the north was the Marcus Whitman Hotel which was eleven stories tall and unimaginably grand. Oliver and his family didn't go there, though later on Oliver carried papers to Mrs. G. who lived on the top floor in a special place people called a penthouse.

Mrs. G. was a source of unfulfilled ambition for Oliver. He faithfully carried the paper to her penthouse apartment for two years. That was a trial, for she was lonely and would wait, and as soon as he slid the paper under her door, she would pop it open and invite him in for graham crackers and milk. Oliver couldn't say no even if it delayed his deliveries by twenty minutes. Then the day came when he told her that at the end of the month he would be leaving his downtown paper route for a longer one in the suburbs. She seemed very concerned and told him to be sure and stop by her apartment the following Friday, for she would have something very special for him. In the days between, Oliver first thought that she would give him a good tip, like maybe five dollars. But by Thursday he had decided that since she had no children of her own -- she had told him so -- Mrs. G. probably was going to present him with a college scholarship, or maybe even make him her heir. On Friday he ate the graham crackers and drank the milk and finally said that he had to go. Mrs. G. Went into her bedroom and came back with a little box. Inside was a rosary!

"This is for you," she said. "Be sure to use it every night."

Oliver stood there waiting for maybe a manila envelope to follow the rosary, but that was all. He was a polite boy and thanked her and said he hoped that she would be happy with the new carrier, and she kissed him on the cheek. In the elevator he pushed the down button, which took him away forever from the graham crackers, and the milk, and the college scholarship, and the inheritance.

Oliver could hear his Irish grandmother saying, "If wishes were horses, beggars would ride."

VI

Across from the Marcus Whitman -- no one ever added the word hotel because it was the Marcus Whitman and that was that -- was the United States Post Office which his mother did visit to buy stamps and get their ration books during The War. South of the Book Nook on First Street was the Stage Depot where the Greyhound busses came and went. Notice that it was still called the Stage Depot and not the Bus Depot. Stage coaches had come there not too long before and the name had stuck. There were a lot a old things like that around town if you looked for them.

So that is Main Street, which will figure in this story a lot more. But right now it's the place where on Saturday night Oliver's mother and grandmother would drive in and park with Oliver in the back seat and watch the people walk by on the sidewalk for a couple of hours, and then they would go home and sometimes, if there was *the money*, stop at the Triple XXX Root Beer Stand and have a root beer and maybe even a root beer float in mugs which had frost on them and nothing has ever tasted better.

VII

If you went farther up Main Street it split and became East Main and Boyer Streets, and if you went to the right within two blocks the world changed again. There was Whitman College with its Conservatory on the right and academic buildings off to the left. Oliver knew all about the Conservatory, even knew the word while he was still living in the country, because that was where his mother went to take piano lessons and singing lessons and got an MFA in Voice and another in Piano and that was very special and he remembers going to recitals there where she sang "My heart is like a singing bird," which she said was Christina Rosette, and "Spink, spank, spank, the bobolink," which she said was not.

Across a little pond was a wonderful place which was a museum which had the tusk of a mammoth in it which a farmer had dug up and some arrowheads. Oliver was taken there once or twice, but not often enough, so Oliver made a museum of his own in a small cupboard in the basement of the house on Whitman Street, but that will come later. It was a very small museum but it was his and it was special.

That was about as far as Walla Walla went for Oliver until they moved into town after they lost the Chicken Ranch because of *the money* Oliver's mother didn't have.

VIII

Maybe there's something else you should know. There was a prison in town, a penitentiary, *the* penitentiary. Nobody liked to admit it was there. It was out on the northwest edge of town, maybe not even in the city limits; at least it wasn't in the city limits in the peoples' minds. It was said that many years ago when Washington and eastern Oregon and northern Idaho were all considered the INLAND EMPIRE that there was a debate that the INLAND EMPIRE should be a state named Lincoln just like Washington got a state named after him, but Oliver and his friends in school thought Lincoln was more famous than George Washington, but that was in school, and the grown ups couldn't agree. There were a lot of people living over on the west side of the state; enough people to prevent Lincoln from being formed. So they gave the people in Walla Walla a consolation prize, the choice of the state penitentiary or the state university. The leaders in Walla Walla thought all those students would be rowdy so they chose the penitentiary, but later they regretted the choice, or at least their grandchildren did because no one, even today, will ever admit what those buildings are on the edge of town.

During the War, though, Oliver's mother did go out there and teach the women in the women's prison First Aid in case the enemy bombed the prison and they got hurt. Which they never did, not the enemy nor the women.

CHAPTER FIVE
GOD AND THE EASTER RABBIT

I

Oliver started school when he was six, before they moved to town. His mother enrolled him at St. Patrick's which she thought was a good idea, two for the price of one: learning to be a good Catholic and to read and write. Every day she drove Oliver in from the country and left him at the little kids entrance to the red brick building.

What a change! Days running naked and alone through dusty fields, then suddenly, halls smelling of damp mops and crowded kids. Sister Doreen, his first grade teacher, white wimple, clumpy black shoes, smelling of Clorox with a touch of Lysol. Clean.

Oliver didn't like school, dreaded the other children's pushing, hated all the shouting and fussing, missed his dog, Boots. When you grow up alone, without playmates, everything has to be relearned. It didn't help that Oliver's eyes were bad; his mother never seemed to notice. He didn't get glasses until the second grade. Big people like Sister Doreen were always pointing things out to Oliver. "Oliver it's right in front of your nose!" "Oliver, pay attention to what I show you!" But Oliver couldn't see things people showed him, not even neat things like the hawk his grandfather saw. "Look, Oliver, there's a hawk!" But he couldn't see the hawk, which he really wanted to. His eyes went all funny. Oliver had what is called a *nystagmus*. It is a condition where the muscles in your eyes short out and your eyes wiggle back and forth. He could control the movement by putting his chin down on his chest and looking out from under his brows. Someone once said he looked like a little billy goat charging around. Why not? His birth sign was Aries.

Maybe that was why he and Sammy B. got in the fight. Sammy B. was in the first grade and sat one row over and two seats back from Oliver. He was as small as Oliver, smaller, which was why he noticed Oliver's eyes right away and nicknamed him "Wiggle eyes." That was very hard on Oliver, who threw a rock at Sammy because it seemed the only thing to do. The rock hit Sammy; Sammy told.

Sammy's father talked to Oliver's mother about it. As things proved, Sammy deserved it and then again he didn't. Oliver was giving a very stern lecture about hurting people, which he silently took under advisement. There'll be more about Sammy when Oliver's in the sixth grade and later on when Oliver's mother has her operation.

Even though he managed to hit Sammy with a rock, Oliver had no depth perception and couldn't catch a ball. He wasn't popular at recess, so he did a lot of reading and drawing pictures. There was the time he drew two pictures. One was of all the animals that live in the ocean and the other was George W. cutting down the cherry tree. Sister Doreen took him to the high school and had him explain to the juniors and seniors about the sea creatures and about George W. All the attention confused Oliver who was shy and proud at the same time.

II

Oliver's desk had black cast iron legs and a slanting wooden top. It had a groove across the top which held pencils and in the right hand corner a round hole into which a little glass ink bottle could fit. First graders didn't use ink; big students used ink, and that would come later. So Oliver would sit and look at the empty ink well and make himself very small and get down in it like he would get down in the holes that he and Boots dug, and he would stay there hoping that sister Doreen wouldn't see him. But she did.

"Oliver, sit up!"

Sister Doreen was small, even the first graders knew she was small and that's small when you think about how small little kids are and how most things and people look big to them. But Sister Doreen, small or not, maintained discipline in her class room. She had a picture of the Holy Family over her desk with a dove hovering above Mary and Joseph and the baby Jesus like that kind of light bulb when someone gets an idea in the newspaper funnies. That was the Holy Spirit.

Well, one day she was asking the class about the picture and when Oliver's turn came, he referred to the Dove as "that bird up there" and Sister Doreen smacked him across the face, maybe for being blasphemous, although Oliver didn't run into blasphemy until later.

That evening Oliver's mother noticed his face was pink on one side, and he told her what had happened. So his mother, who by that time had a job as a teacher in the public schools, took him out of Saint Patrick's and next year he went to Sharpstein P.S. right across the street from where they had moved on Newell Street, which was easier on everybody.

III

Before we talk about Sharpstein School, we should explore Oliver's religious education which came right along with the first grade and continued for a bit after he left Catholic School. There was Catechism class and all that stuff about his failing to be an altar boy. But first there were prayers. Oliver's grandmother taught him about his guardian angel and how the little dimple in the center of his upper lip was where his own personal guardian angel had touched his finger there so that Oliver wouldn't tell lies. That was nice to have a guardian angel when you were so lonely most of the time. Sometimes Oliver would talk to his angel, though the angel never answered and was invisible, even to Oliver. Just before going to sleep at night he would say the prayer his grandmother taught him:

Angel of God
My guardian dear
To whom His love
Commits me, here,
Ever this day
Be at my side,
To light, to guard,
To rule and guide.

Oliver doesn't believe in angels anymore, but sometimes late at night he still says that prayer. His guardian angel has stuck to him like a little limpet. *Limpet of God, My guardian dear . . .* Well, as we said, the sea is rising.

Then too, there was "Grace" before meals:

Give us this day
Our daily bread
Which we are about to receive
Through the bounty of Christ,
Our Lord, Amen
Pass the butter.

Which was the way his grandfather said it with a little smile, which for some reason made his grandmother mad.

There was a morning prayer at school. Sister Doreen stood in front of the class to say it. If she was in a hurry, it was simply a straight assembly line Hail Mary, but sometimes she spoke to God or the Virgin Mary about someone in the class who needed help being quiet. Once she spoke to God right in front of all the kids and asked Him to help Oliver stop fidgeting.

Of course, there was *real praying* when the whole school marched out the front of the school and went next door to the church where the students sat quiet and quivering and full of secret giggles. Almost every kid, at one time or another, went through an apotheosis when suddenly he or she became aware that God was up there behind that little door in the middle of the altar and could see right through the metal to where you were sitting. But most of the time it was just giggles and the silent squirms, which wasn't so bad unless you really had to go number one, which most little kids have to more than their teachers think.

There were special catechism classes which Oliver went to on Saturday morning.

"Who made God?" "God always was and always will be."

"Where is God?" "God is everywhere."

"Who made the world?" "God made the world and everything in it."

Which pretty well sums up the Catholic Big Bang Theory.

Catechism was preparation for First Confession and First Communion. Those were the two BIG firsts, but for Oliver they opened the front door of the church and pushed him away forever.

Father Calahan felt it necessary to reinforce the First Confession class's sense of fear and retribution. He thought about this as he smoked his morning cigar, and then sent his acolyte to tell Sister Doreen to bring the first grade class over to the church at recess so he could talk to them.

It was a very serious time for Oliver's group. They were sitting in the pews facing the altar, their legs dangling from the wooden benches. Father Calahan stood in front of them. It was a cold spring and a week day and the church wasn't heated. Oliver could see the sleeves of Father Calahan's long winter underwear sticking out from the cuffs of his black coat. Father Callahan cleared his breath and began:

"It is very important that children are truthful when they go to confession, especially their first confession. It is very important that they make a complete *Act of Confession* and a sincere *Act of Contrition*." His voice went all low when he said the last words. Oliver wasn't certain what an act of contrition was, but it seemed to him it must be a good thing to do if Father Callahan said so in a voice like that.

"You must tell the priest every bad thing you have done, and said, and thought. That way the priest can ask God to forgive you and when you die you will go to heaven instead of to the other place." Oliver knew the other place was called *hell* because his grandmother had told him that was where sinners and Protestants and the British went when they died.

"If a child makes an imperfect confession, if he leaves out anything," and again Father Callahan's voice went low, "the Act of Contrition will be ruined and if you take communion in a ruined state of grace you will commit a mortal sin, and when you die you will go straight to the other place."

The little girl next to Oliver began to cry. Sister Doreen who was in the row behind leaned forward and shushed her.

"Here is what happened to a little boy who made an imperfect confession, didn't tell the priest something he should have, and this is what happened to him.

"There was this little boy who one day stole and apple and ate it." Father Callahan put his hands on the front of the first pew and leaned forward. He seemed to be staring straight at Oliver. Did he know about the peanut at Kidwell's Grocery? Was eating a peanut as big a sin as eating an apple? It was smaller, and maybe didn't count as much. In the midst of Oliver's panicky thoughts Father Callahan continued.

"Now this boy didn't think stealing the apple was all that bad, but it is a sin to steal even an apple, and when it came time to go to confession he didn't confess about stealing the apple, and so he made a faulty confession and said his penance and then went to communion."

Father Callahan paused for effect. "He hadn't confessed stealing the apple, so his confession didn't work, and he took communion in a state of sin which made it a mortal sin!"

Father Callahan looked up, shot his arms forward so that his long underwear popped out of the wrists of his black coat, and then settled forward again for the rest of his story.

"Later on, the boy forgot that he hadn't confessed to the priest about stealing the apple, and when it came time to go to confession again he still didn't confess to the priest about the apple and the bad confession he had made. He had forgotten it completely. So that confession was just as bad as the first, and the next time he went to communion he committed another mortal sin."

"The years went by and the boy turned out to be a very, very good boy. In fact he was such a good boy that he became a priest himself and did good deeds for his flock . . . for his flock." Father Callahan repeated the phrase, rolling it around in his mouth, and smiled a secret smile to himself.

"And all his life he did good things and was a good, good person and priest. BUT," and the word rang through the church, "he never confessed about his bad first confession and the mortal sin he had committed by taking communion in a state of sin."

Father Callahan was talking faster now. "Well, the years went by and the priest grew old and died and everyone was very sad because he was such a good man, and everybody was planning to go to his funeral.

"The day before the funeral his body was placed in front of the altar so that everybody could come and see him and say good bye. The whole town came, even Protestants!" And Father Callahan's voice grew shaky taking the risk of saying that word inside his church, but this was a special case to prove just how good everybody thought the priest had been.

"Well, everyone said their good-byes and went home to bed in order to get up early for the funeral the next morning. But when they came back to the church the priest's body was gone! Disappeared! And nobody could think of where it had gone, but then they saw foot prints, the priest's foot prints burned right into the marble floor of the church! Those footprints led out the front door and right down into the earth outside and disappeared."

"You see," and he leaned forward again, he seemed to be looking straight at Oliver, "You see, that priest had made a bad act of confession and committed a mortal sin by taking communion in a state of sin, and he never confessed the thing he had done, and all the good things he did after that didn't count because he was in a state of mortal sin, and when he died the devil came and took him to hell!" That word! In church!

Father Callahan was breathing hard. He swept his gaze across the pews of terrified children, nodded at sister Doreen, turned and opened the little gate that led to the altar and disappeared through one of the side doors into the back of the church. Sister Doreen crossed herself, fingered the rosary at her waist, and herded the children back to their classroom. Everyone was very quiet except for the little girl who was still sniffling.

Oliver was in turmoil as they walked back through the echoing halls. The terror he had felt when father Callahan looked straight at him and talked about the consequences of an imperfect confession disappeared as soon as the file of students cleared the dim interior of the church. He would confess about eating the peanut and that would be that. But another, greater, terror came to mind. The boy had forgotten about stealing the apple, forgotten about the bad confession. What if he, Oliver, would forget something when he went to confession? What if right now there was something he had forgotten that would years and years from now make the devil take him to hell?

Now contrary to adult-think, children aren't born stupid and then grow up maybe intelligent. They are very bright all along. If they end up stupid it is because some stupid adult made them that way. Kids seem to do dumb things not because they aren't intelligent, but because they don't have all the facts and experience to make adult level stupid decisions. Did a kid ever start a war?

By the time Oliver had settled behind his desk he knew something was wrong with the story. First of all, he knew about rocks. There weren't any around the farm house where he lived, but when they went other places he saw lots of rocks. He brought rocks home with him in his pockets. The quartz crystal he had found in the attic had a rocky base. One time they had gone on a picnic up near Kooskooski and had built a fire by the river and roasted marshmallows. That fire had been in a circle of big rocks, rocks that hadn't melted no matter how hot the fire was.

On the other hand, the marshmallows caught fire and you had to blow them out right away or they'd turn all black, not just brown which tasted good, and be spoiled. Well, he had gotten some hot marshmallow on his bare foot and it had hurt something awful and there had been a pink spot and a blister. So if a marshmallow could burn your foot and the fire could burn marshmallows and not burn the rocks, then why had the priest's feet burned holes in the marble floor which was a rock, too?

That bit of child logic (not childish logic!) was the tip of a wedge which quickly split Oliver's mind wide open, split open what he thought, and what eventually he would do. Oliver sat there looking up at the picture of the Holy Family over Sister Doreen's desk. Take Jesus. Jesus loved little children, although why had he said, "Suffer little children to come unto me," which to Oliver seemed a very odd thing for Dear Jesus to say. "Suffer?" Why did he want little kids to suffer if he loved them so? But even that question disappeared if you thought about God, because somehow or other Jesus and God were the same, but were different, or at least seemed to be very different, because God had punished the little boy who really hadn't meant any harm, and God made apples as well as everything else, so why couldn't God make another apple to even things out? So how could God be that terrifying fierce God and Sweet Jesus at the same time? Something was wrong.

Oliver's thoughts went tumbling until Sister Doreen rapped her knuckles on his desk and he sat up and stopped thinking about it all. That evening, he asked his grandmother about it, but she hushed him and said that he shouldn't worry about such things, that he would understand when he grew up.

"You're grown up. Do you understand? Tell me." But she just kissed him goodnight and walked out of the room.

That is all Oliver remembers about Catholic school; Sharpstein School and the second grade is where his school memories begin again. As for religion, he still had to be "confirmed," which by then he didn't want to be, but that came later. It didn't matter, the tip of the wedge had entered.

IV

There was another small thing, the Eucharist. Oliver would receive communion, kneeling there at the railing in front of the altar and open his mouth and stick out his tongue as he'd been told to in the first grade. His knees were bony and the cold marble step hurt. He knew he should be thinking about the bread which had been made into a piece of God by the priest, but his knees hurt and he would get strange itches while waiting his turn. It was distracting. But the worst was after he'd been given the little wafer.

"Don't chew the wafer!" he'd been told by Sister Doreen.

The notion of ritual cannibalism being incorporated into the greatest church in Christendom didn't occur to Oliver until years later. It was just the thought of chewing Jesus, or God Himself, that bothered him.

At every single communion he would shift the dry little wafer round on his tongue, trying to get it to go down easily, but *zap*, it would stick to the roof of his mouth. It wouldn't come loose! It would plaster itself there. This necessitated working the clinging piece of bread free with the tip of his tongue.

"I'm sorry Jesus, and you too, God" he would say to himself, and little by little try to get God free. But in getting the wafer off the roof of his mouth, it would get crumpled and mushy. It was Oliver's notion that God should be swallowed whole, not all crumpled up, and Oliver could never resolve this tight rope struggle between piousness and blasphemy. Eventually he would have to mix what was left of the wafer with some saliva and swallow it anyway he could. The problem didn't drive Oliver away from the Church, but when he did leave, he felt relieved of a great theo-masticatory burden.

One good thing did come out of all this. Oliver was on his way back up the aisle from his first communion. He was having a terrible time seeing which pew his mother was waiting in. His eyes were jiggling back and forth at a great rate and he had his chin down on his chest trying to slow them down. A friend of his mother who was sitting next to her noticed Oliver's odd gaze and asked, "What's wrong with Oliver's eyes?"

'Nothing," she answered. "Why do you ask?"

After church, outside on the lawn, they drew Oliver to one side and talked to him and looked at his eyes, and his mother decided that maybe she should take him to the eye doctor. That was how Oliver got glasses. That didn't help the *nystagmus*, but he was also near sighted and glasses did help that. So that's how God helped Oliver, except when he laid his glasses down and lost them which he did all the time, much to his mother's despair. That's when his grandmother told him to pray to Saint Joseph who helped people find things they'd lost. St. Joseph apparently didn't approve of Oliver, because no matter how much Oliver asked St. Joseph, his glasses usually stayed lost.

V

Oliver still had to be confirmed, which means you are Soldier of God, or at least that's he was told. Even then, Oliver found it odd to match God who needed soldiers with God who could do anything He wanted.

After confirmation there came an unsuccessful attempt to be an altar boy. Oliver was of two minds about this. He really wanted to swing that thing which smoked and smelled of incense, but he didn't like the idea of wearing those silly clothes. He never got that far. First he had to go to the parish house on Saturday morning and sit in a big leather chair in a dim room while Father Callahan talked to him about the mysteries of the church. Father Callahan smelled of old cigar smoke and coughed a lot and frightened Oliver, though as far as Oliver can remember Father Callahan wasn't one of *those* priests that they send to New Mexico to metaphorically dry out.

Oliver learned, *Ad Deum qui latificat juventutem meam, et nunc, et semper, et sacula saculorum* (at least that's the way it still sounds to him like it should be spelled), and that was about it. He went on two Saturdays, and then never had to go again. No explanation. Maybe Father Callahan decided he didn't need a little billy goat stumbling around God's front porch.

VI

That's the extent of Oliver's indoctrination into Mother Church. That still left myth to be dealt with. That Easter on Newell Street Oliver's mother, in a round about way, helped Oliver solve the problem of Santa Claus. It was late and she was tired. She waited until Oliver was asleep and then boiled the eggs, decorated them, and stumbling around outside in the dark, hid them. The bunny would not disappoint Oliver! Her work accomplished, she went slow step by slow step upstairs to bed.

Morning came and Oliver, eager for Easter and eggs, climbed out of bed and ran through the kitchen heading for the back yard which he had been told the Easter Rabbit particularly favored. At the zinc topped work table he paused. Strainers, cups of colored liquid, an empty egg carton. She had forgotten to clean up the signs of her work!

Oliver looked at the labels on the egg dye envelopes. He eyed the surviving unused, flower and little chick decals. Deception! He forgot the Easter Rabbit, forgot the eggs and the tattle tale evidence. There was something more important! He bolted out of the kitchen, up the stairs and into his mother's bedroom, jumped on the bed, and landed shouting to his sleeping mother, "There's no Santa Claus!!"

The Easter Rabbit quickly followed St. Nick into oblivion. Oliver had put two and two together and found eight!

VII

The issue was finally closed when Oliver was in the fifth grade at Sharpstein. For some unaccounted reason Oliver became very religious during the fifth grade. He didn't tell anyone, he just silently negotiated with God and the Virgin Mary, and set himself the goal of one hundred "Our Fathers" and one hundred "Hail Marys" per day. This was hard to do when you were studying and beginning to worry about what was happening to your weenie, and playing and reading a lot. So day by day Oliver failed to fill his quota. He never tried to start over or to write off unsaid prayers. Instead, he kept a tab of what he owed God. The tab got bigger and bigger. After a while Oliver owed God over a thousand "Our Fathers" and the virgin Mary about seven hundred "Hail Marys."

The burden was too much and something snapped inside Oliver. At first, it was just plain escape from overload, a kind of Chapter Eleven spiritual bankruptcy. But the wedge was driven deeper and allowed all kinds of skepticism to filter into Oliver's brain. So he left the Church.

Later in college he tried Unitarianism, and actually became president of the Channing Club -- mainly because he was wearing a bright red shirt and stood out in the crowd at a meeting he went to out of curiosity. He didn't mean to join the Unitarians nor to be president of the Channing Club, but he was the only one nominated, and also the vice president elect was a coed with truly remarkable breasts, though he never saw them except well clothed at meetings. She moved to college in another town at the end of the first semester and Oliver resigned at the end of the year, partly because he missed seeing her breasts, but also because he thought it was silly of the group to argue whether or not they should include the Buddha and Albert Einstein in their prayers.

After that, Oliver floated along the shallow stream of agnosticism for years until he finally made up his mind. But that's another story.

CHAPTER SIX
GEOGRPAHIES

I.

As Oliver grew, his personal geography, the frame of space and time that defined his world changed. First, there was the dark warm wet. Then blinding light, lung burning air. Fingers, toes, ME! Looking up: crib bars blank ceiling looming faces. Standing, crib rail walls doors room, came later. Hall, carriage, spinning blue green, more faces, looking straight up their nose holes. Every face has two dark holes right there between the eyes and the mouth; stroller walk.

Next came certain rooms but not every room, kitchen high chair MY spoon bowl potty seat toddle-romp CRASH tears. A chicken wire play pen.

Now, Oliver's exploring. Outside, a green patch yard, fields beyond, dusty yellow dusty. Wearing clothes only when the weather insists; naked in the dust. Nobody to see, nobody to care, only grandmother in the house. Exploring under the yellow rose bush, adventuring with dog, animal think. Not Me, Boots, into the wheat stalk deep dirt world. Beginning to put it together. Oliver and Boots, Oliver think. Little by little, "I am not Boots, I am me."

Just in time for First Grade. An in between time, part country, part town.

When they moved to Newell Street Oliver's geography expanded again. There was across-the-street-to-the-far-end-of-Sharpstein with its steps and halls, the little kids play ground on the east end. Peeing in the funny wall stalls in the boys room. And the empty-on-weekends big kids playground right across the street from his house, and ball games, always being chosen last being littlest and unable to catch or hit because his eyes wiggled, wouldn't stay still. Over there where his nose got broken.

He tried to catch the ball, he was catcher, and stepped right into the swing of the bat. It caught the tip of his nose, knocked it right onto his left cheek. He ran home across the street and Dr. Campbell made a house call and gave him ether as he lay on the living room couch and apparently did a good job putting it back. It doesn't look broken today even though when he pushes it, one way it is stiff but when he pushes it the other way he can make it flat on his face.

That "Oliver's world" was a patchy kind of world made up of sidewalks and part of a play ground and a part called on-the-way-to-school which really wasn't far, and other places way off called Auburn, and "Back East" where Aunt Mary lived, and the chicken ranch gone forever. But his world wasn't yet a neighborhood. He hadn't figured out about neighbors. That came when they moved to Whitman Street and he was in the third grade.

A neighborhood is a patch of territory with people you know but who aren't family living in it; good, friendly, indifferent, and hostile people, who know you. It has edges, big people call them boundaries, some very distinct, some blurred. It is where you are welcome and also where you know whom to avoid and where to hide and the fastest way home if Bobby Jarman is going to beat you up. It has houses and a school building and the corner grocery store on Whitman Street kitty-corner from Sharpstein School, at least that's what Oliver's first neighborhood had when he was in the third grade.

His neighborhood centered on the upstairs apartment on Whitman Street. Pioneer Park at the end of Whitman Street; Sharpstein School two long blocks the other direction. His geography defined by line-of-sight. He could see his friends' houses, the places where he played, all within sound of his mother's voice. When she was home.

Oliver's voice, too. He and his friends would never go up on the porch and ring the door bell and say, "Can Jim, or Bill, come out and play?" No, all those little boys would stand out in the street and call "JIMMYYYYY," or "BIIIIIL!" And if Jimmy or Bill was at home he would ask his mother could he go outside and play. Oliver still can't understand why parents allowed all that yelling, but they did.

II

Sharpstein P.S., the lodestar of Oliver's new world, was a big building made out of rough cut stone. By the time he was in the third grade they had moved from Newell Street to the place on Whitman Street east of Sharpstein. That was OK because the lower grades were on the east end while the sixth, seventh, and eighth grades were on the west end. It was sort of like East and West Germany during the Cold War though there wasn't any wall you could see. Little kids at recess just didn't go past a certain line, or else. Not *or else* from the teachers, but *or else* from the big kids. On still another planet, girls played on the south side of the school, boys on the north. They never missed each other; no thought of gender segregation.

Miss Green whom Oliver's mother called a spinster taught the second grade. She was a nice lady, but Oliver didn't know what a spinster was. He thought that maybe she made things with a spinning wheel but when he asked her, Miss green just smiled, said "No," she didn't.

Next came the Third grade with Mrs. Jensen who drove a big old coupe with a fabric top and milk cans strapped onto the running boards. She lived on a farm. She was big and smelled of hay and was tough but fair. Oliver sometimes got in trouble in her class because by then he could read as well as the big kids and when the third grade reader was handed out at the beginning of the year—it was *The Open Road to Adventure* — he read it all the first day. It was supposed to last the whole year, so when reading time came he mostly day dreamed and forgot to follow as the really slow kids labored along, and his turn came and he didn't know the "place" where they were in the book. Mrs. Jensen knew his problem, but discipline is discipline, especially with third graders, and so he would be told to pay attention.

A lot of growing up things bothered Oliver when he was in the Third and Fourth grades. His mother went off to teach school early every morning and Oliver would wash the dishes and get dressed by himself. He was never sure whether you should tuck your sweater inside your pants or leave it outside. Going to school, which was three blocks away if you went down the right side of the street or two long blocks away if you went down the left side of the street, he used to tuck it in and pull it out three or four times, and sometimes he'd arrive at the Third grade with it tucked in and sometimes it was out. The same thing for his shirt. Did you button the top button or leave it unbuttoned? Oliver was miserable and nobody ever told him which was the right way.

Combing his hair. Maybe he didn't. After his class picture was taken the principal called him into his office and showed him the picture before anyone else had seen it. There he was with his hair standing straight up. "See yourself as others see you, Oliver," is all the principal said.

Keeping your pants buttoned was a problem, too. Oliver wasn't the only little kid who had to learn to be sure to button up after going to the bathroom at school. If you didn't, then some kid who noticed that you had a button or buttons showing would shout "One O'clock" and point at you if you had one button undone, and "Two O'clock" if you had two open. Some of the bigger kids, not necessarily Big Kids, it was just kids who were bigger than Oliver, would walk by and swipe their hand at your pants and rip open all your buttons and then yell "Four O'clock," which was pretty awful if it happened to you.

There was another thing on the play ground that was even worse. It didn't happen often, but when it did, you wanted to die. A bunch of kids would gang up and "Pants" you. That is, they would pull your pants right down around your ankles.

This happened almost every time Oliver's mother made him wear knickers to school. He had a pair of knickers which bunched in at the knees which made you look like a chicken with skinny legs. That was when Oliver got "pantsed," until one time the fly got torn and his mother didn't want to mend them and threw them out, which made Oliver very happy.

But there were good things, like on the way to school right near his house were some mountain ash trees with orange berries in the fall. Oliver would pick a bunch and take them one at a time and throw each berry ahead of him and then walk up to it and throw another one and see if he could get all the way to school on one bunch of berries. And on the other side of the street going home was a hollow tree that if you hit it with a stick it sounded hollow though Oliver never did find a secret hole where you could hide messages and stuff like that.

The Fourth Grade remains in Oliver's memory as the Palmer Method. This was when pen and ink became serious. Each student was equipped with a pen holder, a set of steel pen nibs that were inserted into the pen holder, a bottle of ink that fit in the little well on the upper right corner of his or her desk, and a small packet of pen wipes. Pen wipes served two functions. Of course, they were to wipe the ink off the pen nib once the writing exercise was done, but they were also to help get the oil off the new nibs before they were used. The oil on the new nibs kept the ink from clinging to the nib when the pen and nib were dipped into the ink well. This meant that you couldn't get a clear line on your exercises. The little flannel pen wipes didn't help much, and Oliver discovered that the best way to get an oil free nib was to put it in your mouth and suck it clean. He can still taste the oil and the acidic tang of steel in his mouth.

The exercises were to make long lines of mechanically even "O"s, all overlapping and all exactly the same. Then you had to make long lines of straight lines slanting from upper right to lower left. After that came lines of old fashioned end-of-word "T"s, which didn't look like "T"s, they weren't crossed, but were curving arcs, each one joined to the next.

There was a Palmer Penmanship book for each student. A picture of Mr. Palmer was on the cover. He had a very high forehead -- some might say he was bald, and a full beard and mustache. He stared out from the cover with a stern gaze as if to admonish each boy and girl to do as well as he did. That is, if he really had penned the perfect examples on the pages inside.

That was clearly impossible. The book, and the teacher in turn, explained that the secret of penmanship success was to slide your fore arm back and forth from the elbow, NOT from the wrist! This seemed genuinely against the laws of human ligature and nature, and no one except a girl named Vera, who sat two rows away, was ever able to do it.

Oliver's papers were among the messiest. He seemed to blot more than he wrote, and his consumption of pen wipes was excessive. For years, his cursive style was big and looping, sometimes on the lines, sometimes not, until he taught himself cursive printing after a year of engineering drawing in college. Most people have forgotten Mr. Palmer and his method, or have never heard of him, but sometimes even now Oliver, exorcising his past, scribes a line of imprecise Palmer "O"s or end-of-the-word "T"s, with his felt tip Sanford Onyx.

III

There were bigger questions, too, part of the wedge that Father Callahan had helped to create; call it skepticism. Why should the big kids lord it over little kids? So Oliver organized all the fourth and fifth graders on the east side of the school. They made snow balls and ran around to the west side and pelted the big kids and got back in line to go inside just as the bell rang. The big kids were really mad. Somehow or other they found out that he was the one who organized the little kids, and after school that day they were waiting for him. He got ahead of them and hid in the bushes. It was like *I Love a Mystery* on the radio. That was an adventure program. There was a person on it named Reggie who was being hunted by bad guys one time and hid just like Oliver hid. Oliver could hear the big kids hunting for him, but they didn't find him, and after a while he was able to sneak home. He had to be careful going to school for the next few days, but he felt like he had done something that should have been done.

IV

Oliver was still a little squirt -- some of the big kids called him that. This brings us back to round two with Sammy. Somehow Sammy ended up at Sharpstein like Oliver. Just like at Saint Patrick's he teased Oliver. Oliver was called "Science" by the other kids, and sometimes "four eyes" because by now he was wearing glasses. That wasn't good, but Sammy made it worse by still calling him "Wiggle Eyes," in front of everybody.

Oliver's mother was always telling him that he had to set an example because she was a teacher and that he had to show how good a student and how good a person he was. Not only smart, but good. Well, Oliver had to do something about Sammy and his teasing so he went to Mrs. Shaw, his sixth grade teacher.

Mrs. Shaw was Oliver's hero. She was the only married female teacher in the school. It was all right for the men teachers, there were two of them, to be married. Somehow or other, if you were a woman teacher, it wasn't fair if you were married.

Oliver knew a lot of what the teachers in the Walla Walla Public school system talked about because his mother sometimes gossiped with her friends when he was around. Little pitchers have big ears, his Irish grandmother used to say. He knew that Mrs. Shaw was disliked by most of the spinster teachers. She had, he heard, unfair advantages, though Oliver never found out what they were.

Mrs. Shaw seemed to understand things better than the other teachers. Maybe it was because she wasn't so worried about losing her job. Anyway, Oliver explained the Sammy situation to Mrs. Shaw, and asked her permission to beat up on Sammy. Yes, he actually did that, and what is more amazing, Mrs. Shaw gave Oliver permission to do it.

So that recess Oliver found Sammy on the school grounds and told him why he was going to beat up on him, and knocked him down on the ground and sat on him. Oliver was a very determined little squirt and Sammy was even smaller than Oliver. Sammy told his father again;, and this time Oliver's mother and Sammy's father and Mrs. Shaw and Sammy and Oliver all met face to face. Oliver never told anyone about Mrs. Shaw's giving permission; that was their secret which neither of them ever mentioned. Sammy said Oliver had two other kids hold him while Oliver hit him. That wasn't true, and somehow or other all the grownups knew that it wasn't the truth. Sammy's father got very serious and had a talk with Sammy who never bothered Oliver again.. That's not quite the end of the Sammy story as you will see.

V

Real bullies! Every little kid knows about bullies, but Oliver never understood when he was in grade school why he got picked on by bullies. Later he figured out it was because he was small but had a big mouth. For example, there was Bill Baxter, a great big kid who would stop Oliver on the way home and hit him. Oliver got so he could stop Bill Baxter five feet away by just saying some things that made Bill cry. Or maybe Oliver made Bill cry, and then Bill would hit him. Bobby Jackson, on the other hand, lived several blocks away, really outside Oliver's neighborhood. Bobby would sometimes wait for Oliver on the way home, even though Bobby's house was in the other direction. Oliver would see Bobby and run. He had the advantage of home territory and could usually hide before Bobby caught him and knocked him down. It still wasn't any fun.

And then there was the time Kurt and Oliver got in a fight on the playground at recess. Kurt was stronger than Oliver, but somehow or other as they were rolling around on the ground, Oliver caught Kurt's head in a scissors grip between his legs and held Kurt there. Kurt's voice was muffled but very angry. He kept telling Oliver that he would kill him when he got loose. The bell rang and all the kids lined up and went inside except Oliver and Kurt who just lay there on the ground.

Oliver wanted to go inside, but was truly afraid to let go of Kurt's head. Ten minutes passed and then Oliver's teacher came outside and found them there. Oliver doesn't remember much about what happened after that, or what the teacher said. He does remember that there were creases all over Kurt's face where the corduroy of Oliver's knickers had pressed in. Strangely enough, Kurt never bothered Oliver after that.

When Oliver got to high school the bullying stopped. In his sophomore year Oliver grew about five inches and gained forty pounds and managed to care for himself. That story's still to come.

VI

Sixth grade Shop was a trial. Oliver wasn't very good at it, and while the other boys were making bird houses and tables and stuff, Oliver was trying to make a shelf for his museum. This shelf was a very simple affair, just two long boards held apart by two shorter boards to form sort of a rectangle. It was his own design. The only thing was that Oliver couldn't get the two sets of matching boards to be the same length. The corners of the boards were supposed to join at right angles and all fit together, but he never could make them straight. So he finished the year with a kind of uneven shelf that things slid off when you put them on it. He kept it in his museum for a while, but later on he took it outside and used it as a toy fort along the stream that flowed behind the house on Whitman Street.

Just the same, don't feel too sorry for him. He must have been a pain in the ass. One day in the seventh grade Miss Ashley was out of the room and then came back just as Oliver was throwing a paper airplane.

"Oliver," she said, "what are you doing?"

"I am experimenting with flollysoids, " he told her. "That is what scientists call paper airplanes."

Miss Ashley was a meek teacher and just said, "Well, don't do it during class time."

Oliver could be a real smart Alec.

Oliver also made model airplanes from kits. There were sheets of balsa wood with the parts printed on them. You cut out things like wing ribs and aerlions and stabilizers and then fastened them down on a newspaper with pins, where you glued them all together with airplane cement which smelled of acetone and stuck to your fingers until it dried and you could pull it off with your teeth. The airplane skeletons were covered with tissue paper and sprayed with banana oil that made the paper shrink. Inside the fuselage of the plane was a long rubber band that attached to the propeller at the front and to a thick piece of balsa wood near the tail. You wound the propeller around and around until the rubber band was really tight, and in theory, when you let go of the propeller; the plane would fly off just like a real plane, though most of them simply crashed. That year, Oliver thought about why the planes crashed and decided they were too heavy for the rubber band. So he made a model plane with regular wings and tail but just a balsa wood stick for the fuselage. There was an airplane contest at school. He flew it out of the second floor window at Sharpstein and it really flew and he won the prize. That was the first time that he really understood what his being called "Science" meant.

VII

The apartment where Oliver lived had a front yard where Oliver never played. Mrs. Abernathy, the landlady, made it very clear that little boys weren't welcome there, nor were they in the back yard. Fortunately for him, beyond the heavy post and wire fence far back behind the old barn that served as a garage, there was a large meadow with two streams. The near stream puddled along at the base of the fence and supported a head high crop of water cress which Oliver would chew on for the tart taste, just like nasturtium stems. The stream on the other side of the meadow was larger, but was cordoned off by a dense growth of berry bushes with fearful thorns. This was one of Oliver's most secret places, but we'll talk about those later.

VIII

Oliver's next geography was defined by his bicycle. Suddenly he could go everywhere! The country outside town opened to his pedals. The edges of his neighborhood blurred. He could make far forays, speeding past kids he didn't know, who didn't know him. He has a lot more to say about his bicycle days and bicycle world.

IX

Later came cars! and Oliver's first driver's license, when he reached the Big Sixteen. Those times when he was allowed the family car, his geography was defined by being home by a certain hour and money for the gas. Back then, high school kids didn't take off on jaunts to far places, at least not the kids in Oliver's high school. Graduation changed that when some kids left home and drove to school on the other side of the state. Their world expanded thanks to wheels and being older, and earning money of their own. For Oliver the army came first.

Oliver has thought about his changing horizons. When you're grown up the world's your oyster. Airplanes now, if you can afford them; back then, steamships. (Not cruises; that was a time when you still crossed the Atlantic or Pacific on a steam ship). Grownups take vacations, go to visit *their* children. If you really want to, you can cut your traces and visit Timbuktu! Which Oliver eventually, actually did.

Age comes on and on. Now, your spouse or your children worry about your driving skills. You tire more easily. The body, the you-machine you're in begins to need repairs and replacement parts. One day, you sell your car; you really can't safely drive it any more. Before the used car dealer comes to pick it up, you go outside and sit in it for maybe an hour, thinking of the trips you've taken, the freedom these four wheels gave you.

The car's gone. You depend on friends to take you to market or the movies. The horizon is now back to line of sight. Sure, you take walks, around the block, to the end of the block. Maybe with a walker. Meals on Wheels? The front door is your portcullis protecting you from the no longer accessible, more and more frightening world beyond. Your window is barred by "can't."

Will you live long enough to study the mountains that your knees make under the white sheet on your bed? That's the way our personal geographies go, tiny territories, growing bigger, big, growing smaller, tiny, gone.

But we're getting way ahead of our story. Back to Oliver, at play in the fields of Sharpstein School.

CHAPTER SEVEN
AT PLAY IN THE FIELDS OF
SHARPSTEIN SCHOOL

I

Toys feed our fantasies; games lead us into life. These were the toys Oliver played with, toy trains and tiny cars, and toy soldiers with toy guns. Today the guns would be phasers, but the idea was the same back then as now. Some day you're going to have to zap your enemy or he'll zap you. Today little girls get Barbie dolls; in Oliver's time they were given tiny china tea sets. The message is still the same: some day you are going to be somebody's toy in a tiny little life. Oh yes, and squirt guns, then and now. Even little girls like squirt guns.

Getting them all ready.

Later on there are big toys for big people. Mostly for men. Shiny convertibles, the more expensive, the more likely to be driven by a balding pate. And toys for the bedroom. Will Viagra diminish the need for fun? Unlikely; all that talk about "mowing the lawn," instead of plunging into bed, means we'll need all the toys we can find. At some point, television even makes certain kinds of games into toys. All those couch potatoes fantasizing themselves onto the playing fields. Wow! Despite all this flab, I just made a touchdown!

And what about frustration and failure? Somebody must be responsible. Not me! The Commies used to be behind it all, or the

Jews. Now it's terrorists and Osman bin Ladin. Oliver once met a woman in Michigan who said it was a conspiracy driven by the Dutch living around Holland, Michigan. The simplest way to resolve this is to join the American Rifle Association. Every man needs his special toy, an automatic weapon, just in case *they* come. And of course, if you're really put upon, there are elaborate games to play called Militia and the KKK. Or the legal, honorable ones, like the National Guard, which politicians have transmogrified into a kind of Gotchya!

All kinds of games, children's games, board games, ball games, Olympic games, war games, playing the game, the games people play. Children's games teach about choosing sides. Oliver learned not to show how it feels to be chosen last. He learned about team work and not complaining when you're "it." Board games like checkers and chess and Go, hone your intellect and quicken your competitive sense and give you the thrill of acceptable aggressive behavior. It's not all bad. There's a lot of that in the grown up world. You've got to get used to it. War colleges everywhere play board games before going out and playing war games, before playing the game of war.

Take Chess and Go. Go was very important to Oliver though he didn't learn about the game until years after he left Walla Walla. Nevertheless, because of Go, Oliver escaped high school and went to Japan. Before World War II, they played chess at West Point, Go at the Japanese Imperial War College. To win in chess you capture the king after elaborate and formal maneuvering. To do so, you move pieces from square to square, space to space, all laid out evenly on an eight by eight board. If you win, you are given the privilege of toppling the king with a flick of your finger. To win in Go, you place white or black stones on a seventeen by seventeen lined board at the intersection of the lines, not on the spaces they define. The lines are somewhat unevenly spaced if the board is well made. Once put down, the stones do not move; they jostle one another as their numbers increase. The idea is to surround "armies" of enemy stones, so they have no empty interior intersections on which to breathe. If you succeed in capturing an army, you remove the prisoner stones until the summing up after the game.

The amazing thing about Go, at least to western minds, is that there is no formal end to the play. As the game progresses towards its close, its outcome becomes apparent to both sides. At last, one player or the other, winner or loser, will say something like, "four more moves?" and the other will almost always quietly agree. Then the empty intersections each player has protected are filled in by his opponent returning captured prisoner stones to the board. The player with the most enemy stones left over is the winner. The best game is where the winner wins by only one stone more than the loser.

Why speak of this? In Oliver's youth there was war in the Pacific, When you think of those island battles, substitute real islands for Go intersections, for chess spaces read open sea. Little by little the Japanese garrisons on the islands were isolated. The Americans took as few islands as possible, leap frogging across the great Pacific space, cutting off whole archipelagoes, leaving the Japanese garrisons to starve. As the Americans came closer and closer to winning; they demanded "unconditional surrender." They wanted to topple the Emperor-king. Why wouldn't the Japanese surrender? Couldn't they see they were finished? The Japanese wanted to lose by only one stone. Only atomic mega-force resolved the impasse.

Who was right? The way you play the game makes all the difference. Later, in another life, Oliver escaped high school and went to Japan in the army of occupation and learned about a culture different from his own. Meanwhile, Oliver was growing up in the land of "Topple the King" and "Unconditional Surrender."

II

Oliver was given toys for Christmas and his birthday. He remembers a pedal airplane he had admired in the toy department of a store he went to with his mother. He never got it as a present, but it didn't matter, he still remembers how disappointed he was when he sat in it in the store and pedaled and it didn't fly. Toys sometimes help you fly and sometimes tell you that you can't.

Oliver began to sense the deceitfulness of toys. Lincoln Logs were kits of small brown rods and poles and tiny boards with which you could build miniature houses and forts. Tinker Toys were all spools and sticks from which you cold make machines that actually worked! Tinker Toys came in a round tube with metal ends and pictures of the incredible things which you could build. Lincoln Logs came in rectangular boxes with similar pictures. At least that was what the pictures on both kinds of boxes implied. There weren't any Leggo sets back then.

Oliver never got beyond very simple stuff like little bridges and a log cabin that not even Lincoln would have lived in. It was very much like what happened later on in shop class at school. Maybe the lesson to be learned was that no matter how fast the sport cars go in the advertisements, you are never going to be Al Munser in the Indianapolis 500.

Oliver wasn't allowed to play with toy guns when he was little. His father, when he was a kid himself, had shot and almost killed a friend when they were out hunting rabbits. The message burned bright as blood. Oliver under the parental eye was never allowed to point even a stick at someone and say Bang. Later when he was in the Sixth grade and his mother lost track of him, he bought a be-be gun and shot lead soldiers with it. Down in the basement, alone with his loneliness and his anger, he showed entire armies how vulnerable they were.

One awful day he shot a neighbor girl in the leg as she rode by on her bike teasing him. It left a welt, didn't penetrate the skin. Thank God! The angry, anguished parents, his mother mortified, shaking him. "What do you think you were doing?" The police came. A quiet talk with his mother, Oliver sitting alone in the patrol car. Afraid. Jail!

The cops came back to the car. Sat there. Didn't say anything. It seemed to Oliver that days passed. He began to cry. The policemen made him promise never, ever to do that again. They took his be-be gun. Nothing more came of it.

What would have happened today? Would the air gun have been 22? Or a pistol Oliver bought from a big kid on the school grounds? These are the days of kiddy militiamen, minor murderers. Would Oliver be doing time until his 18th birthday for manslaughter? He has no idea how the times might have caught him up, brought him down. The step between a toy air gun and a rim fire weapon is only a millimeter wide.

III

There were little kid toys, really stupid toys like a cup on a stick and a wooden ball on a string attached to the stick. You were supposed to catch the ball in the cup and even Oliver could do that after a few tries, and then what were you supposed to do with it? And yo-yos which Oliver could make go up and down a few times but could never make sleep or get started without winding them up first, or spin around your head and then come back into your hand, which was called *Around the world* which is very different from the *Around the world* played by grownups which Oliver found out about much later. Needless to say, after an hour or two Oliver abandoned his yo-yo.

IV

Games outside with the neighborhood kids were better. Playing outside games is what children did before television. On warm evenings after dinner, Oliver or someone else would go to a friend's house and call for him, never knocked on the door, just stood in the street and called. Other kids in other houses would hear and come outside. After a while there would be enough kids to play a game in the street until it got too dark and their parents made them come in because some one might get hit by a car, although there weren't any cars on the streets where Oliver lived except those of parents who were already home.

Girls who could run fast were welcome to play, but nobody wanted to be *it*, especially when parents began to call and time go in came along because the person who was it when the game ended had to be *it* the next time they played. So the game would go on after dark until some one's parent got cross and then the kids really did have to go inside.

Everyone, boys and girls, played kick the can, annie annie over, hide and seek, icebox, and mother-may-I. Only boys played bottle caps, marbles, and keep-away, which Oliver hated since it was usually kept away from him. Boys also played good guys and bad guys which were sometimes Nazis and soldiers, sometimes Japs and soldiers (sorry, but that's the way it was). When they were old enough, they pretended their bikes were fighter planes.

M a,a,a,a,a,a,a,a,a,a,a,a,chine guns! VRRRooommmm!

Colin Kelley right down the smoke stack of that Jap carrier. They were all heroes.

There was one boy up the street who would climb up on the chinning bar suspended from a tree limb in his back yard and jump down yelling, "I'm paratrooper and I'm beating up on all those Jews!" Oliver wondered where he got that idea. Not because Oliver even knew about what was happening in Europe but because nobody really ever spoke of the Jews except how cheap they were and how they would cheat you. (Oliver insists that he never heard his own mother say anything like that, ever, though maybe his grandmother did when she took care of him.)

Oliver doesn't recall ever playing cowboys and Indians. This was curious considering the Indian Wars that had washed over the Walla Walla valley a few decades earlier, and the number of redskins, except Tonto, who did mean things in the movies at the Roxy theater every Saturday morning.

Oliver didn't play ball much. He couldn't see the ball, no depth perception. Remember how he got his nose broken off? Also, Oliver was too little, was usually the last kid chosen. Nobody played football, not even touch, two hands below the belt.

Inside games, when it was cold and rainy, were Chinese checkers, once in a while checkers, no chess, no cards, Oliver doesn't know why no cards.

Here's how the outside games worked.

Kick the can. There's a can in the middle of the street, one person is *it*. Every one hides except him. He hunts for you and if you're caught you have to go and stand in a pen by the can. If one of your friends runs in and kicks the can, whoever is *it* has to run get the can and put it back. Meanwhile the prisoners can escape. This is very discouraging if you are *it* and small. When Oliver was *it* too long he would begin to get frantic and then maybe someone else would take pity on him and take his place. When that happened and all the others were out hiding, Oliver and his benefactor would yell "allee allee auksin free" or maybe "allee allee oxin free." Which meant they wouldn't be caught and have to be *it* if they came out of hiding.

Mother may I? is when you line up and the one who is mother tells you "You may take ten baby steps", or "You may take six scissors steps," which is putting your right foot over beyond your left foot and ditto with your left foot over beyond your right foot, or "You may take five, or six, or ten, or however many mother wants you to, but never more than ten GIANT steps." And you must say, "Mother may I?" and if you don't then you are the mother. But if you do it right and don't forget then you cross the finish line and get to sit around and tease the others who forget to say *"Mother may I?"*

With *annie annie over* you need a ball and a building that isn't too tall and you get teams on both sides and then the team with the ball yells "annie annie over," and throws the ball over the building and the kids on the other side have to figure out where it's coming over and then spot it and catch it. It teaches kids about being honorable, because for the game to work, you have to admit that you didn't catch the ball, if you didn't, and then you throw it back over. The side with the best catchers wins. That is one of the games where Oliver was chosen last since he couldn't see the ball coming and one time got it POW! in his left eye, which wasn't the time he broke his nose.

Hide and seek is just hide and seek and they didn't play it very much. Oliver can't remember what *ice box* was but it is a variety of *hide and seek*.

Bottle caps was something different. Milk used to come in glass quart bottles with thick paper caps inserted in the top. These caps had a little hinges you could lift up and use to pull them out of the bottle top. A cap good for *bottle caps* didn't have the tab disturbed. All bottle caps had pictures of cows and stuff on them with the name of the dairy.

The way you played bottle caps was for each player -- it took at least two to play -- to put a bottle cap on the ground. That was the ante. Then you stood over them and laid your shooter bottle cap flat in the palm of your hand and slammed it down on the ground as hard as you could, but it wasn't fair to touch the ground with your hand. You had to let go of the cap and let it flatten itself on the ground. If you were good at bottle caps your cap would overlap one of the ones on the ground and you got to keep both of them. If you missed, then you had to put another cap on the ground exactly where your shooter landed. Sometimes you might actually cover two caps on the ground with your shooter, just parts of them, and you could keep all three. A good shooter was very limp and didn't bounce around but would stick, but it couldn't be sticky like with glue or honey but just sort of naturally sticky. It's amazing how soon Oliver got tired of playing bottle caps.

The only thing Oliver can remember about marbles is a glazed green crockery shooter he had which he really liked and that his thumb nail was sore when he played marbles a lot. There all kinds of marbles; the best ones were the clear ones with a spiral swirl of color inside them.

V

Most of the games Oliver played disappeared in the Sixth grade. There were some other things that vanished about the same time, things like penny candy and falling in the water while wearing your street clothes, which drove Oliver's mother crazy. Earning money for bikes and stuff came along, and Oliver's and his friends' bodies began to change in strange ways. They spent a lot of time trying to figure out what was happening because nobody would tell them. But let's talk about Penny Candy first.

CHAPTER EIGHT
PENNY CANDY AND OTHER CRIMES

I

Penny candy was addictive, maybe little kids' coke. (It isn't any longer; the supply has dried up. No more penny candy.) Oliver doesn't know if there was hard stuff in Walla Walla at that time or not. (An old timer told him about an entire town in Oregon that was addicted to snow. That story's still to come.) Of course, there were those little bottles he found in the park, so maybe there was and maybe there wasn't. But even penny candy can be a crime. It depends upon how you define addiction, or possibly what drives addiction. It can be psychological or physiological. Little kids grow fast, crave high octane fuel, sugar hits. Combine that with loneliness, feeling ignored, whatever, and you've got a problem. An addict's an addict, and whether it's coke or penny candy, it can drive a person to crime.

Oliver became a penny candy criminal when he was in the third grade living on Whitman Street. Kitty corner from Sharpstein on the way to school was a small grocery store. Oliver can't remember the proprietor's name. Maybe he didn't have one, because everyone just called him "the grocer," sort of like "the man," and his store, "the corner grocery."

The store was like Kidwell's Grocery only smaller. If you needed four eggs, the grocer would split a dozen for you. Oliver and his friends had a joke about going in there and asking for three tablespoons of flour, a pinch of salt, a spoonful of sugar, and a tiny piece of chocolate. When the grocer asked, "What are going to do with this?" They would say, "We're going to make a cookie!" But of course they never did; that was just a joke among little kids. Like any good corner contact, if a kid came in and bought candy, the grocer never asked.

At the back of the store was a glass case full of penny candy. Oliver would stand there eyeing what it held. Long sticks of twisted licorice, red and black, and licorice whips which had maybe a third of a licorice stick for the handle with a long, thin, untwisted string of licorice of a different color for the whip. You couldn't really crack a licorice whip like you crack a whip, because the string part almost always flew off without a sound. Next to the whips were little wax milk bottles full of sweet juices in different colors, red, orange, green. You bit into them and got a squirt of sweet color in your mouth and then you chewed the wax like gum until you got tired of it. But you didn't swallow the wax.

Then there were jaw breakers which Oliver didn't care for because they were really HARD and it took forever to suck one smaller and smaller. You couldn't bite into them, they were that hard, but if you were patient and sucked long enough then they would change color. They were layered like an agate. The very center was black, but didn't taste like licorice. Oliver can't remember if it even had a taste.

And tiny Baby Ruth bars in wrappers that cost a penny just like the big ones that cost a nickel. There were strips of wax paper with little dots like flowers and other decorations on them and you got maybe ten dots for a penny. You scraped them off the paper with your teeth, it wasn't really biting, and they tasted dusty and sweet. Oliver still wonders how anything can taste dusty except dust, but they did. And marzipan fruit sometimes, but they cost two cents and weren't worth it. Tootsie Rolls in wrappers, penny ones and nickel ones. Whistle for Captain Tootsie! They were chocolate and good, and had a secret sweet taste which was something more than chocolate. Even today, Oliver's mind searches around inside that case and sees sticks of gum, Black Jack, that was licorice, and Tutti Frutti, which was his favorite. Nobody ever bought a whole nickel pack, just penny sticks, one at a time.

Kids most often didn't have nickels. Parents sometimes bought their kids nickel bars for treats. Things like Idaho Spuds which were potato shaped and had chocolate and coconut shreds on the outside and a kind of chocolate mousse inside and were good. There were Uno bars from the Cardinet Candy Company which were in silver wrappers and were also a kind of light chocolate mousse and also were good. And Cotlets which tasted like apples or apricots and were actually lokum, but Oliver didn't know that until many years later when he lived in Turkey. And Almond Roca which is still around and came in flat round tins and was meant for times like Christmas. Those were special things kept in boxes on the shelf behind the glass case, not in it.

It wasn't those grown up candy bars that got Oliver into trouble, It was thinking day after day about the stuff in the glass case that made him dishonest. It was penny candy.

One Saturday morning when Oliver's mother was away, the need was on him. Like de Quincy and his laudanum, he could imagine laying out rows of candies and deciding which he would eat first. He wouldn't hurry. Should it be a Tootsie roll for a quick rush, so that the juices under his tongue would gush? Or maybe some licorice that you chewed and chewed? His pockets were empty and his mind was full.

Oliver went to his coin bank which was a glass mason jar where he was supposed to save up for special things like a bicycle and college. Oliver was in the third grade when this happened and hadn't really thought much about college, but his mother kept saying "when you go to college . . . " not "if you go to college." For Oliver, a bicycle was immediate desire. Neither mattered that Saturday morning. He counted out fifty pennies from the jar -- Oliver had been told he was on the "Honor System," but that didn't matter. It took time to make the count, and Oliver felt the double thrill of guilt and maybe being caught. It seemed to him that FIFTY CENTS WORTH OF PENNY CANDY was the ultimate. Many years later Oliver would understand what Sting meant when he said, "Too much is never enough." Oliver loaded the coppery weight into his two front pockets and headed for the corner grocery.

He walked in trying to seem innocent, casual. He stopped in front of the glass case.

"I want a licorice whip, five licorice whips."

The grocer smiled, a big spender.

"And five Tootsie rolls, and , and, some of those wax milk bottles, five of those." Oliver rushed on. The grocer began to frown. Little kids didn't have that much money. He dropped Oliver's order piece by piece into a brown paper bag.

`Finally Oliver was done. He shuffled over to the cash register counter and began unloading the pennies from his pockets. He didn't count them out.

"Fifty pennies, fifty cents! I counted them at home. They're all there."

He grabbed the bag and ran out the door. The grocer stood looking after Oliver. He didn't count the pennies, just scooped them off the counter into his hand and dumped them into the penny bin in the cash drawer. He stood there thinking and then went to the phone on the wall. Oliver's mother wasn't home, but later that day she answered.

Oliver ran all the way home, the crumpled top of the paper bag getting all sweaty in his hand. He ran right past the steps to the apartment, right to the barn-garage at the back of the property. Climbed the ladder to the dusty loft and sat there on the buckled flooring out of breath, clutching his bag of treasures.

That evening, after supper, Oliver's mother sat him down on the sofa.

"Oliver, I want to have a talk with you." She only spoke like that when something special had happened. He knew he was caught. They talked. He confessed his crime, the pennies, about not being honorable, buying penny candy. Oliver can't remember what his mother said to him, but he went and got what was left in the bag and gave it to her. After that he had to go cold turkey for a month.

Oliver wonders if he would still think that penny candy is as wonderful now that he can buy as much candy as he wants. But if he were offered the opportunity to have some more penny candy, he wouldn't, he tastes the memory in his mind.

II

Oliver grew up during the Great Depression. Of course, it didn't seem like the Great Depression to him because that's the way life was. There were curious customs that he took for granted back then that he wonders about now. If he or one of his friends were eating something, you know, chewing so it could be noticed, then some non-chewer would always say, "Watcha eating?" Many times the questioner would launch into the second standard sentence without even asking the question.

"Bites!" or "Halfers!"

Unless the chewer were quick enough to say "No bites!" he had to share whatever it was he was eating. That was the unwritten school kids' law. "Halfers" was more devastating than "Bites!" but "Bites" was bad enough if you only had one piece of candy. Many kids Oliver knew would even insist on pieces of sandwich.

The question is: was this simply a custom in small town America? Or was it peculiar to Walla Walla? Or was it really based on the fact that a lot of kids didn't have that much to eat and no candy?

You may think this last interpretation too dramatic, but one day Oliver learned something about candy and who had some and who didn't. It was the first day of April and the grocery stores were selling April Fools Day candy, chocolate coated beans and bon bons with cotton fillings. Oliver bought some of each and took them back home. There was a family of poor kids who lived across the street. That evening when every one had come outside to play before dark, Oliver offered the trick candy to them. He didn't even wait for them to say "Bites!"

They grabbed every single piece, which this time didn't bother Oliver who was going to have a big joke on them. But those kids sucked the chocolate off the beans and then cracked the beans with their teeth and ate them, and gulped down the bon bons without even noticing the cotton. He stood there watching them and began to feel like he'd done something wrong but didn't know what. Later that night he thought about it and decided that those kids didn't get as much candy as he did, and maybe not even enough food considering they had eaten the beans. What good was a joke if the person you played it on didn't get it and was grateful instead? April Fools Day passed, but every once in a while Oliver thought about what had happened and felt uncomfortable. Little by little the wedge in Oliver's mind was creating new spaces.

III

There was something even better than penny candy! Fire works! The little kid's answer to the grown up kid's ultimate boom toys. Fire works weren't easy to find, only just before the 4th of July. When he was little, Oliver was allowed to buy sparklers and roman candles and snakes which were little cubes that when he lit them swelled up and oozed out and made a kind of snake out of ashes. Roman candles were the best. They went off with a pshhhhhh, pop! followed by a glowing ball that went up into the night sky. When it came to REAL fire works, little kids could shoot off lady fingers which came altogether in a bunch. It was nearly impossible to separate just one and light it and when and if Oliver did it wasn't very loud and not worth the trouble. Pin wheels were what other kids' folks would tack on a fence post and light and they would go around and around. Rockets were usually too expensive. And there were Zebras which were big, and cherry bombs which were black and wicked looking and dangerous. Oliver was never allowed to shoot off Zebras or cherry bombs. It was also considered very stupid to put a zebra in a bottle. Oliver's friends never did because there were stories about kids who hadn't listened and had eyes put out and fingers blown off, and who set wheat fields on fire, which was even worse in Walla Walla than having your fingers blown off.

Of course, Oliver and his friends yearned for the mythical explosion, that dramatic release, which never seems to go away, even when you're grown up. Think about all those new, post nuclear, nuclear weapons, the toasts raised to India and Pakistan around Los Alamos dinner tables. It's all the same.

When Oliver and company were young it wasn't easy to find the right stuff, but Oliver was clever. He had heard on the radio about Molotov cocktails. World War II was raging and Russia was our ally, but they didn't have any weapons. A brave Russian named Molotov had figured out a way to stop the German tanks. It was called a Molotov cocktail in his honor. Oliver listened and then went and found an empty quart whiskey bottle in the neighbor's trash. He filled it with gasoline bought at the neighborhood service station -- no one seemed to notice things like a kid buying a quart of gasoline. After that it was easy. He and two friends took their Molotov cocktail into the parched creek bed behind his house. They stuffed some rags in the neck of the bottle, and when the rags were damp with gasoline, struck a "lights anywhere" kitchen match and lit the bomb. They were so excited they almost dropped the bottle at their feet, but Oliver threw it onto a pile of rocks thirty feet away. The billow of flame was more than they expected and scared them. There in the smoking creek bed they talked it over, and though they were proud about knowing what to do if the Japs came, they never made another cocktail.

Now kids consult the internet to learn how to make pipe bombs. With a little effort they can move on to bigger stuff. Oliver might well have done that if there'd been computers and an internet when he was young. Why? What is it that makes fireworks and bombs so appealing? Is it the sense of being ignored, wanting to say I am I!! Or is it anger, pure and complex? It wasn't Oedipal rivalry where Oliver was concerned. He had no paternal competition for his mother's affection. That would all come later when she discovered boy friends. The question remains open.

The best time Oliver had with fireworks was studying catalogues which he thinks were put out by Johnson and Smith, but he may be wrong on that. Anyway, these catalogues listed incredible marvelous unattainable fire works like sky cannons and multiple rockets and bombs bigger than cherry bombs. Oliver made long lists and planned to save up and get all those things sent him, but he never did get enough money to place an order. It's just as well he didn't.

IV

Earth, air, fire, and water. The four primal elements. Palouse country loess, the great Chinook, the foothills glowing hot with burning stubble, the waters of Walla Walla.

For Oliver it was running plunging into deep dust, the dark house shaking in the wintry night, a gasoline bomb in a dry creek bed, and getting wet all over.

By the time Oliver was in the third grade he was always getting wet. Water fascinated him, and after all, wasn't Walla Walla the place of many waters? When he lived on Whitman Street he would go out back to the stream and wade in it. The water cress grew over his head so there was this little green tunnel where no one could see him, which he liked a lot. Even on school days he would dam the stream when he came home after school, and though he didn't mean to, he would always get wet, which was like losing his glasses and sometimes his jacket, which also happened a lot. His mother must have worried about him.

But maybe she didn't, because by then his sister was older and went out with her girl friends, and his mother was away evenings at meetings and maybe with boy friends, and if Oliver lost his key which happened, then he would sit out under the street light and wait for someone to come home. And if he was wet, he was just wet and that was that.

There were other waters. A block east on Whitman Street was the southwest corner of Pioneer Park. The park was a neat place and in the fourth grade Oliver was old enough to go there by himself and play because kids didn't disappear in Walla Walla back then like they do now all over the country. The park is a square about four blocks on a side. There was a fish hatchery on the southwest corner where Oliver usually played. A stream there came from the hatchery and went under the street and then on behind his house. There were trout that had escaped from the hatchery in the tunnel where the stream passed under the street. BIG ones! Oliver tried to catch them, which was against the law. It was the catching part, not the eating, that intrigued him.

If you went north along the west edge of the park you came to a small pond which Oliver fell into. He can't recall why, but it always seemed to happen. Beyond that pond was a rounded hill which used to be a dump for the city until the mound was covered with dirt and grass. Oliver wanted to be an archaeologist and excavate that hill and find all kinds of interesting stuff inside it like old bottles and pioneer guns and wagon wheels. The street after the hill was East Alder. Four old 75 mm field guns from WW I were ranged along edge of the park, their barrels intimidating the houses across the street. Oliver and his friends used to climb on the guns and twirl the elevation wheels, and snap the little oiler caps that remained. One time, under one of the guns, he found four little bottles and a needle thing that his mother called a hypodermic when he showed them to her. She said he should never, ever, play with things like those he had given her. She called the police and gave the stuff to them. Oliver has no idea what the police did with the needle and the bottles but he never found any others.

Back inside the park in the center of the circular drive at its center was a bandstand on which Oliver never saw a band. Beyond that was another lake on the same stream as the fish hatchery. It was more formal and had ducks and an island and a bridge, and for some reason Oliver never fell in there.

Oliver and his mother and sister moved to East Alder Street because their land lady on Whitman kept looking in their garbage can and telling his mother that she peeled her potatoes too thick, or at least that was the story Oliver heard.

Lots of things happened in the new house, but we're still talking about Oliver and water. The first winter there, Oliver went to Mill creek across the field out back to play on the ice in the stream. The WPA had put gabions, huge wire sacks filled with boulders, across the bed of the stream. A plunge pool formed in front of each weir when the snow melt of spring filled the stream bed from bank to bank. Even when the flow dried to a spastic trickle, the pools remained full, sometimes four or five feet deep. It was on their wintry surfaces that Oliver slid, or tried to crack through the ice with tossed boulder bombs.

One bitter day the ice gave way beneath his weight. Suddenly he was up to his shoulders in icy water. Lucky for him his feet touched bottom, so there was only a desperate scramble through shattered shelf ice to the pool's snowy edge. There was a cold wind blowing, no Chinook this, and he could feel his clothes getting stiff as he stood there. Ran for home; just made it. The house was empty and Oliver was able to shuck off his frozen clothes and huddle by a floor vent until he warmed up. Oliver never told his mother about his icy escape.

V

Two blocks away across the fields of summer was the Natatorium, a commercial swimming pool where Oliver spent most of his time in the warm weather except when he was working. At first, work was mostly delivering papers and mowing lawns, like the time the woman next door gave him a nickel for cutting the grass on her huge lawn. Nobody, not even his mother understood that it was unfair to get so little for so much effort. When he was sixteen he started working nights at the cannery. This meant that Oliver could spend hours baking in the sun by the pool.

Why he didn't get skin cancer he doesn't know, because all the teen agers used to put iodine in baby oil and rub it on to get a quick tan. People used to throw pennies and nickels and sometimes dimes and quarters into the water and Oliver got very good at staying under holding his breath and hunting for the coins. Usually he could find enough on the bottom to pay the admission price.

Oliver was learning about sex and was still uncertain about almost everything. Grown ups made it clear to kids that sex was somehow or other dirty. It was dirty to touch yourself, and much dirtier to jack off which felt really good. This was also called beating your meat, or in a pamphlet the parents of one his friends gave their son and which Oliver read, "self abuse." To do this you held your weenie when it got hard and moved your hand up and down until you squirted white stuff, which was called *jizzum* and made babies. But as soon as that happened you knew you'd done something you shouldn't have. Some older guys said it gave you pimples, and since Oliver and every other boy he knew were getting pimples it seemed that everybody was doing dirty stuff. Oliver also learned from someone that it grew hair on the palms of your hands, but it didn't. The pamphlet said you would become insane if you masturbated, which it was also called.

Along with all this misinformation came a growing fascination with girls. That's where the local swimming pool came in. Swimming there in the summertime gave Oliver a chance to look at girls in bathing suits. This was somehow or other about sex, which made looking at them dirty and probably illegal, though Oliver just looked and pretended he wasn't looking and never got fresh.

One time, the life guard and an old man, really old with gray hair, not little kid old, and a bunch of kids including Oliver were sitting around looking at the girls in their swim suits and trying to decide which one they liked the best. At least that was what the kids said, but the old man - who came to the pool nearly everyday - said what he wanted was different. He said, "You know which one I'd choose?" And Oliver said "Which one?" And the old man said, "That one," and pointed to a little girl five or six years old, and said, "That one, because I could train her to do exactly what I wanted." Oliver and his friends didn't understand what he meant, even though by that time Oliver was thirteen.

This shows you that there were some odd people in Oliver's town, which became clear to Oliver later on, although he didn't think that the man from the Natatorium would ever actually do anything like that. But Father Callahan used to say *a sin of desire is just as evil as a sin of commission,* which was one of the reasons Oliver left the church, because by the time he was thirteen he figured he was doomed anyway. He was a curious mixture, well on his way to growing up Walla Walla.

Well, those are Oliver's early crimes, which brings us to personal stuff and Oliver's secret sadness.

CHAPTER NINE
STUFF!

Stuff. What a wonderful word! The world is made up of stuff. The stuff the world is made of is transient and permanent, material and intangible. And what is stuff? Anything, and everything, undesignated, hard to classify. You have all that stuff in your closet that you don't want to throw away, but don't know what to do with. Or there's all the stuff that happens in a love affair gone sour, or a presidential election, or growing up. So here's some of the stuff that happened to, clung to, Oliver, building around his life like one of those little chrysalises that May fly larva in summer streams put together out of tiny stones, and little bits of wood, and bits of shell. Shelters for their edible, tender bodies. Part of changing into May flies

I

After Oliver's mother earned her teaching certificate she drove all over eastern Washington and Oregon trying to get a job. Sometimes Oliver went along. They went to all the little towns, but when the school board members found out that she was Catholic, somehow or other the jobs would disappear. Oliver remembers her crying, leaning her head against the steering wheel of the Chevy, before driving on to the next town. Stuff. Oliver was little, and couldn't understand why her being a Catholic made those men so mean.

Then her luck changed. She got a job teaching at Edison, a new school on the east side of Walla Walla. It was considered revolutionary for it had only the first through the sixth grades. There were microphones in each room and the principal could listen in to each classroom and if necessary speak into the room. Oliver's mother was made principal, which was a coup for her. Principals were supposed to be men, which shows how persuasive Oliver's mother could be when she wished.

The job in town made it possible for them to move to Newell Street. Oliver entered the second grade at Sharpstein; his sister was stuck at St. Patrick's right through grade school. It turned out, after they'd been living in town for a while, that dogs were not allowed in the house on Newell Street, so Percy took Boots to live with him in Auburn. Oliver was very sad to say good-bye to Boots but he knew that his grandfather was lonely and needed Boots for company and would take good care of him.

After Percy fell in the snow drift and Oliver's grandmother went to Auburn to take care of Percy, Oliver and his mother and sister moved to the apartment on Whitman Street. But there was a big old barn there made into a garage that Boots could live in and a field out back where he and Oliver could run. So for a while stuff worked out for Oliver and Boots.

II

So, stuff was happening to Oliver, events, strands slowly weaving themselves into a life. Hard to classify, impossible to ignore. The entrance to the apartment was on the side of the house. The stair top opened into the living room which was in front. On the right was Oliver's mother's bedroom. Next to it, all the way in back was the bathroom, and beside it on the other side, his sister's room. Continuing on in a circle you came to the kitchen and then back to the living room. You may wonder where Oliver slept. Oliver still hesitates to say that right through the Fourth grade he slept in his mother's bed, even though he was way too old for that.

Why she kept him there he doesn't know. It's odd when you think about it. There was Oliver, feeling left out, and sometimes truly left out under the street light if he lost his key. (His mother was irregular about what hour she came home, and it was clear to him that if he lost his key and had to sit out there it was his fault and no one else's.) On the other hand, having no place to be alone inside the house became more and more difficult for Oliver the older he got, because strange things were happening to his body. The worst part of it all was his wetting the bed. No matter how hard he tried not to, Oliver would wet the bed. His mother was long suffering and gave him gentle lectures about how big boys didn't wet the bed.

"Oliver, what am I going to do with you?"

Oliver tried and tried, but It wasn't until they were living out on East Alder Street when George, his mother's cowboy boy friend, insisted that Oliver needed a room of his own and made him one in the basement opposite the furnace that his problem suddenly stopped. Oliver was very glad when that happened. George's story is still to come.

III

Oliver's grandparents moved to another small town, Snoqualmie Falls. Auburn, Selah, Sumas, all the smallest places, grandfather Percy working the four to midnight shift. It was very damp in Snoqualmie Falls and Percy bragged that there was a mushroom growing on the upholstery of his Ford car. Later on he fell ill. Oliver thinks his grandfather had cancer of the prostate, but that is just a guess because people didn't discuss cancer in those days. It was like VD, which Oliver didn't learn about until he was in the army and the chaplain told the recruits that their right hand was a soldier's best friend. Something a little different than the Walla Walla view of self abuse.

Oliver's grandfather died in the mists of a West Coast winter. Those same mists brought deep snow to the Cascade Mountains. When Oliver's mother learned her father was dying she took Oliver on an automobile trip across the mountains to Tacoma to the railroad hospital. The sign at the foot of Snoqualmie Pass said *Stop -- Do Not*

Proceed Without Tire Chains!! She drove right past the police car which was stopping traffic and started up the pass. Near the summit the car slid into a snow drift. Oliver got out and started tearing at the snow with his bare hands, but it was no use. Then a big truck slid to a stop and skidded into the snow drift alongside their car. The trucker got out and helped Oliver and his mother get out of the drift. His mother was very pretty and Oliver thinks that's why the trucker stopped. Once on their way, they left the trucker standing looking at his rig stuck in the snow.

In those days truckers didn't take dope and were called Knights of the Road and Norman Rockwell painted their picture for the cover of *the Saturday Evening Post*. So it was OK that he was left stranded. That's what knights are for.

Grandfather died. Oliver cannot remember much about that. On the way back home his mother told him that now he was the man of the family and had to take care of them.

IV

When they arrived home Oliver got his first job. It was at the Crescent Drug Store on lower Main Street. Mother knew Mr. Mockel who ran it. Oliver swept the floor and ran errands in town. That was when he got his Social Security Card. Oliver found the bulk chocolates stored in the basement and ate only one or two a day, but "Many a mickle makes a muckle," as his Irish grandmother used to say. Pretty soon the chocolates were noticeably diminished. Mr. Mockel noticed too, and Oliver decided to change professions and have a paper route. But maybe he left because of the older boy who was eighteen and clerked in the store. Oliver and he didn't get along. They would argue and though Oliver was only twelve he would win. He remembers telling the clerk, "Well, when I'm as old as you are, I will go to Brazil and have adventures instead of being a dumb clerk." The older boy started to strangle Oliver and Mr. Mockel had to pull them apart. It was after that the Oliver left.

V

Oliver saved his money, and with the help of a check from his Aunt Mary Back East, bought a bicycle. It was a big red Schwinn with coaster brakes and balloon tires and a metal canister body between the two bars below the seat. Once he had a bike he could get a job delivering newspapers. The first route he had started at Second and Main Streets and covered lower Main. It was actually a walking route with too many stops close together to ride a bike. Among other customers such as stores and law offices, he delivered papers to four of the rumored seventeen houses of ill repute found along lower Main Street. He didn't know they were not nice places, although later on he found out that the men in town called them *houses,* which was short for whore houses, but nice people if they spoke of them at all called them *those places.*

Everyone knew about them and no one said anything. It was one of the town's secrets that everybody kept, even the Chief of police. The Police Station was in the basement of the Town Hall which was just off Main Street at Third. The entrance to the station was in the alley on the left side as you faced the building. The fanciest house in town was on the same alley, on the south side, on the second floor of a building about one hundred feet down from the Police station. People said that house belonged to the chief, that it came with the job to insure that "everything" went smoothly. Or so they said. Anyway, the house was there and it had a Chinese girl named Toy and a Black girl as well as several specialists who did things like "around the world," and "Pabst Blue Ribbon."

Oliver didn't know about any of that stuff until he got back from the army.

VI

Oliver's paper route was an afternoon one. He usually rode his bike down town after school to deliver his papers, but the Sunday edition was delivered very early Sunday morning. He would get up at three o'clock and ride his bike to the Walla Walla Union Bulletin press room where he and a bunch of other kids would go into the crummy basement and fold their papers so they could throw them easily onto the porches without getting off their bikes. Most of Oliver's papers, however, were delivered by hand to businesses and other special places.

The basement room had a window that opened into a well in the sidewalk. The press men would crawl into the window well and lay there looking up through an iron grill on the sidewalk waiting for women to walk over it. Younger kids like Oliver thought this was a crazy way to act, but the older boys seemed to understand.

Four AM one Sunday morning Oliver was near the Marcus Whitman delivering Sunday papers, and a man came out of the lobby and came up to Oliver and said, "Hey kid, where can I find a girl?"

Oliver thought about the man's question. It seemed to be a very strange request. Oliver said, "There are a lot of girls over at the high school, but it won't be open until tomorrow morning."

"Fuck you, kid," the man said and gave Oliver a dollar bill and went back in the hotel. You can see that Oliver really didn't know what was going on. Now, Oliver says that if he had known, he would have told the man there were lots of girls waiting in the houses along lower Main Street.

VII

Mrs. Tithewold ran the Cleveland Arms upstairs on Fourth Street just off Main. She was very kind to Oliver when he delivered her paper. On Mondays, she always had a box of chocolates that some nice man had left her and gave Oliver three or four. That was how Oliver got into the bottle business.

It seems that a number of men stayed there on the weekend and by Sunday morning there were dozens, maybe a fifty or more beer and whiskey bottles piled around the hall. This presented Mrs. Tithewold with a big disposal problem. She talked it over with Oliver, and he agreed to take away all the whiskey bottles if he could also take away all the beer bottles. The little ones, stubbies, were worth a penny, and the big ones, quarts, were worth five cents. Oliver years later wishes he knew more about this. It sounds like recycling which is supposed to be new and ingenious. Maybe some people have had sense all along.

Oliver made as much money hauling bottles away from the Cleveland Arms each month as he did delivering papers. This was because if any subscriber refused to pay their paper bill or moved away, and as we would say now, stiffed Oliver, he as a JUNIOR BUSINESS MAN, took the loss instead of the newspaper. The owner of the newspaper explained that this built character and prepared young paper carriers to later on become BUSINESS MEN and not feel bad about stiffing the kids who would work for them.

Back to the Cleveland arms. Sometimes there were so many bottles that Oliver couldn't carry them all on his bicycle, and his mother early Sunday morning would drive down in her new Hudson Terraplane and Oliver would load them in the trunk. He used the whiskey bottles for targets, throwing rocks at them in the dry bed of Mill Creek behind his house.

In order to remove the bottles from the upstairs hotel Oliver used his paper carrier bags. These were big canvas sacks joined together with a hole to stick your head through. You wore one bag in front and the other in back. Oliver would fill the two pockets with bottles and carry them downstairs. One time he was coming down the stairs at the Cleveland Arms with both bags loaded with bottles when he tripped and fell all the way down. He landed at the bottom in a heap of broken glass and spilled bottles. Mrs. Tithewold came running and screaming, but Oliver wasn't even scratched. He says that his fall was much harder on Mrs. Tithewold than it was on him. What hurt more was losing the return deposits on the bottles that broke.

The ladies in the other upstairs hotels on Main street weren't as easy to collect the subscription money from as was Mrs. Tithewold. In fact, sometimes they moved away without telling him to cancel their paper, and if some lady in another room picked up the paper without telling him, Oliver wouldn't know for almost a month that he had been cheated.

What Oliver learned from all this was that people can be nice or not nice whatever they do for a living. This contradicted what he heard when he was in the army and an officer he knew told him every whore has a heart of gold. Not necessarily. It was all very Walla Walla.

--- --- ---+

Oliver also went on his bike with the other kids who hunted for bottles along the highways and at special places where people used to go and neck. He wasn't quite sure what necking was or why people did it. They would drink beer while they necked which was good for the kids. On Saturday morning he might find a dollar's worth of bottles near the Natatorium out east of town where the neckers had thrown them.

VIII

Oliver learned more about bikes and bought another one with hard, narrow tires and a three speed gear shift. It was much easier to pedal and he took a longer paper route that went all over the east side of town. He earned more money that way. By then Oliver was buying most of his own clothes including the red Pendleton shirt he bought at Wades Clothing Store. He still keeps that shirt even though it's ragged. It cost fifteen dollars which when he bought it was a small fortune. Oliver couldn't pay for it all at once and they let him charge it even though he was just a kid. That was Oliver's first charge account.

Oliver also had a charge account at the Bendix Music Store, and when the family radio, the one with the spool legs, broke he bought his mother a new one for forty dollars which it took him a year to pay off. The radio had a laminated wood cabinet and a round dial with a magic tuning eye and sat in their living room at home. Oliver also provided all his own spending money. He felt lucky, though, for the kids who lived across the street had to give their parents the money they earned and only got a little bit back for themselves.

89

His third charge account was at Allen's Ice Cream Parlor on the east end of Main Street. He passed there every day on his paper route and would stop and get an ice cream cone or an ice cream soda if he had the money. One day near the end of the month he didn't have any money – it was Oliver's turn to worry about *the money* -- but he stopped anyway and asked Mr. Allen if he could have a glass of carbonated water free.

Mr. Allen said, "Sure, but why not something else?" Oliver said that he didn't have any money. Mr. Allen said it was OK with him if Oliver charged something, so Oliver did, and after that he had a charge account at Allen's Ice Cream Parlor, which no other kid in Walla Walla had. The adult world of indebtedness opened easily for Oliver.

IX

Oliver ate a lot of hamburgers downtown. There was a diner there, a real railroad diner up on blocks. The man who ran it would say as he served his thick, juicy burgers with tomatoes and lettuce and ketchup, "Hamburgers! The rich man's delicacy and the poor man's staple." They cost a dime. Oliver's never eaten any better.

The hamburger man was a good man and always talked to Oliver, who by then was working downtown every day after school. Oliver remembers one day when a man came in and ordered a cup of tea which came as a cup of hot water and a tea bag. When the hamburger man wasn't looking, the man took the catsup bottle and emptied most of it into his cup and poured in the hot water and began spooning it into his mouth very fast. The cook turned around and saw what was happening and got angry at the man and ordered him out of the diner.

"I can't help it," he told Oliver. "I know he's hungry, but I can't buy tomato soup for every bum that comes in here. If they don't like it, they should talk to Mr. Hoover or President Roosevelt."

Oliver didn't know what to say. The tomato ketchup man was hungry and the hamburger man had to work hard to stay in business.

---- --- ---

Oliver had another downtown friend. He was the boot black at the hotel next to the dry goods store where Oliver worked. He was the only African-American Oliver knew while he was growing up. Oliver didn't think of him as a black man or as an African-American. He thought of him as a colored man, just like his mother had taught him. Many of the people Oliver knew called them niggers, and were afraid of them because they were lazy and stole things.

Oliver's friend wasn't lazy. He worked very hard shining shoes. Oliver would come in and talk to him if there weren't any customers. The colored man had gotten out of the penitentiary and was earning enough money to go home. Oliver learned that he spoke Spanish and told him that he wanted to learn Spanish because he was going to Brazil. (Oliver didn't know they speak Portuguese there. He also had convinced himself that his mother would give him a trip to Brazil for a high school graduation present. She had said no such thing, but Oliver liked to have dreams, and didn't know then that he wouldn't be in town for his own graduation.)

One day Oliver's friend gave him an old, battered beginning Spanish text book which Oliver studied and would come in and practice saying things in Spanish. This was also because there was a beautiful Spanish woman from Roswell, New Mexico, clerking in the store where Oliver was a stock boy. Her husband was a soldier at the U.S. Army Air force base east of town. Oliver thought she was the most beautiful woman he'd ever seen and wanted to impress her by saying things to her in her own language. That was during Oliver's Junior Year, his last year in high school. Later that year Oliver went away to the army, but he remembers his Spanish teacher, and knows he was good man even if other people said he was a black ex-con and couldn't be trusted.

There were so many contradictions, so much stuff. Even though during those years Oliver was busy working and going to school, he was very sad. He couldn't understand why, but he was. It's time now to talk about Oliver's secret places full of tears.

CHAPTER TEN
SECRET PLACES FULL OF TEARS

I

Sadness was like spongy ground under Oliver's feet. It rode doubles with him on his bike when he delivered papers. It came and peered into the bedroom at night when he was home alone. It followed him everywhere; sometimes it had a focus like when Boots was killed, sometimes not.

Boots had come back to Oliver by the time they moved out on East Alder a block beyond Edison School. East Alder Street led in from the country, straight for over a mile. The farm boys came down that road fast in their trucks and jalopies, and one very bad Saturday morning, Boots was struck by a man driving farm truck. Oliver was in the yard and heard the thud and the high last yelp as Boots died. The truck never stopped, never even slowed.

Oliver carried Boots, all limp and awkward, up into the yard. No one was home besides Oliver. He sat for a long time beside Boots crying and wondering what to do. Should he wait for his mother to come home or not? Then he couldn't wait any longer and buried Boots in the alfalfa field beside the house. That evening he his mother what had happened and what he had done for Boots. She went out with him to the mound of fresh earth and they stood there and said good bye to him.

For a while Oliver's sadness had a focus, but as the mound of earth above Boots settled flat with the field and fresh alfalfa grew over it, his sadness spread thin across Oliver's life like dust sifting onto the table in the front room of the farm house. Even when the patch of new alfalfa disappeared into the old growth, Oliver was sad but didn't know why.

Oliver's mother got him another dog, an Airedale from a breeder in Seattle. The dog cost fifty dollars which Oliver was going to save up for before buying the dog, but the puppy arrived early and Oliver's mother said that there was a mistake and the bill was somehow or other already paid. Oliver didn't have to wait and save the money. They called the dog Fifty after that piece of good luck. It didn't occur to Oliver to track down the bill and make sure someone else wasn't stuck with the mistake.

He thinks now that Steve, who was another boy friend of his mother's, and very wealthy, gave her the money, but that is just a guess. Steve used to send Oliver's mother things like a ton of coal in the winter and a big fan in the summer time. The brand new Hudson Terraplane that his mother bought in 1939 on her teacher's salary was probably another of those mysterious and unexplained appearances. His mother told Oliver that Steve was a secret and Oliver understood that he was never to mention him to anyone.

Oliver was sad even after Fifty came, and dealt with his darkness the best he could. He found secret places where he could go and cry. He didn't know why he cried, but he felt better afterwards. The places were secret because big boys and men don't cry. Oliver remembered once when his grandfather cried in a movie, and Oliver's mother and grandmother sat and whispered in the back of the car on the way home.

"I hope he's not sick."

"No, he's like that sometimes."

Oliver's tears were Oliver's secret, and he cried them only in his secret places.

II

Oliver's first secret place was across the field behind the house on Whitman street. This was right in town, but there was a big field behind the house with an old apple tree on one side and two prune trees on the other and an old horse whose prick hung down to the ground. Oliver liked to draw pictures, and one day was sitting under a prune tree trying to draw the horse. He was not having any luck with the horse's jaw and shoulder. Quite unexpectedly a very pretty young woman walked through the field and saw what Oliver was doing and showed him how to get the lines right. Oliver was very embarrassed by the old horse's prick, but the woman paid no attention to it. She just showed Oliver how to draw better. Oliver never saw her again -- maybe she was just visiting -- but he remembers how kind she was and how she knew how to draw things so that they looked real.

On the far side of the field was a raspberry bramble that went all the way to another creek and completely covered a dead tree in its middle. Oliver made a hidden tunnel into all this by carefully breaking off the thorns from the lower vines and squirming in on his stomach. He made a couple of sharp turns in the tunnel so that if anyone chased him and went straight ahead they would get badly stuck. At the foot of the dead tree was a little open space where Oliver spent a lot of time sitting and thinking. That was his first secret place full of tears.

III

Oliver became independent when they moved out on East Alder. By then he had his three-speed bike with the small tires. They lived on the very edge of town, with an alfalfa field right next door and Mill Creek just a block away across the alfalfa. The first mile of East Alder beyond the city limits had one story frame houses scattered here and there along it. Now days they would be mobile homes. There was usually a pickup truck parked in the driveway and penned up chickens or horses tethered in a field. Maybe out back an old refrigerator skirted with weeds.

Another mile and the paved road turned south. If Oliver pedaled straight ahead, the dirt track petered out into a rutted farm lane. This led to the Scout Bluffs where a branch of Mill Creek swung in close to a high hill made entirely of wind blown loess. The stream had cut steep cliffs fifty to a hundred feet high in the loess. There were easy trails and difficult trails up the bluffs and lots of willows and locust trees massed at the bottom. Up on top the surface was plowed and planted in wheat fields that sloped away for miles to a valley at the foot of the Blue Mountains.

One time a farmer was on his tractor out there plowing when a stray fifty caliber machine gun slug from the Air Force firing range to the north came along and hit him. He wasn't killed but he had to go to the hospital. Another time and on another farm a tractor tipped over on its driver. The motor kept running and the engine was in gear and the wheels rubbed the farmer to death. Those were the same fields that Oliver ran down, his steps getting farther and farther apart until he couldn't stop and spilled into the soft dirt. Oliver went to the Scout bluffs by himself, and little by little got up nerve to climb the steep trails and to throw himself down the slopes gouging his own path in the soft earth.

IV

On the way to the bluffs, if Oliver took another farm track he came to an abandoned orchard. That was where he once was treed by a huge sow. Oliver was lucky to get up the tree because the pig could have easily killed him. Oliver's new dog was with him. Fifty ran around and around the sow while Oliver was getting up in the tree, and after a while Fifty nipped the sow's leg and she chased him. Later Fifty came back by himself very proud of saving his master, which he did.

Beyond the orchard was a dense thicket where Oliver made a place to hide his bike so nobody could see it. Oliver would crawl even farther into the bushes and sit there and cry. He used to cry a lot but always so nobody ever found out. Oliver became really sad from the Fifth grade on when he finally could be truly alone. He has some ideas now why he cried so much, but back then he just wanted to cry, so he did.

Once he was sitting in the thicket crying when he heard a rustle and looked around and there was a big porcupine just looking at him. Now there is that story -- Oliver thinks it's *The Secret Garden* where the little girl is crying, and a porcupine says to her, "Don't waste all that salt." Well, Oliver was crying and this was a real porcupine but it didn't say anything, and after a while it waddled slowly away. Porcupines don't have to rush anywhere for anyone. Skunks don't rush either, but porcupines are more thoughtful about it all. Having a friendly porcupine to share tears with made Oliver feel better.

V

Oliver's most secret place was out in the country beyond the turn off to the Scout Bluffs. There was a high hill, and from the top of it he could see all the way to the Horse Heaven Hills west of the Columbia River thirty miles away. On really clear days he could see Mt. Adams sticking up at sunset over two hundred miles away. The hill was lovely and deserted. Oliver could hear the wind far off, or was it the soft whickering ghosts of Indian ponies? Now there are big suburban ranch houses sitting there with lawns and cars and RVs parked in front.

When Oliver was a kid, though, there wasn't anything on the hill except wheat and dirt and he could go way down to its foot where another stream had cut a deep, deep gully through the loess. It was twenty, maybe thirty feet deep in places, filled with all kinds of trees and bushes. There were a couple of places Oliver could get down into the ravine, and once there he could half wade, half scramble along the creek bed to some really neat places where the shadows were green and the sun came through little chinks in the leaves up above and little gnats would circle up and up the shaft of light and then drop right straight down and do it all over again. There were even tiny fish in the riffles of the stream and if he ran his hands along the banks just under the water he could find holes which crawdads dig. Oliver didn't mind getting his fingers pinched and pulled them out and looked at them. But he always put them back in their homes, and didn't find out about eating them until many years later in New Orleans.

Even though Oliver cried there in the gully, the nice thing about that place was that it was so deep and greeny dark and peaceful that after a while he didn't feel like crying any more and could get on his bike and go back to town trying to think up some excuse to tell his mother about why he was wet up to his hips and covered with mud which she wouldn't believe anyway.

VI

When Oliver came back from the army some one asked him, "Weren't you ever homesick?"

Without hesitation, without thinking about his answer, he replied, "No, I had a foot locker and a bunk of my own."

After the army, Oliver never cried again without knowing why he was crying, but that is another story.

CHAPTER ELEVEN
WEEDS, PLANTS, AND PEAS

Weed n. 1. Any common, unsightly, or troublesome plant that grows ...on cultivated ground. 3. Any worthless animal or thing. --- v.t. 3. To remove (anything regarded as harmful or undesirable): with out. Standard College Dictionary (Harcourt Brace & World, 1963).

--- --- ---

In the beginning was rock and water, energy and air. All necessary but inedible. Vegetation transposes that primordial stuff. Oliver's first playground was a field of wheat. Then brambles by pastures, bicycling to bush havens. Oliver grew up green. Let there be weeds!

Plants defined Walla Walla: weeds and wheat and peas, and asparagus on the truck farms west of town. But where were the *Walla Walla Sweets*? Fifty years later, wonderful sweet onions, better than Vidalia Onions, fill valley fields. Were they there when Oliver was young? He doesn't know. And grapes and fine wine! Half a century ago no grapes grew near Walla Walla. Now, some of the best wines in the United States come from the hills outside of town, and west around Pasco are the vineyards of St. Michele and Columbia Crest wineries. Grapes, nourished by water from Columbia River reservoirs, vintify the desert where once sage brush grew.

When Oliver was young, the only wine Oliver heard about was the "Dago Red" that the winos drank on lower Main Street. (Yes, Oliver knows that "Dago" is not PC, and probably 'wino" isn't either. There was even a time when "Lower Main Street" wasn't PC to mention. But does that matter to a weed child?)

I

So begin with the weeds.

Indian Tobacco: Not really tobacco, but in the fence rows between the fields reared up long spikes covered with crumbly brown seed that looked like tobacco to small boys in search of forbidden adventure. Oliver and his friends lighted it in little rolls of news paper, but puffed in vain for any intoxicating, forbidden fumes.

The men in Walla Walla smoked real tobacco. Most of the farmers and cowboys rolled their own using sacks of Bull Durham and cigarette papers. Some show-offs made cigarettes one handed. Oliver's grandfather used a little machine that held a bit of tobacco and a paper and when you pulled the lever out came a cigarette. Sometimes he let Oliver roll cigarettes for him. But smoking cigarettes wasn't important to Oliver. Maybe he hadn't seen enough advertising, No TV. On the other hand, his mother smoked, which Oliver hated. He argued with her, telling her to stop because it made her smell bad, but she wouldn't. Many years later she died from emphysema in a hospital in Seattle, but that is another story.

Nettles: Weed magic; if Oliver held his breath when he handled nettles they didn't sting.

Water cress. Great mounds growing along the stream behind the house on Whitman Street. Oliver munched on it for its peppery taste. His mother knew it was there for the taking, but never used it in salads. Salads were a quarter of a head lettuce with bottled Thousand Island on top. Oliver also ate nasturtium leaves which taste like cress, but were flowers and shouldn't be eaten.

Clumps of grass. Grab a bunch, pull it up and heft the heavy dirt clod held together by the roots. Oliver would swing the clod by its grassy tail. When he let the missile go it arched high in the air and came down with a satisfying thump. The kids used to have grass clod fights; it was considered unfair to use rocks. Just *thump, thump,* go home dirty.

II

If ferns are weeds, ferns should come next, but in order to talk about ferns, the pea fields must come first. When Oliver was eleven, his mother and sister got summer jobs working as book keeper and as a kitchen aide for Sam, a friend who farmed peas in fields high in the Blue Mountains east of Waitsburg. Sam had originally farmed wheat up there on rented land, but peas paid more. His own ranch was outside of Walla Walla. Oliver's mother had met Sam at Red Cross preparedness meetings held because of the war. All the farmers were short handed that summer, so the women's help was welcome during the three weeks that the mountain fields were being harvested.

The pea fields, scattered through the woods, were planted on defunct natural pastures, which like natural forest and alpine pastures all over the American west, are full of ferns or skunk cabbage as a result of over grazing, grazing fostered by the greed of people who run too many cattle on government land, and encouraged by Forest Service officials educated in university Departments of Forestry dominated by Business School ethics.

Back to our story. Sam, the women and Oliver, and the cook, lived in an abandoned farm house across the county road from the biggest of the fields. The house still had glass in its windows, old bluish glass with little bubbles in it. The wood on the porch side of the house, which faced the road and was exposed to the north winds, was silvery gray. Trees scraped the back of the building and bushes leaned against the rear door until the cook cut them away. The wood on the back side was brown and peeling and splintered, but the rooms inside were still usable after a good sweeping. The cook got the wood stove going. For a bathroom everybody used the two-seater in a little house out back, each time carefully pouring a tin can of wood ashes down the hole for sanitary purposes.

The men who drove the trucks and Caterpillar Tractors, who ran the swathers, the loaders, and the viners, slept in a barn converted into a bunk house by the addition of rickety wash stands and beds made from 2 X 4s and ply wood. It was rough living but only for three weeks and the pay was good.

All the scut work was done by migrant Mexican laborers hired from a labor camp at the foot of the mountains. They were brought to the fields jammed into open trucks, in two shifts, one arriving at six o'clock in the morning and the other at six in the evening. When the peas started ripening work went on day and night, before the peas got over-ripe and tough.

Commercial peas for canning grow on bushy vines that lie along the ground. The problem is to get the pods off the vines and the peas out of the pods. A harvesting machine called a *swather* is pulled along the rows by a Caterpillar Tractor. The swather cuts off the vines and piles them in windrows which are then picked up by a *loade*r which dumps them in open trucks. The trucks haul the piles of vines to the *viner,* a stationary, box-like piece of equipment into which the vines, pods and all, are dumped, pitch fork load by pitch fork load. The Mexican laborers did that. The viner removes the pods from the vines, shells the peas, and spits them into lug boxes which the Mexicans working for Sam loaded onto waiting trucks. When a truck was fully stacked with lug boxes it drove off to the pea cannery, racing to get there before the peas steamed in their own heat and turned sour, which is another story, still to come.

The thoroughly smashed vines and empty pods were ejected on the other side of the viner, and pitch forked into trucks which took them away to be used as fodder. The steaming mess went sour immediately and the stench wafting behind moving pea vine trucks was unbelievably awful. Nobody wanted to be stuck behind a peavine truck on a narrow road! That foul odor was the sign of summer harvest in full swing, as sure as wheat stubble burning on the hills marked the arrival of autumn.

III

Mountain life was more than peas. It was flavored by the people who farmed and worked there. One day Sam and the others were sitting on the front porch of the farm house letting lunch settle before going back to work. Far off across the road at the top of a distant pea field, two figures appeared. Sam said they were scouts from another cannery, not the one to which he sold his peas. They were there to look at his peas and see if they were ripe. Sam felt that his territory was being invaded. He went and got his 30.06 rifle and sat there in his chair and put three shots around the feet of the two scouts. They were at least half a mile away, but they took the hint and disappeared over the crest of the hill. They weren't seen again that summer.

Another evening in the deep violet dusk Sam shot a deer with his 22, one clean shot and it was down. Sam said, "It's not hunting season, but they eat my peas, so it's a fair trade." Next day, venison for dinner.

One morning the labor camp truck stopped by the farm house. The driver wanted to know where to deliver his crew. The day and night shifts of Mexicans brought their own lunches which were provided by the labor camp. A paper lunch bag fell off the truck. Sam said, "Let's see what they give them to eat," and walked over and picked it up.

Inside was a withered orange and two slices of stale bread spread with rancid margarine. That was all. Sam was furious and started looking through the other bags. They were all the same. He stomped inside the farm house, brought out the cook and said, "I want you everyday, twice a day, morning and night, to make a big kettle of meat stew for the workers." He showed the paper bag to the cook, who looked in it, made a face and grunted, and nodded yes. After that, as long as they worked for Sam, the Mexicans ate at least one square meal a day. Sam was a good man.

IV

And now, Oliver and the ferns.

Oliver had no job during pea harvest, and nothing to do. He spent his time roaming the woods that stretched out behind the cabin. No one but Oliver went there. Everywhere in the glades and abandoned pastures the ferns were waist high, and in wet places they were taller than Oliver. Oliver loved the ferns. He took off his clothes and ran naked through those fragile jungles. Their filigree printed lacy tattoos on his body. The rust colored powder on the fronds stained his skin Redskin red. The fronds whipped him as he ran, and he would get a heart on. Then he would sink into the deep shadows. Those places weren't places to cry. Getting a *heart on* was something very special which Oliver will tell about in the next chapter.

V

Wheat, a plant, not a weed. Wheat was the yellow amniotic rustle of security when Oliver was little and wandered the fields surrounding the chicken ranch.

VI

Oliver was growing up, and plants soon meant more to him than weeds. Plants meant money. If mowing lawns counts, Kentucky blue grass was Oliver's first source of plant income. He had failed at picking strawberries. The farmer out towards Kooskooskie assigned picked-over rows to kids like Oliver, and reserved the fresh, berry full ones for professional, migrant workers. That was hard on Oliver but probably fair. He wasn't buying groceries with what he earned.

Asparagus came next. There was the chicken ranch asparagus when he lived on the farm, but Oliver didn't know about money then, except for *the money*. Asparagus and money came together when Oliver was a Junior in high school. He had made friends by then, friends he has yet to tell about. One friend knew an Italian truck gardener, and got Oliver and his buddies jobs cutting asparagus early in the morning before they went to school.

The truck gardener drove into town before sunup, and they all would climb on the back of his flat bed truck and go out to his farm. They learned to cut the asparagus with long narrow knives, notched on the tips, which they thrust into the ground in order to cut the asparagus stalk below the surface. Oliver learned to grab the cut stalk in his left hand and scuttle, all bent over, to the next spike. When he accumulated a handful he placed it beside the row and started another handful. Another worker moved up and down the rows putting the cut bundles in boxes and taking the full boxes to a waiting truck.

Cutting asparagus is *stoop labor*, one of the hardest jobs in the world. After five minutes your back feels as if it is going to break. Being young and supple doesn't help. You hurt and keep on hurting. Oliver and his friends cut and scuttled in the dust every morning until seven o'clock. Then they would be paid and get back on the flat bed truck. On their way into town the farmer gave each of them a cold beer which really tasted good, all bitter. When your throat is coated with dust it helps to drink a beer, and tastes even better when you come to school all dusty and smelling of beer. None of the teachers seemed to notice, which may be part of attending high school in a farm town.

--- --- ---

And peas, the first source of wealth for Oliver. Canning peas at the pea cannery meant money, lots of money. That story is still to come.

CHAPTER TWELVE
GENDER INCOGNITA

I

Oliver cautions the reader not to expect hot and lusty at this point. Oliver was a wheat field kid who first had to learn about playmates. This chapter is about girls and sex as Oliver first experienced those mysteries. All the exciting stuff came later in his life, and this chapter may be skipped if the reader chooses.

Girls were around before sex became the question. They simply were there. It wasn't like those cute movies where Spankie says, "Ahhh girlzz!" Not at all. There were no other girls or boys out in the wheat field where he played alone. In the first grade at Saint Patrick's the girls sat on one side of the room, the boys on the other. At recess the girls were magically disappeared. The nuns were careful to keep temptation at bay -- who knows what pale cave-fish swam within their midnight robes?

Oliver didn't really notice girls until the second grade, and then they were simply different. Mrs. Green, the Second grade teacher at Sharpstein, kept such a tight rein on her charges that nothing happened in her class. She was a spinster, one of the harem eunuchs of the school, a guardian of blossoms yet to flower.

At recess the girls played in the yard on the south side of the building, boys on the north. When the lines formed to come in from play the boys and girls seemed to be two different species, like those African herds with all the different animals grazing side by side, the boys zebras and the girls gazelles.

Oliver believes that in those early years *gender defined by sex* was an idea imposed on little kids by grown ups. Of course, boys and girls did interact and things sometimes happened. There was the time that Johnny, another Third grader, did something strange. Oliver was part of a giggle of third graders on their way home. Johnny was with them. He was different from the others and had difficulty keeping up in the reading class. He was bigger too. That was because he had been held back twice. Johnny was shambling along with the group when suddenly he pushed one of the little girls onto the grass and pulled her panties down. He looked at her privates – Oliver remembered that that was what his grandmother called those places between your legs -- and touched them and then stood up. The other kids gathered in a mute circle and did nothing. They were more curious than shocked. The girl got to her feet, smoothed down her skirt, sniffled once, and then tagged along with the group as the kids straggled home. She never said anything to her parents. The other children whispered that Johnny was a bully, but no one thought what he did was sexual, just mean.

Oliver had one friend in the Third grade who was a girl. Her name was Janet; she sat across the aisle from Oliver at the back of the room. In the third grade girls were generally bigger than the boys, and Oliver was small for his age. Janet towered over him, but she was friendly and thoughtful and didn't tease him like some of the other kids did. It wasn't that Janet and Oliver ever said much to each other, but Oliver really liked her. He still does though he hasn't seen her since the Eighth grade when suddenly to his surprise he was taller than she was. Life was simpler then.

II

The Fifth grade is when it all seemed to happen. At that time, body functions became important. Of course, there was shitting, which before then had been "going moochee" as Oliver's mother called it, or "kaakaa" according to his grandmother. They made up special names for anything that wasn't nice. Since shitting was done near your privates and since you peed out of your weenie which kept getting stiff, it was natural that Oliver and his playmates were confused.

Then there was masturbating, which was called either "beating your meat " or "jacking off." Oliver called it jacking off when he found out about it -- it took years for him to discover that it was masturbation, and more years to find out it was OK, that it didn't make you feeble minded and give you pimples or grow hair on the palms of your hands.

Fucking was the third thing. Oliver and his friends didn't do that. They weren't even sure what it was. Big boys fucked girls. Now when Oliver thinks back, he feels they really didn't, or not nearly as much as they said they did. Maybe sometimes. There was that girl in high school who took a mid-term trip, some people said to Switzerland. Her parents were wealthy and Oliver really envied her having such a swell vacation.

Fucking seemed to Oliver and his friends to be different from making love which grown ups did, like when Oliver's sister said to her friend Amy, once when he was listening though he wasn't supposed to, "Did you see the way Clark Gable made love to her!"

Oliver had been to that movie, too, and making love as far as he could tell was hugging some one and kissing them on the mouth.

III

The first thing that happened to Oliver, along with the other guys he played with, was getting a *heart on*. That's the way they heard it said, not getting a *hard on*. Later in the eighth grade, Oliver was set straight on this by a classmate who had an older brother who knew about such things. Oliver was very embarrassed when he got corrected.

Anyway, they got hearts on frequently. Once Oliver and Alan who lived in the next block, and Alan's little brother, Bobby, rode their bikes out to the Whitman Memorial which was on a hill west of town. There wasn't anything there at that time except a stone marker, not like now when it is a National Monument with exhibits and paths that you are not supposed to step off. They went out there expecting to find arrowheads and maybe pieces of skeleton or something, but they didn't. They got tired of searching for "artifacts" as Oliver called them, and went to a small creek nearby and found a bushy place by a pool and took off all their clothes. It was dusty beside the water, the same dust that was everywhere and Oliver lay down on his back and heaped dust on his stomach. His heart on stuck up through the dust, and Alan lay down and he also had a heart on. Alan said to Bobby "Jack me off."

Bobby didn't know what that was so Alan showed him, and he did it to Alan and then to Oliver. That was not being gay, and not being dirty. That was being uninformed and experimenting and that was the only time it happened. Oliver remembers that it felt good and his stuff squirted onto the dust. Afterwards, they got into the pool and washed off and got dressed and rode back into town. That wasn't exactly sex because they had no clear idea what sex was.

Oh yes, Oliver also took a shit and Alan and Bobby got down and watched and Oliver asked, "What does it look like?" And they said it sort of pushed the skin around his ass hole out puffy for a minute. They weren't sure whether or not shitting had something to do with sex. Which maybe it does, but not for little kids and not for most grown ups either. It became clear to Oliver and his friends that shitting and jacking off and sex were all kind of dirty but they still couldn't leave jacking off alone. Or at least Oliver couldn't, though he didn't tell the others how much he did it. He got into the habit whenever things went wrong which was quite often.

IV

There was one time on East Alder before Oliver had a room of his own in the basement. His mother had been out late, and he had been jacking off into one of his socks. He was in the upper bunk in the bedroom he shared with her. At that time, they had bunk beds. She slept in the lower one and he had the upper one. His sister had a room of her own at the back of the house. When Oliver finished, he fell asleep without getting under the covers. When his mother came home, there he was on the bed, naked. Oliver has a big hole in his memory at that point so he doesn't know what happened next. Maybe that was why a short time later George, his mother's boy friend, built him a room in the basement out of wall board and two by fours.

Oliver liked having a room of his own. He liked it even though there was the time when his mother forgot to pull the plug in the deep laundry sink on the wall next to his room. There were some clothes soaking in it, and his mother asked Oliver to go downstairs and let the water out of the tub. Meanwhile, she had put out Warfarin which kills rats by making them terribly thirsty. The water was murky -- the load held Oliver's clothes which as usual were muddy -- and when he reached into the water he grabbed a drowned rat. He still remembers how its slimy tail felt slipping through his fingers. The drowned rat didn't have anything to do about sex, but it was part of having a room in the basement.

V

Oliver read a lot and found a very technical book hidden in his sister's closet. The book was about women's sex and had cross section views of the female breast and the uterus which was how Oliver found out about those female things. But there weren't any views of the prick or weenie, and nothing in the book about getting a heart on.

The next thing Oliver did to learn about sex was to look up words in the unabridged dictionary at school. That didn't help much. Naturally, sex was never discussed by his mother or grandmother or sister, or his teachers. Later on Oliver learned a lot more about sex from older guys who called it fucking.

Sex still didn't make much sense until Oliver was a Junior in High School and fell in love. The girl's name was Molly; she was a Senior, a year ahead of him. Oliver loved her and by then thought that fucking was what you did when you loved some one. But sometimes when you didn't. He had thought a lot about making love to Molly, but Oliver was very shy and didn't even know how to talk to her. What he did was give her presents. This was possible because Oliver worked down town and knew a lot about the stores and where to find scarce things.

By then the War was on, and there was rationing and there weren't supposed to be any luxury goods, but Oliver found some nylon stockings in the Bee Hive, the store where he worked, and gave them to Molly. He also went to Bendix's Music Store on Main Street and found a record of Glenn Miller playing *Moonlight Serenade* which Molly said she liked. He gave the record to her, even though he knew Molly dated only Seniors and guys from Whitman College, or at least that is what Oliver thought because he never asked her for a date until he came back on leave from Basic Training on his way to Japan.

Being in the army made you equal to being at least a freshman in college. So Oliver got up his nerve and dated Molly once and had his first kiss which wasn't nearly as romantic as he thought it should be. Then Oliver hugged Molly and felt very awkward even though hugging her was special. He can still remember the surprising combination of soft, warm, sweet smelling Molly, his first grown up hug.

Oliver left for Japan feeling confused because the two of them didn't fuck, didn't even get close to fucking, and by then a lot of the guys were bragging that they were doing it regularly with the prettiest girls in the high school. He didn't know whether to believe them, or not, but Oliver is glad that his and Molly's relationship was exactly what it was.

VI

There wasn't much opportunity for a kid to be exposed to sex in Walla Walla. Oliver's talking about normal times and not about what happened there when he was away in the army. That was different. What he means is that there weren't X-rated movies and stuff like that. Of course, there was the theater that opened over by the Elks' Club south of Main Street which showed only two films before it was closed down. one of Those films was *The Outlaw* with Jane Russell who had very big breasts. She was a girl friend of Howard Hughes who paid to have the film made. It was 1943 and breasts were real sex.

Oliver called breasts *boolahgs* because once when he was very young he had wandered into the bedroom when his mother was half dressed and said "What are those?" And she said, "They are *boolahgs*." Later in high school Oliver told his special friends about that word because by then everyone knew they were BREASTS. They thought it was very funny and made up a call. One guy would shout "Daahh Booolaahgs!!" and the rest of his friends, including Oliver, would shout back "Ng Gha Ng Gha Nung," which didn't make any sense, but to them it did and was hilariously funny.

Back to Jane Russell. Oliver didn't get to see that movie because you had to be eighteen. Oliver also didn't get to see *The Birth of a Baby* which was all about a baby being born. Why that should be considered reason to close down a theater wasn't clear to Oliver, but the theater was closed down. It must be because back then having babies was dirty.

VII

Oliver's last year in high school was his Junior year and some of his friends graduated and pledged a fraternity at Whitman College. One of the special events the fraternity had for its pledges was a talk on sex by a medical doctor. His friends sneaked Oliver in. He was very surprised when the doctor referred to that part of a girl as a *dirty cunt* which Oliver didn't think was the way a doctor should talk not even to fraternity brothers. Oliver is still surprised. It pleases him that after he and his friends returned from the army they never pledged that or any other fraternity.

--- --- ---

So that was what sex and girls were all about until much later, only part of which belongs in this story.

CHAPTER THIRTEEN
GEORGE, WHO TAUGHT OLIVER
TO DOFF HIS HAT TO A LADY

When Oliver was growing up, Walla Walla had a population of 15,000 people, real gritty people. In those days, cowboys met farmers on its streets, bankers and businessmen made fortunes, and lost them, sometimes when the price of wheat fell, sometimes at card tables in the back rooms of respectable stores. Even then, migrant laborers came up from Mexico at harvest time, and drifters struggling through the Great Depression wandered in. And always there were itinerant roustabouts and farm hands.

Those were the men fatherless Oliver grew up around. Weathered men, ready to drink up their week's wages, ready for a fight, men who took off their hats in the presence of a lady, and would do business on a hand shake. They were part of Oliver's Walla Walla. That's why he wants to tell about them. George was the one Oliver knew best.

I

George, was Oliver's mother's boy friend. Oliver learned a lot from him about growing up in the west and just plain growing up. George was born and raised in a cabin somewhere in the hills behind Bozeman, Montana. One room, four children, two boys, two girls, their mother. George never mentioned his father. The winter of 1916 was bad, not enough food in the cabin. George was twelve.

His mother said, "George, you're the oldest, you have to leave."

George understood. His mother loved him but he was the oldest and he had to leave. He rode a freight down to Bozeman and worked two years during World War I breaking mules at two bits a head for the U.S. Army. He sent money home to help.

II

Oliver never learned how George got to Walla Walla. He came into Oliver's life, we should say Oliver's mother's life, during World War II. George was a tall man with most of his height in his torso. He had powerful shoulders and arms, a thick, muscled neck. His Levis rode low on his small hips. His legs weren't particularly long, but long enough to sit any horse alive. He had bright blue eyes and a thin nose with a decided twist to it he had gotten falling off a mule. He had tried to set it himself, but what does a twelve year old know about setting broken noses?

George spoke slowly as though he sampled each word before sharing it. He never swore in Oliver's presence, but Oliver thinks he knew how to. He was always kind to Oliver in his own way. He had never married and had no children that Oliver knew of. George was civilian Fire Chief at the U.S. Army Air Force base outside of town when he came into Oliver's life. Oliver doesn't know how his mother met him. It was probably at the Log Cabin Inn out near the air base. She went there sometimes for a drink. Oliver remembers once she and his sister and he were driving around and pulled in there. Oliver's sister was big and looked older than eighteen, so they went in to the Inn for a drink. Oliver had to sit in the car. Thirteen was too young and Oliver looked about ten.

III

Anyway, George showed up in Oliver's life. He was an honest to God cowboy. He rolled when he walked and had slightly bowed legs though they didn't show because he was well over six feet tall and big all the way up. He seemed gentle, was always good to Oliver. At that time, as Oliver has already said, Oliver and his mother shared double-decker bunks. Oliver's sister had the back bedroom to herself. That arrangement disturbed George. That's why he made Oliver a room in the basement.

George seemed gentle but he had a streak. One time he and Oliver's mother and Oliver were going to go to a movie at the Liberty Theater on upper main street. There was a good parking place just up the street in front of Jensen's department store. George had drawn up alongside it to parallel park when a car with four older teen agers whipped into it from behind. They were laughing. George got out of the car and walked back to them. All four got out of the car in a "what are you going to do about it?" manner. They spoke for a moment, Oliver was craning his head looking around backwards at it all, his mother was sitting very still looking straight ahead. Without warning George knocked two of the four down. They had trouble getting up. The other two just stood there. George came back and got into the car.

"I think we should go to the movie in Pendleton," he said. And that is what they did. Oliver's mother never mentioned what happened that evening. Oliver is certain George never hit her. If he had, she would have dropped him like a hot potato.

Maybe George just had different standards. The Code of the West was still working for people like him. If he were around today and was in a restaurant and there was some dude wearing a big Stetson while he ate, George would walk over and say, "Excuse me, sir, but there are ladies present. Take off your hat when you're inside."

Oliver is certain the dude would do what George said.

IV

Oliver saw the streak another time. His sister had quit college up at Pullman and had gone to work for Smith, Hoffman and Wright, contractors over at Hanford, where nobody knew what was going on. Fifty years later, it was announced that the AEC released radioactive iodine into the air to see where it would go and what would happen. Oliver hopes that was after he left Walla Walla which was down wind from Hanford. The tumble weeds over there are still radioactive.

Oliver's sister was eighteen and while in Hanford met up with some fast talking guy who was not nice. She was naive and he was good looking and they got involved and he wouldn't leave her alone. She came home to Walla Walla one weekend. She was very worried and for the first time confided in Oliver. The creep was coming to visit her. He wanted to meet their mother. He wanted to marry Oliver's sister. She was desperate.

Oliver thought about it and said, "Let's ask George," which they did. His sister telephoned George at work and explained it all. George said, "When he comes over this Saturday I will take your mother out to dinner, but I'll be there when he shows up. You," he said to her, "keep your mother busy in your bedroom when you see him coming."

That's what happened. George showed up early. The man came by taxi and started up the front walk. Oliver's sister got his mother in the back bedroom. George said to Oliver, "You come with me, Oliver; I want you to see this."

The guy knocked on the door. George opened it instantly and stepped outside grabbing the guy by the shirt and jacket collar, pulling him up close and then shifting his grip to the back of the guy's collar and the seat of his pants. George whirled him around and frog marched him down the walk to his car. "Come on along," he called to Oliver, and Oliver got in the back seat of George's car. George pushed the guy into the front seat; the guy was petrified. He wasn't small but George was huge. George told him to shut up and sit still. They drove way out into the country among the rolling wheat hills of the Palouse. In a remote spot George stopped the car and went around and pulled the guy out.

"You leave her alone and don't ever," and he emphasized the ever, "come back!"

George hit the him once so that he cart wheeled backward into the ditch with the dry Palouse dust coming up like a little explosion, making the guy all gray and powdery as he lay there. George got back in the car and Oliver and he drove back to the house. He talked about taking Oliver fishing on the Snake River sometime. When they got back, George took Oliver's mother out to dinner. His sister never saw the guy again, not even back at Hanford.

V

Oliver was thirteen by that time and George would come to the house to pick up his mother and while she was in the bedroom "fixing her face" he would pull a pint of whiskey out of his pocket and say, "How about a drink Oliver?"

He would give Oliver a shot in a drinking glass, and Oliver felt it was important not to let on that he didn't like it and would take it straight and in one gulp like medicine, which made him sleepy. That was probably what George had in mind.

George did take Oliver fishing up on the Snake River at a place he knew. They didn't catch anything but it was interesting. They left very early in the morning to get there and ate breakfast at Lutcher's Saloon on lower Main Street. Oliver had pancakes and George ordered him coffee which Oliver had never tasted and didn't touch which puzzled George, but he didn't make Oliver drink it.

VI

On the way to go fishing, George told Oliver how he and his brother and the family got back together after World War I. "Me and my brother, Bob, we always fought, and I always won being older and bigger. Then, one day, all of a sudden Bob was grown up, and our mother had gone to town, and we fought one last time. Broke all the furniture and almost everything else in the house." George laughed real hard and then pulled out a handkerchief and blew his nose. "Mother made us pay for it. Ever since then me and Bob have been as close as two brothers can be."

Bob was a Highway Patrol officer and dated Oliver's mother until George got interested and because that was the way it was, Bob stopped dating her, although they all stayed good friends.

VII

The Air Force was training pilots at Walla Walla, mostly in B-17s, but also some B-24s. Flying Box Cars they called them. The B-24s weren't as safe as the B-17s. Maybe once a week one of the planes would crash. Sometimes the crews bailed out, sometimes they skidded onto the landing strip and George would put out the fire driving his rig into the flames and spraying foam every where. But sometimes they ran into the Blue Mountains to the east, particularly before the government put a long string of lights up there so the inexperienced pilots would know they were headed for trouble.

One evening George -- remember, he was the Fire Chief at the air base -- was at Oliver's house and the telephone rang. A B-24 had crashed just outside of town. George left immediately and said, "Come on along Oliver." When they got to the crash site there was wreckage everywhere. It was still burning and Oliver followed behind George as he directed the cleanup and they hunted for bodies. Oliver found one chunk which was a rib cage. It was still burning and sputtering. George led Oliver away from it, but it was so totally not a human that it never really bothered Oliver. It seemed to Oliver just like the top of the baby Indian's skull which Dr. Campbell gave him for his museum. That little cap of bone didn't seem like part of a real human until many years later. By then Oliver had lost it somewhere along the way. If he had it now he would bury it in a quiet place way out in the country.

VIII

George bought a ranch east of town out towards Kooskooskie. It was a fairly big spread with maybe fifty cows and pasture which he could run when he wasn't fighting fires at the air base. Oliver loved to go out there. George had a big stallion, ungelded, that had killed a man. The previous owners were going to shoot it but George bought it for the cost of the meat.

That horse loved George. Oliver remembers how he and George stood at the edge of the pasture and George whistled through his fingers. The stallion lifted its head and snorted and came racing. George stepped out into the field and stood there, grass to his knees, the harness in his hands, waiting. The stallion plunged in front of George and reared over him, its front feet churning. George reached up and gentled it down and slipped in the bit. Then he cinched on the saddle and the man and the animal became one galloping around and around the field with Oliver watching from behind the fence. George rode very tall with his elbows akimbo. You couldn't slip a playing card between George's seat and the saddle. He was gentle and kind to animals.

IX

George called Oliver one day.

"Oliver, my cows have broken out of the pasture and are running loose on the Kooskooskie Road. We've got a problem here at the base, and I can't get free. Will you ride your bike out there and herd them back to my place?"

Oliver said yes, and pedaled five miles as fast as he could until he found the cows. He got behind them and shouted and waved his coat and got them going in the right direction. But then the herd came to a T-intersection with the leg of the T heading up to the mountains. Half the herd split off that direction. When Oliver went to head it off, the rest of the herd wandered back the way they'd come. For two hours Oliver ran back and forth, shooing the cows first one way and then the other, but he couldn't keep them together. Oliver was exhausted and desperate, when over the hill came George on his stallion. It took him about two minutes to get the herd together headed in the right direction.

"Thank you, Oliver, you really helped me." That was enough. Oliver grinned all the way back home. He had paid for his room.

X

After Oliver returned from the army his mother married Bill. Oliver doesn't know why she didn't marry George. A lot of men around Walla Walla kept bulls. More than one, like Mr. Roberts who ran the service station, were killed showing off their animals. Years ago, the last time Oliver heard about George, he had been gored by a bull.

CHAPTER FOURTEEN
TOWN CHARACTERS AND OLD TIMERS

The Walla Walla Oliver knew when he was young was a wheat and cow town in the remote southeastern corner of a remote northwestern state. Or at least the town and the state were remote when he grew up there. Perhaps Whitman college and its conservatory made a difference, but its campus was only a place he pedaled by on his way home from work, its museum a place to visit once or twice a year, an auditorium where his mother sometimes sang. Its faculty were another species whom he never met. The men who influenced Oliver were a different breed.

Walla Walla lies between a cool mid-latitude desert to the west and the forested Blue Mountains to the east. To the north, the rolling Palouse Hills yield bumper crops of wheat and peas. To the south around Pendleton, the higher, drier country is better for grazing cattle. The valley land to the west supported truck farms, mostly run by Italians. Walla Walla prospered for a while as a supply point for a small gold rush in Idaho, but the gold petered out. Later on, after the Indian Wars, an army post west of town became the Veterans TB Hospital. There were still a few prospectors who came into town, old desert rats, hunting for a grub stake, and a few others like the Old Timer who told Oliver about the frontier.

I

The Old Timers by now have all bought the farm, nor does the city any longer have any characters. No characters? How can that be? In his off days Oliver gets curmudgeonly and says that it's the media's fault. Radio was regional when he was young, with gentle imports such as "Portia Faces Life," "Fibber McGee and Molly," "The Adventures of Lorenzo Jones and His Wife Bell," and the "Jack Benny Show." Of course, "Amos and Andy" were white men in black-face -- or should we say, "black voice," for they were heard but never seen? And Benny's Rochester was that happy, caring, Uncle Tom, Oliver's grownups all used as an alibi. But Oliver, way back when, was innocent. To him, that was just the way the radio world was, a magic pathway out.

Stations were low powered and no satellite or cable links existed. Television was a futuristic idea hinted at in *Popular Mechanics* magazine. There were no lurid tabloids for sale at grocery store check out counters, and "movie magazines" satisfied any teen age lust for news of fame and scandal.

It's different now. As the millennium expands before us, publications like *People* and *Entertainment* specialize in personalities. Here today, gone today. Talk shows and daytime serials, news bytes, NPR and CNN, bring a processed view of the world into every house. Entertainers with real lives and real talents are replaced with media clones like "survivor shows" which provide the overfed and indolent with effortless adventure.

More than 50,000 CD titles are produced each year. TV viewers may choose from over a hundred channels. The younger population, mobilized by a super highway system and two hundred million automobiles, sloshes back and forth from coast to coast like water in a bucket, while the retired survivors, mired up to their axles in the American Dream, sit in Sun City and watch life go by.

Just as American pop culture won the Cold War long before the Berlin Wall fell, the current rainbow influx of immigrants is rapidly melding into a common feeding frenzy of consumption scarcely leavened by race, ethnicity, or personal character. The homogenization of America through surfeit proceeds full tilt.

II

In a town as small as Walla Walla when Oliver was young, everybody thought they knew everybody. Actually they didn't. Some of the stuff that happened at the high school shortly after Oliver left town made that clear, but since he wasn't there all he knows about it is hearsay. Oh, there were a couple of things for which he can vouch, like when he heard the grownups talking in low voices about an article printed in a major news magazine. It was called "The Wickedest Cities in America" and listed Phoenix City, Alabama, and Gary, Indiana, and also Walla Walla! The magazine told how places like "houses of ill repute" and "gambling dens" were found in those cities. Those were things about which Oliver had only the vaguest ideas though they sounded forbidden and therefore very interesting. But when the grownups realized he was listening they looked sideways at each other and changed the subject.

It was rumored among Walla Walla gossips that the members of the Chamber of Commerce spread out across the Pacific Northwest in their cars buying all the copies of the "Wickedest Cities" magazine off the news stands. Some people said they also raided mail boxes, but that would have been breaking the law.

Oliver doesn't mean those kinds of things. Nor does he any longer question why he had two years of history in high school and never heard about the Treaty of Walla Walla with the Native Americans, and how that treaty wasn't worth a plugged nickel when the white people got through with it. Nor why he heard so little about Chief Joseph, though what happened to the Chief and his people was pretty hard to sweep under the rug. However, Oliver did learn all about Marcus Whitman's being scalped.

There were other odd bits floating around. "Who drank the whiskey off of Pue Pue Mox Mox's ears?" the Old Timers used to say to each other and laugh. It seems that when Chief Pue Pue Mox Mox was finally tracked down and dealt with -- as the Old Timers said (he was actually murdered under a flag of truce) -- some enterprising person cut off the Chief's ears and preserved them in a pint of whiskey which was kept on a shelf in the guard room at old Fort Walla Walla. Well, one morning the sergeant came in and the bottle was empty of whiskey, but not the ears, though they had gone a bit ripe. They never found out who had been thirsty that night.

III

Oliver is talking about the town's share of characters who nowadays would be institutionalized. That means cosmetically disposed of. The ones Oliver remembers personally were Cecil Diesel Tractor Oil, the Cowboy, and a big guy whose name he never knew, but whom Oliver thought of as the Giant, who stood on the corner of First and Main. These people were genuinely, noticeably crazy. That meant they were safe because Oliver and the other kids knew to avoid them, and to watch them from a distance.

Cecil Diesel Tractor Oil hung out near the Roxy Theater on lower Main Street. You might not know he was crazy just looking at him, but if you went up to him and said CECIL DIESEL TRACTOR OIL real loud he'd chase you. If he caught you he would stammer, "Don't you call me that!" But he wouldn't hurt you. When Oliver got a little older he understood about those things and didn't tease him, but each year a swarm of new little kids was there to take up the taunting.

The Cowboy lived somewhere east of town. People said that he had been in the Marines and had gotten brain fever and was never the same after that. He was very strong and could do all kinds of neat things. He could actually throw a nickel in the air and shoot a hole through it with his six shooter. Oliver never saw this happen -- never even saw the Cowboy's six shooter -- but Oliver knew a kid who knew a kid who had seen it done, and that was what really mattered if you were eleven years old. The Cowboy had a bull whip which he could make CRACK! but he never hurt any one with the whip or any other way. In the play ground in Pioneer Park, the Cowboy would climb up the underside of

123

the metal ladder that sloped to the top of the high slide, using only his hands and arms, his arms bent at the elbow, holding his body straight up and down.

The grandest thing he did was to drive down East Alder past Edison School where Oliver's mother was Principal. Her office and her class of sixth graders were at the front of the building. The Cowboy would come down East Alder from out in the country and, well up the street, would blow the horn on his flat bed truck so Oliver's mother could hear him coming. If she was in her class room she would excuse the children and they would all crowd over to the windows and look at the Cowboy as he went by. He had rigged his truck with a brick on the gas pedal and a rope on the steering wheel so that the truck went straight. Then he would jump out of the cab and run back to the flat bed and swing on and off it just like trick riders swing over the rumps of their ponies at the rodeo. Honest to God! Oliver actually saw him do it. When the Cowboy got by the school he would get back in the cab of the truck and drive off to wherever he was going, and the sixth graders would go back to their seats. After a while the Cowboy didn't show up any more. Maybe he was institutionalized.

The Giant at First and Main was scarier. He was very big and needed a shave and was messy, and stood there in the summer sun and the winter cold and rain and smiled at the women who walked by. He lived at the Catholic hospital, but the nuns couldn't keep him home and couldn't get him to shave. Oliver believes the Giant never hurt anyone but scared a lot of people. It's interesting to think about why he wasn't institutionalized. Maybe he was. He wasn't standing there when Oliver returned from the army.

IV

In addition to crazy characters. were other characters the people called Old Timers. A typical Old Timer was the weathered and ancient prospector who once a year would show up at Mr. Marcy's service station on the edge of the business district. The Old Desert Rat -- that's what Mr. Marcy affectionately called him. "Hey, you old desert rat, I thought you'd dried up and blown away a long time ago!" The Old Desert Rat would sit there on the bench in the sun, and when Mr. Marcy wasn't busy pumping gas or changing oil or washing wind shields, the Old Desert Rat would talk to him about the *color* he had discovered, and how he was about to unearth the mother load, and all he needed was enough of a grubstake for beans and a new pick, and then he and Mr. Marcy would be rich. Mr. Marcy would give him some money, and off the Old Desert Rat would go until next year.

V

Oliver was lucky enough to know one Old Timer personally. That Old Timer gave Oliver some of his nicest memories. The Old Timer was a rock hound, and collected and polished agates. Oliver also collected rocks and minerals when could find them. One time he learned about a small deposit of spherosiderite, a rare crystalline form of iron, in the basalt up north of town near the village of Dixie. Oliver pedaled fifteen miles there and fifteen miles back, and collected a specimen of that mineral which sixty-five years later is on the shelf above the desk where he works.

Oliver heard about the Old Timer's interest in rocks and that he had a lapidary outfit, that is a diamond saw and a polishing wheel for cutting and polishing agates. Oliver hung around the Old Timer's house which was a block away down Whitman Street. The Old Timer liked Oliver and gave him half of a cut and polished thunder egg, which is an agate nodule weathered out from basalt. Oliver still has it.

One day the Old Timer said to Oliver, "Me and my wife are going hunting agates in Oregon. Do you suppose your mother would let you come along?"

Oliver stammered out "Yes!" and then ran all the way to his house to ask her even though he knew she wouldn't be home until after dark. That night, after supper, she talked to Oliver about the importance of school work, but finally said it was all right with her, if his teachers at Sharpstein agreed.

It was the middle of the school year but Oliver went to every teacher and they all gave him permission to leave for a whole week. He can't remember how he did the assignments they gave him, except his history teacher's. She gave him a special book to read and when he got back he wrote her an essay on the Congress of Vienna. No other kid in school did anything like that, and he sent a copy of the paper to his Aunt Mary in New York. She wrote him that it was a good paper and sent him a *Scott's Junior International Postage Stamp Album*, and some stamps, and that's how he started his stamp collection as well as having a special trip.

On their way to Oregon the Old Timer talked a lot as he drove, for he was an old man and was reminiscing. Oliver rode in the back seat. They drove through the Wallula Gap and down the Columbia River gorge on their way to The Dalles, and passed the two basalt plugs which people call the Twin Sisters. Oliver called them The Ink Wells because they reminded him of the ink well on his desk in the third grade. Oliver leaned forward and rested his chin on the back of the front seat, and listened to the Old Timer talk.

The Old Timer kept looking back over his shoulder at Oliver, and his wife kept saying "Watch the road." The Old Timer said, "When I was a young man back in the late nineties, I worked all over eastern Oregon and Washington on sheep and cattle ranches. A lot of things happened back then. I'll tell you a couple of stories." By then they had turned south from the Columbia River at The Dalles and were driving through the high, dry country where the Old Timer had grown up.

"When I was in my twenties," he said, "I worked as foreman on a sheep ranch down near Bend, Oregon. One time I went into the little town of Drewsy, which is still there, and went into a bar and ordered a beer. When it came, the barkeep put a little dish with white powder in it alongside the beer. I Said, 'What is that?' and he said, 'It's snow.'" Oliver asked what snow was, and the Old Timer explained, "That's another name for cocaine." That didn't mean much to Oliver, but when the Old Timer tried to explain about cocaine and drugs, his wife fussed at him, and he quickly finished the story.

Anyway, it seems the whole town of Drewsy was using cocaine which found its way there through the Chinese who worked the borax mines at Malheur Lake just to the south.

Oliver remained pretty much in the dark about what happened in Drewsy, for the only Chinese Oliver had ever seen was the old man in Walla Walla who sold him litchi nuts. And besides, back in those days, maybe cocaine wasn't illegal since they used to put it in Coca Cola.

Pretty soon it was noon, and they stopped under a lone tree alongside the road and ate a picnic lunch which Mrs. Old Timer had packed. The old man drank one bottle of warm beer with his sandwich, and then told Oliver another story.

"Another time I was on the stage (He meant the real kind, with horses) going from Bend down to Elko (which is in Nevada) across that wide open eastern desert that stretches off forever. Well, we were out in the middle of it and there was a famous jockey on board who had been born in eastern Oregon but had gone on to win fame and fortune at Saratoga and those fancy places Back East. Well, he was dying of the cancer, and so way out there in the middle of nowhere, he told the driver to stop the stage and he got off without a town within fifty miles, and waved us on and the last we saw of him he was just walking off into the desert."

The Old Timer gave a little smile with one corner of his mouth turned down, and his wife, sitting beside him, leaned over and patted his hand. Oliver has never forgotten those stories.

VI

Then the Old Timer and the Old Timer's wife and Oliver went on to Shaniko in central Oregon. It was a ghost town and completely empty. They went into the hotel where there were sheets and blankets on the beds and dishes on the tables but nobody to care for them. It was spooky. They went out on the hotel's rickety porch and looked up and down the town's one street. Tumble weeds were blowing in the wind and piling up in the corral at the end of town. The Old Timer said, "The last time I was here it was full of people. I brought a herd of sheep here to sell." He shook himself and started back to the car.

If you visit Shaniko nowadays, it is quite touristed up, what there is left of it. Once the little town had been described as an Oregon *ghost town*, the souvenir hunters arrived like carrion crows taking away everything they could, including a lot of personal property from the front yards of the few surviving inhabitants.

After that Oliver and his friends visited the Priday ranch where there were thunder eggs, but Oliver didn't find any. Then they went on to Yachats (pronounced Yahuts) on the coast which then was a tiny town with only one cafe, not like the tourist resort it is now. Oliver found some agates there.

That was very exciting. At Yachats there are wave worn beds of flat rock extending out from the mountains which come right down to the sea. Big crevices have opened up in the rocks and the waves come pounding into them and smash against the boulders at the foot of the hills. In the summer, these long narrow slots are floored with sand, but in the early spring when Oliver visited there, the waves had washed away all the sand revealing mounds of loose gravel underneath. There were agates mixed in among the ordinary rocks! To get the agates Oliver had to wait until a wave had smashed itself and retreated rolling the stones over and over. Then he would jump down into the crevice and paw among the loose rock until he saw an agate which he would grab and then scramble back up the boulders before the next wave smashed in.

It wasn't very safe, but the Old Timer trusted Oliver to be careful. Nowadays that would be considered irresponsible, but the Old Timer helped Oliver grow up a little, to be a little bit proud of what he'd done.

So Oliver's collection of rocks and minerals grew. He kept it in a jam and jelly cabinet in the basement of the house on Whitman Street. That was his museum. Oliver doesn't remember the Old Timer's name, and most of Oliver's rocks and agates and minerals have disappeared, one by one, as the years have passed, but the Old Timer himself hasn't disappeared. He is safe inside Oliver's head.

CHAPTER FIFTEEN
PERCY HIMSELF

Oliver's grandfather was an Old Timer although Oliver never thought of him like that. His name was Percival. Oliver always called him Grandpa Percy to his face, but just plain Percy when he talks about him with other people. The name Percival seemed mysterious and strange to Oliver, something a knight would be called, like Sir Percival. But Grandpa Percy wasn't a knight, he was an old fashioned, steam engine, railroad man, an Old Timer of a different sort.

"Lucky the child who knows his own father," the saying goes. Luckier the child who gets to know his own grandparents. They shape and mold and understand, and feel indebted for their brief contact with the future, for they are the past. We've already met Oliver's Irish grandmother, this is about summers with Oliver's grandfather.

I

School time defines the calendars of kids. Without school, weather calibrates their year. Before school, summer to little kids is simply a time warmer than winter. Winter is when you stay inside most of the time and the litany becomes, "What's there to do, Mom?"

Winter can be fun if it snows, but there are all those clothes, coats, boots, mittens to struggle into. And out of.

"Oliver, How many times have I told you not to track snow into the house!"

The fact is, little kids got bored in the winter and big kids got bored in the summer. During his country summers, before they moved to town, Oliver shed his clothes and ran naked. There was always something to do, dirt to dig, bushes to explore under, houses to build out of boxes. Back then by summer's end, bigger kids actually missed school but wouldn't admit it. In their awkward gonadal transition, too old to play imaginary games, unable to find summer jobs except mowing pinch pennys' lawns, by late August they welcomed school. Malls to hang out in, mind lobotomizing video games were yet to be invented.

For older Oliver there were summers in Walla Walla, and summers when he stayed with his grandparents while his mother attended the State Teacher's College in Bellingham. She took Oliver's sister with her which made Oliver feel unwanted. On the other hand, he came to know his grandfather, and sixty years later that makes it all OK, although then it wasn't.

II

Being away from home, being homesick, gave Oliver perspective on what home was. *Away* became an envelope into which Home began to fit.

Away meant two places for Oliver; the first wherever his grandparents were living, dusty or soggy little railroad towns his grandfather sought out. That's why the next chapter's called "Railroad Days." The second were trips to far places, such as going by automobile to New York City and the 1939 World's Fair with his mother and sister. Oliver will tell about those later.

Memories of the first times away return in bits and pieces. Oliver remembers falling out of the apple tree in his grandfather's back yard and smashing his elbow. He landed on a chunk of wood he used to reach the tree's first branch. That was in Auburn on the damp side of the Cascade Mountains. Oliver can still see and feel the bark all rain wet and glistening slippery. Suddenly he was spinning backwards. Pain! His arm dangling useless as he ran screaming into the house. The blood filled, puffy sack of skin with the shattered bone pressed against it from the inside. The local doctor saying he couldn't do the work, better take Oliver to the Children's Orthopedic Hospital in Seattle twenty-five miles away. The crazy drive there; then black out. That must have been the ether. The long recovery.

III

The first summer away that Oliver clearly remembers was in Sumas, Washington, a tank town right on the Canadian border north of Bellingham. When trains were pulled by steam engines, water for their boilers was essential, and little way-stations developed along the rail lines. These consisted of a water tank by the tracks, a shack of a station for the man who tended the tank, and maybe a store or a saloon to serve the surrounding farms and ranches. Some tank towns, like Sumas, grew a little bigger, but not much. It was a damp little village tucked into the forest with Douglas firs peering over the houses into the town's only street. Actually Sumas was two towns. Abbotsford, just across the border in Canada was its Siamese twin joined by a single Main Street.

Percy was telegrapher-dispatcher there for the Northern Pacific Railroad. Sumas was off the main line and very quiet. Oliver's grandfather tended his gladiolas, cooked afternoon supper, and played his violin. He moved in silent isolation, in attendance to his wife, remote, savoring his hobbies. Some people thought he might have a past, that maybe he was hiding out, but such an explanation was too simple. He wasn't Irish, maybe English. He didn't say. Another mystery. He was simply Percy, himself.

In that isolated spot, Canadian coins found their way into Sumas and American coins into Abbotsford. People considered the two metal currencies interchangeable regardless of official exchange rates. Among the coins were big old Canadian pennies which Percy saved whenever he got them in change. The pennies were much larger than the ones the Canadians use now, and had pictures of Queen Victoria and King Edward on them. When Oliver arrived to spend the summer, Percy gave the pennies to him to keep for a collection. That year Oliver was building roads in the garden for his toy cars. He felt real roads should be cement, and went to the drawer where the big pennies were kept and took twenty-five of them. He went to the hardware store and bought twenty-five cents worth of cement and made tiny cement roads. Oliver's mother was very angry with Oliver when he showed the roads to her and she learned how he had gotten the cement, but when Percy saw them he said it was all right because children ought to build cement roads if that was what they wanted to do. Oliver still has fifteen of the pennies, the ones remaining. Grandpa Percy gave them to him to do with whatever he wanted.

Oliver brought away one special thing from Sumas. He traded something, he can't remember what it was, for a very fine Haida carving of a killer whale that belonged to a neighbor boy. The carving was four inches long and fashioned from very old, dense cedar wood. It was -- and still is, though Oliver doesn't know who has it now -- museum quality. He treasured it until he was a freshman in college. Then Oliver fell in love with his Introductory Anthropology teacher. She was a graduate lecturer, but to him she was a professor who actually attended potlatch ceremonies. The Indians accepted her because her hair was long and straight and blue-black as a mussel shell. Her cheek bones were high and her skin the color of smokey cedar. She was pregnant and when her baby was born during the school term she brought it to class on a cradle board, and propped board with baby against the podium where she lectured. That impressed Oliver very much and he wanted her to notice him, so he gave her the carving. Sometimes he wishes he hadn't given it to her because after that class he never saw her again. But sometimes he's pleased that he did. Many years later a student in one of Oliver's classes gave him a fine Masai spear that his family had gotten when they were missionaries in

Kenya. Maybe that student sometimes wishes, like Oliver, that he'd kept the spear, but Oliver loves the spear and remembers the student. Memory for memory, love for love, once a child, now a grandparent, the ledger balances itself.

One summer in Sumas, they went to Birch Bay, an inlet on the mainland at the head of the Strait of Juan de Fuca. The bay is very shallow at low tide and Oliver would wade knee deep, scuffling through the kelp and sea grass. If he bumped into a crab with his foot, Oliver leaned down, and if he dared, and he did dare, plunged his arm into the slippery kelp, picked up the crab, and staying carefully away from its big claw, put it in a bag to take home. Oliver's grandfather steamed them and the family ate them with butter.

Birch Bay is lined with houses now and is probably polluted. If anyone can find a Dungeness crab -- his grandfather taught Oliver to say *done jen ess* -- that close to shore Oliver would be surprised because everything is getting fished out. It may be selfish, but there are just too many people! Of course, this is Oliver talking now, and back then as a little kid those things didn't bother him.

That is all he remembers about Sumas. The next summers away that Oliver remembers are the ones at Selah which was a hop-picking, apple warehouse and fruit packing hamlet four miles outside of Yakima.

IV

Selah summers seemed endless. Oliver missed his mother and became restless and bored, so he turned to the comics. In those days, comic books cost ten cents each. By the end of the summer Oliver had collected thirty of them. Sometimes he would lay them out in orderly columns on his bed. They just fit, five books wide by six long. The earliest one was about Brick Bradford who traveled through time in a machine that looked like a hot air balloon or a very large top. Then came a cohort of heroes with strange talents and physical characteristics: The Flame, who caught fire and burned without hurting himself; the Flash, who could move so fast that no one could see him;

133

Submariner, who changed into water and had pointed ears, like Mr. Spock's in *Star Trek* years later; Plastic Man whose limbs stretched to impossible lengths and were as flexible as snakes; Hawk Man and Hawk Woman with gigantic wings and raptor masks; Captain Marvel who appeared when Billy Batson said "Shazam!," and of course, those immortals we still have with us in more sophisticated modes: Wonder Woman, Superman along with the Joker and the Penguin, and kryptonite, Superman's mineral nemesis, and Batman and Robin (no sissy stuff like Bat Girl back then). Oliver would be rich if he still had that collection, for they were all first, or very early issues, the stuff that make collectors salivate.

Oliver thinks about comic books and the kids reading them, and realizes that as he avidly devoured them his reading skills improved in the process. So let there be comic books as long as they tell about heroes, and the villains aren't sadistic, and women aren't abused and get to do their share of the good deeds, and people don't get blown away by assault weapons as they are in today's violent video games that need no reading skills.

Hmmm, Oliver always was a dreamer, so maybe, after all, it's asking too much to return to the good old days.

V

Grandfather Percy saw that Oliver was restless, and distracted him by teaching him lore from his childhood. First, he showed Oliver how to make a real willow whistle. He took Oliver down to a stream by the depot and chose a fresh, new willow shoot about as big around as your thumb. He cut a piece of the shoot six inches long, making sure the ends were very smooth. Next, Percy carefully made four shallow nicks along one side of the piece so that they were all in a row. These would be fingering holes when the whistle was done. Beyond the four holes near one end he made a vertical cut about half as deep as the piece was thick; next he made a slanting cut from the fingering hole side so that he could remove a piece of bark which resembled a tiny slice of pie. That was for the air vent, like the mouth of a jug you blow across to make a noise.

Then came the tricky part. He tapped the stick around and around as he rotated it in his fingers so that the bark came loose from the wood. After that Percy carefully slid the tube of bark with the holes in it off the inside wood. The core was all white, and smooth, and slippery. Moving along the core almost to the end away from the air hole, he made a vertical cut to the middle of the wood and carefully, carefully split the upper half away, starting at the air hole end. This left him with a slippery inside piece like half a column, with a full plug at one end. He then slid the white, slippery piece back into the bark tube. A Whistle!

Percy *played Turkey in the Straw* on the whistle, and tried to show Oliver how, but Oliver could only find some of the notes. Then grandfather Percy loaned Oliver his knife to use and helped him select a willow wand and make a whistle which wasn't as neat or as good as the one Percy made. But Oliver didn't mind, because when he got back to Walla Walla he could show the kids how to make a willow whistle, which was something they didn't know.

VI

Most of all, Oliver remembers his grandfather sitting in his captain's chair on the wooden platform of the depot as the sun went down, playing the whistle, playing something low and sad. Back in Walla Walla, Oliver would blow the whistle his grandfather made, trying to remember those sad grandfather tunes. Finally the whistle dried out and didn't work any more. There weren't any willows along Mill Creek from which to make a new one.

Oliver also remembers other nights when grandfather Percy would sit on the platform with his fiddle, he called it a fiddle not a violin, playing those same sad tunes. After that Percy would go inside the depot and read *Astounding Science Fiction* and Zane Grey and the newspaper and listen for his bug to sound. It chattered constantly, but he would know when the message was for him. Then he would sit down at his *mill* and would type the incoming message a fast as it came, which was very fast. Sometimes he would stop and lean over and tap out something on his bug and get an answer and then go on typing.

VII

Percy showed Oliver how to make a Y-shaped sling shot which probably everybody knows. He also showed him how to make and use a sling like the one with which David killed Goliath. He said the sling could be very dangerous and that Oliver should only use it when he went way out in the country on his bike. After that he taught Oliver how to make a rubber band gun which was neat. To make a rubber band gun, you saw a piece of wood into a shape like a small rifle. The wood should be a piece of plank about one inch thick. Then you make a notch at the tip of the barrel. After that you take a clothes pin -- the kind that pinches shut -- and a rubber band with which you lash the clothes pin to the butt end.

You get the rubber bands from an old automobile inner tube that isn't any good. Now days, with tubeless tires, this might not be easy to do. You cut cross-sections of the tube about half an inch wide. They look like limp, blue-black onion rings when you get a pile of them. Then you take one of the rings and wrap it around and around the handle of the gun and when it's almost too tight to pull away from the wood, you fasten a clothes pin to the handle with the last lashing.

The flat rubber bands are also the ammunition. To shoot the rubber band gun you hook one of the rings over the notch at the tip of the barrel and stretch the band all the back along the gun and fasten the other end, pinched shut, into the clothes pin. To shoot the gun you aim and then squeeze the clothes pin and whap! off goes the rubber inner tube band.

This was a lot of fun, and kids would have rubber band gun fights which these days would not be allowed because they could get their eyes put out. Just real gun fights, thanks to the NRA.

VIII

Oliver's grandfather did all the cooking. He used a big wood burning stove with an oven down below on one side and the fire box on the other, and a warming oven with eisen glass windows up above. He made solid mid-western fare, egg noodles from dough which he rolled out and cut in thin strips with a knife. Then he would lay out newspapers on the woodshed roof and put the noodles there to dry in the sun. The noodles were a big temptation to the birds, so Percy would sit on the back steps and scare them away with a sling shot. But he never, never killed a wild bird or hurt one; chickens didn't count. Chicken soup with noodles, Oliver can still taste the soup and feel the lumpy, lovely texture of the noodles.

Percy made Floating Island pudding for desert, which is whipped egg white and orange slices in a sort of custard. He also made Prune Soufflé which Oliver really loved, and chicken pot pie and lemon meringue pie. Oliver believes that although his grandfather prepared only mid-western fare, he learned his love of good food and how to cook it from him.

He and his grandfather also went fishing. Percy would wrap the fish they caught in balls of clay and bake them in a pit under the camp fire. He would also put corn on the cob and potatoes wrapped in newspaper in with the fish. Those meals were delicious!

IX

Grandfather Percy's yard was always full of gladiolas which he called *glad-eye-oh-lahz*, and Heavenly Blues, which were morning glories, and sweet peas, and no yard grass.

One year Oliver worked all summer cutting wood for the cook stove and bringing it in and making an extra pile for after he left for home. He figured he had earned as much as two dollars. On the day he left for Walla Walla, Percy gave him a five dollar bill! Oliver didn't expect that much, which was a wonderful amount of money for a little kid.

Percy also bought Oliver paper and pencils and taught him how to draw so Oliver's scenes looked just like the real world. Percy also had a big carpenter's chest full of tools which Oliver could use if he was careful and put them away when he was through.

When Oliver's grandmother died in Walla Walla, Oliver wasn't there and his mother sold EVERYTHING to an antique dealer for fifty dollars including the family bible, the carpenter's chest, Percy's "bug," and all the heavy old furniture including pictures of stern great grandparents. Oliver didn't get a chance to keep any memento that belonged to his grandfather. But that doesn't matter because Oliver remembers all the things Percy taught him.

--- --- ---

Oliver didn't see his grandfather all that much, but he wants you to know how important Percy was to him. You mustn't judge Oliver's grandfather because they found him once in a snow drift. He was a good man, who for Oliver became a positive part of that contradictory combination, *Growing Up Walla Walla,* inside Oliver's head,.

Here is what, years later, Oliver wrote about his grandfather.

Legend
I followed my grandfather
down the invisible path
to the place where they met.

I was not there. I was
never there. I was never.

They met in the bare dawn,
shivering, pale thighs, pale shoulders,
she in her shift,
so naked, small town naked,
small town, Midwestern naked.

When she moved
I could see she was
not my grandmother.

        I was not there. I was
        never there. I was never.

They did not look;
they did not touch; they eased
into the still river; and the river
was warmer than the air.
Silently, where they swam,
ripples reaching
in among roots,
the willow let loose its hair.

        I was not there. I was
        never there. I was never.

They hid in the green mist
until the sun tore
the under edge of the east,
and she left, cloth clinging,
going up into the day,
where the screen door clicked.

        I was not there. I was
        never there. I was never.

He went another way,
Out along the railroads,
telegrapher, dispatcher,
another woman, my grandmother,
Selah and Yakima.

John Kolars

He took to carpentry, gladiolas, loneliness,
sitting at night on the station platform,
playing his fiddle; odor of creosote;
sitting and reading; passing the time
in-between freights, in the dry hills,
In the dry country.

CHAPTER SIXTEEN
RAILROAD DAYS

Grandfather Percy knew all about the railroad. Oliver's grandfather had the second highest seniority on the NP railroad and could work anyplace he chose. (People with higher seniority could "bump" people with lower seniority and move to better locations.) Percy chose dusty little Selah. He could have moved to the important station at Yakima, but instead took the same kind of job as in Sumas, telegrapher-dispatcher on the four to midnight shift in a tiny tank town. Oliver was older, nine, ten, eleven, and vividly remembers his Selah summers, his railroad summers.

I

Selah was a small town in the Wenas Valley where they grow Delicious apples and hops used for making beer. Selah is at the lower end of the Ellensburg Canyon where the Yakima River comes out of the Cascade Mountains. The N.P. railroad had special, big engines which could pull the trains over the mountains. Once over the summit, the trains would come rushing down, charging out of the canyon past Selah without stopping, their whistles wailing. Those were steam locomotives, not diesels and not electric. They had whistles that went *ooowah oooooooooooooo*! Not the brute blast of the diesels' *aaaaaagahh*! but a delicate, mournful call.

After Oliver's grandfather died and his grandmother came to live in Walla Walla, she chose a little house on the west side of town so that she could hear the *ooowahooooooooooo* when she was lying lonely in her bed. She said it reminded her of Percy and made her feel that he was nearby. No diesel's *aaaaaaaaaghh*! could ever evoke his memory. Even when he was alive, Grandfather Percy was much more mournful, and mysterious, and far away.

Selah was his home, a little rented house he transformed with Heavenly Blue morning glories that shaded the front porch and kept it cool on the hot Selah summer afternoons.

II

Even Percy's work on the Northern Pacific Railroad helped make the house comfortable. Oliver's grandparents had an ice box in the kitchen, not a refrigerator, not electric. Percy would put a big cake of ice in the top of it, and before it melted it kept everything down below cool so the food wouldn't spoil. Most people with ice boxes got their ice from the ice man who came around with a horse and a wagon filled with cakes of ice under a heavy canvas tarp. Grandfather Percy was different; he worked for the NP Railroad and could use NP ice from the NP ice house down near the depot. That ice was cut from a mountain lake every winter and brought there to service the passenger trains and the fresh commodity trains going Back East.

To get ice for his own small ice box, Percy would twice a week before work take his little red coaster wagon to the depot. On special days Oliver would go with him. Percy would take the big, brass, ice house key with a hollow end from the nail on the depot wall where it was kept, and walk along the cindery edge of the track to the ice house. The ice house was a chunky little building with no windows and a low, thick roof. Its style declared, "Here I am, an ice house. Come summer, come heat and drought, I keep the ice for those who need it."

He would carefully insert the brass key in the big padlock and pull open the thick door. The inside of the ice house was very dark. There were no lights, just a huge pile of sawdust with great cakes of ice buried like pirate treasure in sand. Oliver's grandfather would take down the ice tongs hanging on the wall and open them. They were like a weapon you would see in a castle. Then he would swing one of the points down into the sawdust and hit a cake of ice and pull it to the surface. The ice would be covered with little bits of sawdust which Percy would brush off before he put the cake into the wagon. After that, he covered the ice with a ragged old blanket he called his ice-blanket so the ice wouldn't melt on the way home.

Percy would take an ice pick he had brought from home, and chip off a piece of ice for Oliver to suck. The sawdust clinging to the ice made it taste like pine resin. The ice pick was long and sharp and dangerous. That's why he wouldn't let Oliver carry it.

So off they would go, the little red wagon dripping melted ice water as they walked up the dusty street all the way home.

III

Some days Percy would take Oliver to work with him and show Oliver how his work as a telegrapher-dispatcher helped the rail road do its job. In those days there weren't two-way radios on the trains. If the railroad people wanted to tell the engineer on an oncoming train something like *Stop at the next station for a box car of apples,* they would telegraph Oliver's grandfather. He had a little telegraph machine which clicked when a message came in and could be operated by his thumb and finger to send a message in reply. He called it his "bug." A message would arrive and Percy had to get it to the engineer of the freight train coming down out of the canyon at seventy-five miles an hour. To do this he would type out the message on his typewriter which he called his *mill.* Then he would tie the message, all rolled up, to the handle of a hoop made from a length of bamboo cane about ten feet long. The cane was fashioned into a big figure 6 or figure 9 depending on how you looked at it. He would take the hoop and climb up onto the *pulpit,* a little tower which really did resemble a pulpit, located at the very edge of the platform next to the rails. The pulpit was eight feet high and put Percy at the level of the engineer's cab. The train would come roaring, getting bigger and bigger. The rush of wind as it went by could almost pull a person from the pulpit. Percy would lean forward and hold up the hoop by its stem, and the engineer would lean out of the cab window and scoop up the cane as the train raced by. At the same time, the fireman on the train would throw back empty hoops farther down the platform so there would always be a supply on hand for the telegrapher.

Oliver would stand up on the pulpit with his arms around his grandfather's waist, scared in a wonderful sort of way, watching the trains howl by.

IV

Oliver was going on a trip Back East to visit his other grandparents, his father's mother and father in Le Center, Minnesota. Percy arranged the trip -- Oliver's mother, sister and he traveled on a special NP Railroad family pass -- and told Oliver about things he would see and hear on his journey.

"At night when you're asleep and the train has stopped and you're laying in your berth, listen for the *car tunker*," he said. "You'll hear him coming."

Sure enough, during the trip to Minnesota Oliver lay there at night in the sleeping car, and far off towards the end of the train -- in those days passenger trains ended with an observation car -- he heard a faint *tunk tunk* of metal on metal. It kept getting closer and closer until there was a distinct *tunk tunk* outside Oliver's window. Then the sound became fainter and fainter until it stopped up at the mail car just behind the tender, or coal car, behind the engine. It had a strange and melancholy rhythm as if someone was knocking on the door wanting to come in.

Oliver knew what the sound was, because his grandfather had told him about it. It was the Car Tunker at work. This had to do with the heavy metal train wheels which ran on big bearings. Those bearings supported the weight of the cars and had to run very smoothly. In order to keep them oiled, the cars in those days had a box or small compartment on each wheel which was called a *journal box.* There were oily rags in the journal box to keep the wheels and the bearings lubricated. If the rags fell out, or became dry, wheel friction could set the journal box on fire and it would then become a *hot box.* If the wheel got too hot it might crack or grind right off the car causing a train wreck.

In order to check the condition of the journal boxes and the wheels, workers would walk along either side of the train when it stopped, tapping each wheel with a metal rod. If the wheel were cracked from the heat of a hot box, or in some other way not properly aligned, the sound coming back would be a **thump thump** instead of the musical *tunk tunk*, which Oliver heard on those railroad nights. When he heard the sound, laying there in his berth, he thought of his grandfather sitting on the platform playing his violin.

V

There was other railroad lore that Oliver's grandfather told him. He explained how track inspectors, men who walked along the rail lines examining the cross-ties and steel rails, wore lengths of stove pipe like leggings from their knees to their boots when they were in rattlesnake country. The rails would absorb the sun's heat and on chilly nights the snakes would lay along the lengths of warm steel to keep warm. In the morning the inspectors might disturb the rattlesnakes which would strike at their legs. Thus the metal leggings.

Once when Oliver was visiting the depot his grandfather took a chunk of carpenter's chalk out of his pocket and walked over to the siding where empty boxcars were lined up. He selected smooth sided car that had *Atchison, Topeka and Santa Fe* stenciled on it, and choosing a big surface free of numbers and graffiti wrote a special name on the wall.

He wrote the name in one grand sweeping movement from left to right creating part of a giant signature, and then without lifting the chalk, back again from right to left completing the name: J B King Esq.*

Oliver was entranced, by his grandfather's fluid movements. "How did you do that? Whose name is that?"

Percy at down on the edge of the platform. So did Oliver. The platform was built of rough hewn timbers and smelled of creosote. Oliver's legs dangled over the edge and he could feel the splinters right through his pants.

"Nobody knows exactly who Mr. King was," Grandfather Percy explained. "Every hobo who's a traveler, not just a tramp or a bum knows how to sign that name."

"What do you mean, a traveler? We travel; we traveled all the way here from Walla Walla. We went on the train to Minnesota, when you helped us, and my mother says we're ⟵————————⟶ going to drive all the way to New York City next year and see Aunt Mary and a big fair that's going to be there."

"That's going on a trip." Grandfather Percy stared at the piece of chalk and then slid it into his jacket pocket.

"But it's not the same as traveling. Some of these men you see sitting in the box cars that go by are hunting for work, want to go home. But there's others who have sand in their shoes. They want to see everything, go everywhere. They're the true travelers."

"How'd they get sand in their shoes? Why does that make them want to travel?"

---

*Thanks to Larry Penn <cookeman@execpc.com> for providing a beautiful example of this signature.

"It's just a way of speaking, meaning they want to go on forever. They are the hobos. They even have a king."

"You've traveled out here all the way from Michigan. You've been to Sumas and even Auburn; are you a hobo?"

"I might have been, but things change . . . . " Grandfather stood up. "I hear my bug. Somebody's calling." He walked into the depot and leaned over his telegraph key.

Though Percy and Oliver talked together on other summer days, Grandfather Percy never again mentioned his traveling. He did help Oliver learn to draw J B King Esq's signature, but Oliver could never make them look as graceful as they should.

Oliver wonders if J. B. King, Esq. was a relative of Kilroy. Or did he himself fight in World War II, and keep his true name, his peaceful, traveling name, secret?

VI

There is another thing Oliver remembers about his first trip Back East on the train. He was looking out the window of the train when it stopped at a small station in Montana. There alongside the track was a gang of workers repairing the rails on a side track. The rails were perhaps fifteen feet long and solid steel and very heavy. Damaged rail segments had to be lifted off the wooden ties which were placed one after the other at right angles to the gravel railroad bed, and new rails had to be lifted back onto the ties to replace the bad ones.

In order to do this heavy and dangerous work -- a dropped rail could crush a man's foot -- a row of four men stood on either side of the rail segment to be moved. Each man held a pair of heavy metal tongs in his hands, and at a signal the entire team would move in unison in a swaying, rhythmic, strangely beautiful dance. They would step up to the rail, reach down and grasp it with their tongs, lift it with a single move and carry it to its destination. The eight men moved as one, their gait was slow, almost stately, a pavan, lifting and walking and lowering the bar as though it were an extension of their bodies joining them all.

These men were *Gandy Dancers.* They danced the railroads into skeins of iron connecting America together, coast to coast. They're gone now, fork lifts and cranes dumbly do the work the Gandy Dancers danced. But Oliver saw them once before they waltzed away forever, moving to their own silent music.

CHAPTER SEVENTEEN
BACK EAST

I

This chapter is not about Walla Walla. It is about the world Walla Walla and Oliver were embedded in. It's first about another world called Seattle. Oliver's Seattle trips were made from Auburn, where he broke his arm, or on the way to Sumas, where he spent the big Canadian pennies, when he was very small. In Seattle, his mother took him to the *Ye Olde Curiosity Shoppe* on Alaska Way. Getting there was exciting. Oliver and his mother had to walk down the steep sidewalks on Columbia Street, so steep that you had to lean backwards to keep your balance. Then they crossed the pedestrian bridge that arched over the railroad tracks and Alaska Way, and scrambled down a crooked flight of stairs to the Shoppe's front door. (There was no Alaska Way overpass at that time.)

The Shoppe was built out on a pier where sea-going ships could dock. It was a remnant of earlier sailing days. Even when Oliver was a child sailors would bring their scrimshaw and souvenirs from the Seven Seas to sell there. Its front door was framed by giant whale bones and genuine totem poles. The glass cases inside were crammed with sea shells and shrunken heads, the rafters were hung with Indian baskets and sword fish swords, and South Sea Island spears. Even inexpensive souvenirs like tiny totem poles were hand carved by Indians along the British Columbia coast -- not churned out by the thousands in Taipei or Hong Kong as they are today.

Now, the *Shoppe* is a travesty of itself. The best exhibit pieces have vanished, sold to collectors or museums. The counters are loaded with Asian sweat shop junk. The dream survives only in Oliver's mind, but *Ye Olde Curiosity Shoppe* was Oliver's first gateway to the world.

After visiting Ye Olde Curiosity Shoppe, his mother took Oliver to the pet store. One time a parrot in a cage said, "Oliver," to Oliver. How did that happen? How did the bird know Oliver's name? Despite that magic bird, it made Oliver uneasy to see kittens and puppies in cages, and tanks full of little turtles with *Souvenir of Seattle* stenciled on their shells. After visiting the pet store, his mother went shopping at the Bon Marché, and Oliver rode on the escalators. That was Oliver's view of Seattle, incomplete. but a catalyst, one of the grains of imagination around which his life formed.

II

Oliver's next world was Back East, where his relatives lived. His father came from Minnesota and had attended Notre Dame. Other paternal relatives lived in New York. Oliver's mother and the Irish side of the family sprouted like potatoes from Michigan soil. Years later, after Oliver had grown more upwards, after the army, Oliver lived *Back East*. But those are stories for another book. When Oliver was little, he took trips Back East to a still different world.

Just like *Out West, Back East* is part of the American experience. The pioneers who settled the American West sometimes returned to their starting points to visit, or in retreat from the harsh frontier. They went back where they started from, that is, Back (to the) East. A word about the frontier illustrates this.

Maps in history books show the advance of the frontier across America. They define the frontier as the dividing line between those areas having "more than two people per square mile" and those that didn't. Of course, the advance of the frontier marked the advance of English speaking, white people from east to west. There it is again! The People! Of course, from an Anglo point of view, the Native American pueblos, the Spanish towns, and the concentrations of Northwest Coast tribes didn't have anything to do with real people. Long live the frontier!

Anther example of the cultural blinders imposed on geography is the case of the Pacific *Coast* and the Eastern *Shore*. These are land and sea terms. You set sail for a distant shore. The Easterners, with their ties to England and Europe, real or imagined, think in terms of the shore that their ancestors approached. The offspring of these Easterners, transmuted into Americans by the continent they crossed, approached a coast, the Pacific coast. Seas have shores, continents have coasts. The coast was way Out West; the shore was back home, that is Back East. Oliver's mother took him Back East, not to *the* Back East.

Oliver's *other grandparents* -- that is how Oliver still thinks of them -- lived in a big house in a tiny town, Le Center, in Minnesota. A silent aunt and uncle, never heard from, seldom seen, lived in Nyack, New York. They were Oliver's father's brother and his wife. Why didn't Oliver's uncle write to Oliver, tell Oliver about his father? Aunt Mary, his father's unmarried sister, lived in New York City. She was the magic aunt who sent Oliver chemistry sets and geology kits, and books about reptiles and dinosaurs by Raymond L. Ditmars. All those relatives were remote, almost imaginary figures. Oliver's mother sometimes used Aunt Mary as a threat. "Oliver, if you're not good, I'll write and tell Aunt Mary!"

The *other grandparents* had information about Oliver's dead father. But they never told. Odd. Oliver was their only grandson. Four sons and a daughter from the house in Minnesota and only one grandson. If so, why so little contact with Oliver? A trip to Minnesota, two more to New York City; one by car with a stop over in Minnesota when Oliver was ten, the other by train when

Oliver was sixteen. Different times, different permutations and combinations; but only Aunt Mary sent letters. Or were there other letters to his mother? Oliver will never know.

III

The first trip to Minnesota was on the train. Oliver's mother was train sick and stayed in her berth day and night. Where was his sister? Was she sick, too? He doesn't remember her being there. Oliver was taken to the diner by the conductor. Oliver liked the diner, liked the conductor. He sat a table with a linen table cloth and a linen napkin, and a special glass for water that the waiter kept filled. Oliver ate a big baked potato, and a Swiss steak and some green beans, The conductor told Oliver that the Northern Pacific Railroad was famous for its baked potatoes. There was lemon meringue pie for desert. His mother didn't want to hear about it. He remembers sleeping in his own berth at night listening to the *car tunkers* whom you already know about.

Then the big house in Le center. Not so big years later when Oliver went there after being in the army. A house with Bohemian cut glass windows over the side board in the dining room and a chandelier in the living room and a horse hide sofa on the glassed in front porch. The street in front was paved but not the side street which was the quick way to the court house square and tiny business district. If you went straight out the front door and kept going you came to the fair grounds two blocks away. Gypsies sometimes camped there and would steal you if you went there by yourself. At the county fair one time his *other grandfather* bought him an X-ray tube which if you looked through it at your finger and there was a bright light behind, you could see the bone in the middle of your finger. But it wasn't really your finger bone but a feather; which Oliver found out when he took the tube apart because he was curious.

All the other memories:

"You mean you don't know how to bat a ball?" That was his other grandfather in the big living room, who turned to Robert R., the second cousin once removed who lived in the house and was a traveling salesman, "Bob, do we have a ball and bat?"

"No, but I can make one."

Bob rolled up a newspaper and put a rubber band around it and crumpled up another sheet to make a ball. Then Oliver's *other grandfather* tried to show Oliver how to hold the newspaper bat and hit the newspaper ball as Bob pitched it gently to him. Oliver missed again and again because he had no depth perception. Finally the two men gave up and Bob took Oliver to the soda fountain in town, the one where Oliver's father had worked as a boy. He bought Oliver a *Dr. Pepper*. Oliver called it "Dahktoh Peppah." Which Bob thought was very funny.

Aunt Mary came to visit while eight year old Oliver was in Minnesota. Oliver went into her room and took two pieces of her costume jewelry and buried them in the sand pile that his *other grandfather* had had delivered for Oliver to play in. Oliver "discovered" the jewelry and announced his find to everyone. He thought that they wouldn't know it was Aunt Mary's jewelry, but they did. Aunt Mary was very understanding and asked Oliver's mother not to punish him. So she didn't, but his mother was "mortified" at Oliver's behavior, whatever that meant.

Another day, Oliver locked himself in the upstairs bathroom and panicked, not knowing how to work the dead bolt. Second cousin once removed Robert had to climb up a ladder and come in the bathroom window and help Oliver unlock the door.

There was, of course, the incident of the ghost dog. In later life, things have happened to Oliver that run counter to his training as a physical scientist, events beyond scientific logic. As Oliver says, "There are no coincidences." There was the affair of the Jolly Hotel in Sardinia, not easily explained; or the fish poison in Turkey where he became one with the living dead for half an hour; or the time in Tanganyika when he was hexed by a witch doctor. The ghost dog was an omen of things, other stories, for another book.

Before world War I, Oliver's father and uncles played together as young boys on the streets and lanes and fields of Le Center. Their companion was Tag, a nondescript setter mix with a happy face and a happy tail, the sort of dog boys need to tag along. War came. Joe, the eldest, left home under a cloud and died in France. Frank and John joined the navy and shipped together, eighteen crossings of the Atlantic. John was Oliver's father. We know what happened to him. Charles was in the service, but never seemed to appear in stories about Le Center. In the years after the war Frank and Charles lived their lives. Enough said.

With all the boys away from home Tag mourned. He sniffed the empty rooms and scrambled onto the low platform the boys had built in a tree beside the house. Eventually Tag died, people said of a broken heart.

Years passed and Oliver arrived in Le Center. He and his mother were there for two weeks. On the third day Oliver went outside and found a dog waiting for him. It was a non-descript setter mix with a happy face and a happy tail. Oliver's *other grandparents* and his Aunt Mary commented on how the dog could have been another Tag. The dog followed Oliver everywhere and insisted on coming into the house when Oliver was called inside. On the second night Tag-two slept on Oliver's bed. Oliver loved his friend and the dog loved him. The two weeks came to an end and Oliver left for home. That day Tag-two disappeared. Oliver's *other grandfather* was curious and searched for the dog. It was nowhere to be found. He advertised in the local newspaper which he owned and ran. No dog. He asked his farmer friends and clients. No dog. It was never seen again. Oliver still has a black and white photograph of him and the mystery dog on the front steps of the house in Minnesota. Yeah sure, it was just a stray dog passing by.

That was the first Minnesota trip. There were more visits after Oliver returned from the army, after his *other grandfather* died, but they are about *another Oliver*.

IV

And now the automobile trip to the New York World's Fair in 1939. This is where Oliver's mother appears as what some now call a *liberated woman.* Oliver can only wonder about what motivated her to load him and his sister into the big, brown Hudson Terraplane -- which was brand new and a puzzling acquisition considering his mother's frequent reminders concerning their poverty -- and undertake a three month drive to the east coast and back.

The trip was amazing; there were no four lane highways to ease long distance road travel. Two lanes all the way with motels best summed up as "oil cloth and linoleum." Oliver loved it! The landscape sliding past. A stretch of road near Snowflake, Utah, that went on forever without a bend. The Mormon Tabernacle and the Seagull Monument. Como Bluffs, Wyoming, with the dinosaur quarry, where Oliver was able to buy a piece of fossilized dinosaur bone for his museum. Outside of Laramie, the house they passed with a man sprawled head down on the front steps. Oliver's mother stopped a few miles down the road and called the local police. Oliver's terror and refusal to enter the Cave of the Winds in the Black Hills of South Dakota was what his Irish grandmother would have called "having a squeal worm sideways". His Mother and sister had to forgo the excursion. Oliver felt terrible, like he was a real coward. But the women did visit Duhamill's Sitting Bull Crystal Caverns nearby. They parked Oliver in the gift shop where he bought a piece of dog spar crystal. They visited the Mount Rushmore Memorial, with workmen clustered like eye-flies on George Washington's granite lids. Then, Pierre, South Dakota, which they discovered was pronounced "pier," not "Pea air."

Minnesota, the beginning of the Mid-west, where the horizon is defined by groves of trees no more than a mile away. No distant, western rim of the sky there.

After Minnesota, Elkhart, Indiana, home of his mother's old college girl friend. Oliver caught a tiny fish in the river behind her house. Battle creek, Michigan -- they visited the Kellogg breakfast food factory. At the end of the tour visitors were given a ten-pack of different cereals in little boxes. His mother and sister were given miniatures just like big boxes of cereal, while Oliver was handed a set with Mickey Mouse pictures. He refused it and caused a scene until he was given a grown-up set. Not a pleasant or a happy child, a Walla Walla.

The excitement of driving through the tunnel from Detroit to Windsor, Canada. A day later, Niagara Falls seen from the Canadian side, pulsing at night under flood lights. Oliver's mother parked in a no-parking area. When a Canadian Mounted Policeman came up, she smiled at him and he let her park there. Later when she returned to Walla Walla, she sent the Mounted Policeman a huge Delicious Apple grown in Yakima -- the apples were still good back then. The Mounty sent her a big Ontario apple that was bruised and mealy by the time it arrived in Walla Walla. On the American side, wearing bright yellow rain coats, they went on cat walks along the foot of the falls, gasping for breath in the heavy mist. When Oliver's daughter was twelve he took her on the same excursion, so history does repeat itself.

Nyack, New York, and the country house of Oliver's aunt and uncle the ones who never wrote letters. They lived in a converted, old colonial mill. The visit was fun because of the stream in back and how Oliver showed them water snakes in the pool where his uncle would sit and write the text for comic strips like *Skippy*, and *Superman* and *Polly and her Pals* and *Out Our Way,* for all of which he ghosted. After learning about the snakes his uncle didn't want to sit in the water. Oliver's mother disliked his aunt because she came from The Main Line in Philadelphia and talked about "single footer" horses and was something of a snob. Looking back on the *other grandparents* and the aunt and uncle who didn't write, it occurs to Oliver that they probably thought his mother was common, being Irish and all that.

And next, New York! Excitement. Aunt Mary lived at 10 West 33rd Street just off Fifth Avenue in a fifth floor apartment across the street from the Empire State Building! She was a Latinist who worked coordinating the efforts of numerous scholars who were making the modern English translation of the Roman Catholic version of the Bible. She was a formidable intellect with an eidetic memory.

"Let me see, I can remember sitting in the canoe with my braid in my lap reading *Pride and Prejudice*. It was, hmmm, page 129 . . . " and fifty years later she would read the quotation to Oliver from memory.

Aunt Mary engaged Oliver in his first intellectual conversations. She took Oliver everywhere, the Statue of Liberty, and to the top of the Empire State Building. (Which Oliver didn't like. He eventually overcame his acrophobia, but that story is not for this book.) They visited the Museum of Natural History, and the Metropolitan Museum of Art where Oliver fell in love with a painting, "The Gulf Stream," by Winslow Homer. Another door opened for Oliver.

They ate at the Automat, and at Schrafts which was considered special, always talking about what they'd seen.

And when the waiter came:.

"Madam will have?"

"The young man will have." Very firmly.

Aunt Mary insisted she order first for Oliver, and that she and the women would come after. The waiter demurred. That was Aunt Mary; no one told her what to do. She championed Oliver, being championed was a new experience for him.

While they were in New York Oliver and his sister and his mother visited the 1939 World's Fair. That's where Oliver saw the Trylon and Perisphere, the fair's logos. Why Trylon and Perisphere? The Trylon was a tall, three sided pylon, *ergo* the name. Beside it was a huge white ball, a Perisphere you could actually go inside of and see what the future would be like. That was the Fair's theme, the future, with futuristic exhibits everywhere. He remembers the Russian Pavilion full of tractors and beaming youth. Was Nazi Germany represented at the fair? Oliver can't remember, and doesn't care. This isn't a travelogue. It is an Oliver-logue.

What Oliver remembers most vividly is his mother taking him to the Bronx Zoo and the Reptile House where Raymond L. Ditmars, the great herpetologist -- a word Oliver already knew and used -- was curator. They looked at all the snakes in the glass fronted cages. She asked a guard if they could see Dr. Ditmars and he said "No," but

Oliver's mother smiled at the guard and pushed behind the cages and walked into Dr. Ditmars office. He was there and was very nice to her and very kind to Oliver and told him that what he needed was a king snake for a pet. Then he autographed Oliver's copy of *Reptiles of the World*. Oliver and his mother left the reptile house and went to look at the Giant Pandas and the electric eel. He had shaken hands with Dr. Ditmars! That was the nicest thing Oliver's mother ever did for him.

After the Bronx Zoo and New York, came the long trip home. Oliver doesn't remember it as clearly as the trip out. Instead of a king snake, Oliver's mother bought him a salamander which he kept in a small aquarium. It was hard to care for in the car and they decided to let it go in a roadside swamp in Pennsylvania, which made Oliver sad, but he knew the salamander was happier and that was what counted.

The last bit he remembers of the trip was how the rear and side windows of the Hudson Terraplane were covered with decals which essentially said "We've were there!!" wherever *there* happened to have been. Later on, his mother took a razor blade and scraped them all off.

CHAPTER EIGHTEEN
AUNT MARY IN MANHATTAN

And then there was the trip to New York city when Oliver was sixteen, when he visited Aunt Mary by himself and began to know her as a person, not only as the Magic Aunt who nurtured his interest in rocks and shells and stars, who sent him books on reptiles and dinosaurs, and Gilbert Science kits: a microscope, another kit about mineralogy with an array of samples from apatite to zircon, and a chemistry set that showed him how to mix simple elements to obtain unexpected results. (Oliver doubts she anticipated the odorous classroom tricks he played with hydrogen sulfide.)

That first time he and Aunt Mary were alone together, no hovering parent or persistent sister present, she gave him the best gift of all. She listened carefully to what he had to say, and challenged his ideas.

I

Oliver was sixteen. His sister was twenty-one and involved with a naval cadet whom she'd met in Walla Walla. One of the blue serge Whitman College crew you've heard about. He had been ordered to a base in Florida and she was determined to follow him. Her mother objected to her going alone, so they compromised; she would go with her as chaperon. How times have changed! Oliver went with them as far as Chicago, and then continued to New York City by himself.

The trip was by train. The war was still on and though Germany had surrendered on May 11, the Pullmans were full of military people headed in all directions. Oliver arrived in the Big Apple for a ten day visit. His mother and sister followed later from Florida.

Aunt Mary had moved from her apartment at 10 West 33rd Street and taken up residence in the National Arts Club in the old Samuel Tilden mansion on the south side of Gramercy Park. It is on 21st Street at the foot of Madison Avenue. The Club, back then, was old and genteel and rickety -- today it is very posh and smart and ultra-in. Oliver is a member although he seldom goes there. It was and is full of paintings and Victorian furniture and a beautiful bar with a cut glass ceiling and window embayments in which he used to sit and watch people walk by. Sometimes he would gaze at the trees across the street in the park, and muse about what he and his aunt had discussed at dinner the day before.

Oliver was old enough to spend his days wandering the city by himself. Again, the round of museums kept him busy until they met in the evening. They attended musicals; *Oklahoma!* and *South Pacific* were the best. It was summer 1945 and everyone knew the war was coming to an end. Germany had surrendered, but a great battle still lay ahead in the Pacific.

II

It was during this trip that a catastrophe happened in New York City. One Saturday morning he and his aunt ate breakfast at the basement Automat on 45th Street. Aunt Mary didn't have to commute to her work in New Jersey, and they were on their way to the Museum of Natural History. They had finished eating and climbed the stairs to the street. Suddenly the orderly world of automatic little windows offering salads and pieces of pie ended.

Sirens everywhere! Crowds rushing to Fifth Avenue, milling, staring south towards the Empire State Building, the tower's upper floors appearing and disappearing in a morning shroud of heavy mist.

Everyone pointing up, shouting. "There! There! See it!" Near the top, Oliver made out a ragged hole punched in the wall of the building. Smoke was spilling from it, but the great tower still stood.

Police were setting up barricades blocking Fifth Avenue, keeping the crowd from moving toward the accident. Someone said a U.S. Army Air Force bomber had plowed into the building, in the heavy fog. Later, Oliver learned that one of the plane's engines had cut straight through the tower and out the other side. It landed on the roof of 10 West 33rd, gutting the apartment where Oliver's aunt had recently lived!

Oliver's memories focus on Aunt Mary. He remembers her, tiny, determined, accosting a very large, well dressed man who was looking at the ragged hole in the building through a pair of expensive binoculars.

"My good man, I wish to borrow your binoculars for one minute," she said.

The man was astonished and meekly handed the glasses to her. She peered through them at the carnage and then handed the glasses to Oliver. He took them as though they were red hot, stared briefly at them, not through them, and in great embarrassment handed them back to the man. This was a very self conscious time in Oliver's life. His aunt's directness embarrassed him, and he was grateful when she turned away from the scene and led him to Times Square and the west side subway.

"There's nothing we can do," she told him. "It's best we go on about our plans."

III

Oliver remembers Aunt Mary with pride and affection, but back then she led him a merry chase through the wilderness of his emotions.

Nothing seemed beyond her. She fed stray cats which lived in the park across from her club, and brought them scraps from her own dinners, dinners always eaten out at some restaurant. She did no cooking of her own.

One evening Oliver was with her in the Automat when a man at an adjoining table departed, leaving a full pork chop on his plate. Cat food! She reached over and was dropping the chop into a plastic bag she carried for such purposes when the man returned with the utensils he had forgotten.

"Here, my good man, please accept this as recompense for your dinner," she said. She handed him a five dollar bill and walked out, bagged pork chop in hand, Oliver in her wake. The man stood gaping after them. Aunt Mary always called strange men, "My good man." Oliver believes it intimidated them.

Aunt Mary didn't restrict her crusade to stray animals. Case in point: She and Oliver were on their way to a Broadway play near Times Square after dinner at the Automat. It was 7:30 on a warm metropolitan evening and crowds were ambling through the streets. As Oliver and his aunt came into the square they saw a circle of a hundred or more people. Aunt Mary, with Oliver in tow, pushed her way to the front. In the center of the circle three sailors were teasing a bindle stiff. The old man was dressed in trousers but no shirt, shoes but no socks. The sailors had grabbed his ragged coat and pulled it off. He was trying to thread one bony arm into a sleeve, but the sleeve was inside out and his efforts were futile. Just as the old man would get the sleeve adjusted, one of the sailors would jerk the cloth away and the man would begin again.

The crowd stood voiceless, not a word of protest.

Aunt Mary took one look and stepped into the circle with the bindle stiff and the sailors. She took the coat from the old man, reached her arm up the scrofulous sleeve and turned it right side out.

"Here my good man, let me help you," she said, assisting him into his jacket. She turned then to the sailors and pinned each with a carborundum gaze.

"You should be ashamed of yourselves."

The chastised sailors escaped into the crowd, and the circle of gawkers scattered like guilty children. The bindle stiff thanked her and offered her a cigarette that had been stuck to his lower lip throughout the teasing.

"Lady, would you like a drag?"

"No thank you, my good man, I do not smoke," she replied, and then to Oliver who stood there in mute embarrassment, "Come on, let's go. We'll be late for the show!" Grabbing him by the hand, she raced them off to the theater.

Oliver felt that the scene had somehow called attention to him. He was aware of his acne and his inadequacy. But all that is past now, and he has come to appreciate and admire his fierce, spinster aunt who marched through the world doing what she could to set things right. Little by little her shade -- she's dead these many years -- has taught him not to give up the good fight.

IV

There was more that Oliver learned from Aunt Mary. As they hurried through the streets of Manhattan from museums to the theater and on to restaurants, she might spy a bag lady or a teetery old man pushing a shopping cart loaded with junk, or a half drunk beggar. "Excuse me," she'd say, and thrust a folded bill into their hands.

"That one almost got away," she'd tell Oliver, smile, and drag him along to the next place on their full schedule.

"Why do you do that," Oliver complained. ""You know that man will just buy wine, Or that old woman won't know what to do with what you gave her." All the Calvinistic Walla Walla voices critical of ne'er-do-wells whispered in his head -- how often he'd heard that such people were just plain lazy, and that "the Lord helps those who help themselves."

"It isn't for us to judge others," Aunt Mary quietly explained. "What matters is for each of us to feel for himself, to find out what makes us feel better. What those people do is up to them. We don't know their stories, what difficulties they've had to face. We should do what we can to help them, but we have no business judging them. It is up to each one of them to use the money as he or she chooses."

She didn't sermonize, and changed the subject, asking Oliver what he thought of the musical they'd just seen or what he thought of an exhibit they'd visited. She left the seed she planted to sprout in its own time.

V

There was another part of Aunt Mary which slowly revealed itself. Oliver learned most of her enigmatic side later in life, but two experiences from his first independent visit stick in his memory.

Aunt Mary was a scholar and a Latinist and worked for the Saint Anthony Guild Press in Paterson, New Jersey. She was the coordinating editor for the Roman Catholic translation of the Old and New Testaments. As such she had frequent contacts and many friends among the Catholic clergy. Some of this washed onto Oliver during his visit. For example, Oliver had the unique experience of going to Radio City Music Hall with a Jesuit confessor, a close friend of his Aunt's. Father O'Brien expressed interest in seeing the Rockets, the famous chorus line, and since Aunt Mary was busy during the week, he took Oliver as his guest. Noting profound happened. No proselytizing took place. They both enjoyed the show. It was a very "Jebby" approach to life, and one that made Oliver realize not all priests were cut from Father Callahan's cloth.

That summer Oliver met another priest who introduced Oliver to the idea that science may not be able to explain everything under the sun, and that intelligent people may harbor strange notions.

One evening, Aunt Mary invited a friend, Father Alexader, for dinner at the Club. Although he was a Franciscan who had spent much of his life in Brazil, he arrived looking disarmingly secular in a well cut suit. Not even his tie and collar revealed his calling.

The old Samuel Tilden mansion was creakingly quiet. The Victorian bar was empty, the fading evening light barely revealed its stained glass ceiling. In the dining room next door only two tables were being served. Aunt Mary, Father Thomas and Oliver were seated near the arched opening to the bar. Oliver was seated in such a way that he looked directly into the gloom of the bar which was made more mysterious by dark mirrors lining its walls.

Despite its somber setting the meal, filled with humor and stories and intellectual repartee, enchanted Oliver. He listened as Father Thomas and Aunt Mary reminisced over times past, and discussed New York City politics with its Mayor, Fiorello La Guardia, "The Little Flower." They were *Commonweal* Catholics and very liberal.

While waiting for dessert, Aunt Mary asked Father Thomas about his service in Brazil where he sometimes traveled far up the Amazon and Rio Negro Rivers. As he spoke he became quite serious and told of the difficulties he had encountered, how once he had been present at an exorcism and had seen levitation take place.

"What was this, evil?" Aunt Mary questioned Father Thomas.

"What can I say? I saw it happen. There are instances in the Vatican records. But I have chosen not to report it as such." Father inclined his head slightly toward Oliver.

Aunt Mary caught his gesture. "Things may happen, but are best left to others. There are a hundred rational explanations. Perhaps you were mistaken."

"Perhaps." Father Thomas smiled and changed the subject.

The conversation shifted and desert followed. Oliver's gaze was drawn again and again to the dark mirrors in the bar. He shivered; a chill along his back. To him the notion of levitation was absurd. He had clear opinions about fact and fantasy. The Easter Rabbit had started it all, and the undeniable force of gravity was discussed in his science books. Yet here were two brilliant people seriously talking about the impossible! It was absurd! Oliver didn't try to contradict them, but how could he believe them?

--- --- ---

As his life has since unfolded Oliver has seen things beyond his power to explain. His theories are not dramatized by religious myth making, but the mystery that confronted him that night at the supper table has persisted. An even greater mystery is how rational minds can entertain such contradictions.

Those were Oliver's childhood trips. The discovery of his aunt's complexities, his seeing thousands of people crowding the streets of New York, his savoring the kaleidoscopic array of art and history both in the museums and on the streets, the possibility of the unknown or perhaps the unknowable.

All those spectacles and events made Oliver aware of an expanding world, a world that tempered the pain and boredom of growing up Walla Walla, that made him able to leave, to put the town behind him. But before his departure, only months away, new friends and new jobs were still to come.

CHAPTER NINETEEN
THE BEE HIVE

Oliver's first real job where he worked scheduled hours and received a monthly pay check came in his Sophomore Year. He worked after school as a stock clerk at the Bee Hive, an old fashioned dry goods and notions store located across from the Book Nook on the corner of First and Main. Mr. Allen, The Bee Hive's owner, allowed it was possibly the oldest store in town, older than Gardner's Department Store, which had "From 1860" on its logo along with a covered wagon. But Gardner's had changed with the times. It had a modern façade and a new fangled X-ray device downstairs in the shoe department so that Oliver, pressing his stomach against the front of the machine, could look down through a viewing screen and see his toes tucked all skeletal into his shoes and learn if his new oxfords really fitted. Oliver wonders now how many customers used that machine and just where all those random X-rays went.

The Bee Hive hadn't changed; it looked old. It had no logo, not even a bee hive; it was simply The Bee Hive, and everybody knew it. It was the spirit of Walla Walla past.

The store was built of worn Victorian brick, two stories tall, with narrow, high windows on the second floor that peered down on Main Street like supercilious spinsters all draped in faded tulle curtains. Show windows on one side of the entrance displayed men's shirts on dummy torsos lacking heads and arms. On the other side, women's gloves on porcelain hands gestured to passersby. Around the corner on the First Street side of the Bee Hive was a solid brick wall without openings save for a small rear door with one show window offering yarn and spools of thread and a few bolts of cloth. There was no alley entrance, and goods were unloaded onto the curb on First Street and then into an old elevator that came up through the sidewalk when two ancient iron doors flush with the pavement gaped open.

The Bee Hive had an aroma all its own. There was a tinge of must that underlay everything, just as ambergris serves as the carrier for attar of roses. Intertwined with the must were scents of soap and hints of perfume from the lady's counters. A suggestion of unbleached cotton drifted down from the dry goods on the second floor. The plank floors gave off their own odor of oiled sawdust and old wood, and a reminder of damp earth seeped up from the basement. All these merged into a special scent, richer to Oliver than all the perfumes he has come to know.

I

Oliver's job was a real job. He had worked other places, swept the floor at the Crescent Drug Store, carried papers and mowed lawns, but being a stock clerk at the Bee Hive involved many new and serious things. For the first time, he had to punch a time clock. This turned time into money. If his card wasn't punched, no pay. At first Oliver thought of this only as money lost or money gained, but there was another side to it all. The store depended upon his being there to fill the shelves and unpack the crates and boxes of incoming merchandise. Some days Oliver felt that being late to work after school was worth the lost pay/time, but Mr. Allen talked to him about promptness and reliability. He pointed out that if Oliver wasn't reliable, the clerks couldn't make sales, and if there were fewer sales there would be less money to pay salaries, and that Oliver could lose his job. By that time Oliver was buying all his clothes, and earning all his spending money. Oliver knew he needed the job at the Bee Hive, and he heeded Mr. Allen's advice.

Mr. Allen and the staff had other expectations. Oliver learned to follow directions and to be accurate in filling stock orders. He also had to check the incoming invoices against the goods received. For the first time, he couldn't fudge his accounts as he did when he carried papers. With papers, he was the only one who lost when his books didn't balance. At the store, Oliver had to account for every item, and those times when he was a substitute counter clerk he had to balance his own cash drawer. It was good training.

When Oliver was asked to wait on customers, he worked at the men's counter selling shirts, and socks, and work gloves, and sundries. This meant he met all types of customers, friendly ones, irritable ones, impatient ones. Personal relations were important, and if you were behind the counter you couldn't put off the contact to another day, like you could when making monthly collections for the newspaper. There were no excuses, and so Oliver learned to "get along," as his mother called it.

"Oliver, you just have to get along!" Little by little he did.

II

Mr. Allen, the proprietor, came from New Zealand. His son, who was born in America, helped him run the store. Oliver doesn't know whether Mr. Allen bought the Bee Hive from someone else, or if he started it himself. The store seemed older than its owner, and probably was there when he came from New Zealand.

The inside of the store was even more interesting than the outside. When a customer came in the front door he or she had a choice. On the right was the men's department with a long counter behind which were boxes of socks and handkerchiefs and shelves with white shirts. The dress shirts were only white and there was no such thing as button down collars. If you were very formal you used a little piece of wire called a *collar stay* which fitted behind your necktie and had two sharp pointed prongs that fit into the tips of your collar and held it in place. Of course, there were blue work shirts and stacks and stacks of Levis with copper rivets and button flies. Kids and young men would buy them tight and then get them wet and wear them dry so that they fitted like skin.

In the center of the store was an island filled with men's dress gloves and work gloves where customers could try them on by themselves, because men don't want help like ladies do when they are trying on gloves. There were also boxes of strange things like celluloid collars, elastic arm bands to keep men's sleeves up, and green eye shades like Night Editors on newspapers used. Such things hadn't been in fashion for years and years, but the Bee Hive still carried them.

Oliver was fascinated by the stiff old collars, and would buy them -- they cost only a few cents each, the only sale of them in years -- and carefully printing addresses on them, would mail them to confused and bemused friends and relatives. He had discovered that the post office would accept almost anything as postal fare if it were properly labeled. He once mailed a coconut in its basketball size, fibrous husk to an unwary friend.

Farther back, beyond the celluloid collars was a table filled with washing powders and soaps, and one time, big brown paper bags of kapok, which is a story in itself. On the left as customers entered the store from Main Street was the women's counter with stools in front on which they could sit while they tried on gloves. The stools had little round wooden seats hinged on single, movable iron rods. The rods were fashioned in such a way that when a lady wasn't using a seat it could be folded up against the counter out of the way. In addition to trying on gloves, ladies could buy needles and thread, and buttons and corset stays, and brassieres and panties, and corsets, but that was unknown stuff which the lady clerks guarded from stock boys. There were boxes of *Kotex* in discrete green wrappers under the counter, but nobody admitted what was there except when ladies asked for it.

The floors were very worn, unpainted wood. Each day, after the store closed, Oliver would scatter red sawdust soaked in oil on the floor.

That was to keep the dust down as he swept the store with a big push broom. The sawdust would lodge in the cracks between the boards and in the places where the softer grain of the planks had worn away, so he swept the floor and then swept it again to make sure it was clean.

At the back of the store was a wide stairway leading to the second floor. Under this stair was another stair to the basement where the stock was stored. On either side of the stairway at the back were two doors to the toilets. They were painted plain white and were unmarked. If you worked there you knew which was the *men's* and which was the *women's*.

Upstairs was one large room which ran the length of the store. At the end of the room behind the stairs was another storage space piled high with boxes of bulk toilet paper and bulk Kotex. The individual Kotex boxes weren't wrapped, which was considered very indiscreet. They each had to be wrapped in plain green paper before they were sold. That was one of Oliver's jobs when there wasn't anything else to keep him busy. There was a counter there with a big roll of discrete green paper and a tape dispenser, the kind with water in it and a brush. The dispenser would get gummed up so that the tape would jam in the machine. Then Oliver would have to stop and unstick the tape so that the handle would work, the boxes could be wrapped, and discreteness could prevail.

Oliver stacked the bulk boxes in such a way that there was a cubby hole up on top of the pile where he could hide from Mr. Allen. Oliver also made the stack so that he could climb up stepping only on the toilet paper boxes which held his weight, and not on the bulk Kotex boxes which did not.

The front two-thirds of the room was public and lined with shelves that held hundreds of bolts of cloth of all kinds, as well as mosquito netting and lengths of lace. There was also blue striped ticking for sale, from which customers made mattress covers. Two elderly women sold these materials to lady customers who came upstairs. Oliver never saw a male customer on the second floor. The women who clerked were nice to Oliver, but did not approve of his wrapping Kotex boxes when there were lady patrons present.

Far below, the store's basement was dark, lighted only by tiny, dim light bulbs with visible glowing filaments. The floor was made in part of crumbling brick, and in other places, packed earth. On the right side, as you came into the basement was the freight elevator worked by hand with rope pulleys. That was where Oliver and another stock boy named Gene unloaded freight.

Mr. Allen never threw anything away, and there were shelves sagging with thousands of boxes of free soap samples, boxes of cleaning powder labeled *The Gold Dust Twins*, who were pickininies -- which would not be at all PC now -- and *Bon Ami* with a little chicken on the front and a label that read "Hasn't Scratched yet." Those are the names Oliver can remember, but there were dozens of other labels from before his time which he didn't recognize. All were free samples never given away.

During World War II there was a soap shortage and Mr. Allen saw an outlet for his hoard of samples. He directed Oliver and Gene to undo all of those sample boxes and packets and to mix the scouring powders in small bags, and the soaps in bigger bags. Presto! The Bee Hive had a special sale of scarce soap and cleansing powders.

Mr. Allen thought of another answer to wartime shortages. A huge crate made of flimsy plywood stood in the basement near the freight elevator. Oliver didn't know what it contained until one day Mr. Allen had the two stock boys push the crate onto the freight elevator and haul it to the sidewalk where they opened it. It held a mass of compressed kapok. Kapok is a natural material very much like thistle down which is used as pillow stuffing and for filling life jackets. It is very light and very fluffy, and when the crate's lid was removed the contents billowed out in a great mushroom shaped cap.

The box was at least six by six by six feet, and as Oliver and the town found out, that is a lot of kapok. Mr. Allen planned to have a pillow stuffing sale, and told Oliver and the other stock boy to stuff the kapok into brown paper bags, one pound per bag, and seal the bags with sticky tape. That was not an easy task; one pound of kapok is a lot of kapok.

During the War, the Navy was training V-5 and V-12 sailors at Whitman College. The cadets, with afternoon passes, would walk downtown dressed in their blue serge uniforms. Oliver and Gene were hard at work, kapok was flying everywhere. Main and First looked like a snow storm in September. The kapok had a natural attraction to all fuzzy cloth, especially blue serge. The *attack of the super lint* hit before the cadets could beat a retreat. It took weeks to de-kapok their uniforms, and the other shop keepers on Main Street laughed and said that Mr. Allen had set back the war effort.

III

Mr. Allen was conservative but very nice. One time Oliver and Gene turned off all the lights in the basement and were having a pea shooter fight, stealing through the dark aisles and surprising each other with sprays of peas. Meanwhile, Mr. Allen came quietly into the basement to see what was happening and why the lights were off. Oliver, thought the shadowy figure before him was Gene and sprayed him with a fusillade of saliva wet peas! Mr. Allen calmly cleared his throat, reached over and turned on the lights, and frowned at Oliver. But all he said was, "Is that all you have to do?" He didn't fire Oliver or Gene. They learned their lesson, though, and were more grown up employees after that.

Mr. Allen and Oliver discussed geography. Oliver studied maps and dreamed of traveling to far places, and was fascinated knowing someone who came all the way from New Zealand. Mr. Allen once said to Oliver that Timbuktu was in Asia; Oliver said, "No it is in Africa on the south side of the Sahara Desert." Mr. Allen brought Oliver into is his office where he kept an Atlas and the two of them found Timbuktu in Africa just as Oliver claimed. Mr. Allen said, "Good for you, you are right and I was wrong." That made Oliver admire Mr. Allen even more.

IV

Sometimes Oliver waited on customers at the men's counter. He remembers how the Indians, who are now Native Americans, would come in and shop. There was one Indian he waited on who bought a pair of socks. Oliver made out the bill and wrapped the socks and put them in a paper bag. The Indian paid, and then said "I want a handkerchief." So, Oliver got out a big box of cowboy kerchiefs and the Indian chose one. Oliver wrote out the bill and wrapped up the kerchief and his customer paid. Then the Indian said, "I want a work shirt." They went on like that for five different items, but that was OK with Oliver, because how many people have ever gotten to wait on a real Indian.

There was one old man who came in and bought green eye-shades which he still wore. He died the year Oliver worked at the Bee Hive, but Mr. Allen still kept the eye-shades in stock just in case somebody else needed some.

V

Oliver wasn't completely cured of being a kid, or maybe he just wanted attention. After he stopped working at the Bee Hive, he returned once to play an elaborate practical joke. He went in the side door on First Street, rolled up his sleeves, stuck a pencil behind his ear and walked out the front door with a big ball of twine, a piece of chalk, and a six foot tape measure. Once outside on Main street, he marked an X on the sidewalk and began measuring around the corner from Main Street to the First Street side. He used the twine to mark his path, but it kept slipping off the X. People began watching his unsuccessful effort until Oliver asked a man, who had paused to look, to help him. He explained that the Bee Hive was planning a store front stand for a sale, and would the man please hold the twine on the X for just a minute while Oliver measured around the corner. The man was very helpful and held the twine on the X with his foot. Oliver then measured around the corner, made another X, and asked another passing man, would he hold the end of the twine on the X while Oliver went in the store and got some tape to hold down the twine. When the man put his foot on the second X, Oliver didn't go into the store but sneaked away and ran around the block and went up on a roof across the street. From there he watched as the two men became impatient holding the twine and each began to follow it around the corner until they confronted each other.

Oliver was not the first person to play this joke. He had read about Jim Moran, a famous practical joker, who thought it up. Oliver thinks now it wasn't so much the joke's being on the two men that excited him, as the feeling of danger as he approached each man and got him involved.

VI

The more Oliver looks back, the more he misses the Bee Hive. It's gone now. The wonderful odors and the plank floors with red sawdust in the cracks, and the celluloid collars, and the discrete green boxes of Kotex, and nobody knows what all was in the basement, and the little stools where ladies sat to try on gloves, and the ladies, and Mr. Allen, a real gentleman from New Zealand, are all gone, and Walla Walla is the poorer.

CHAPTER TWENTY
FRIENDS

I

In his sophomore year Oliver moved from the house on East Alder, with his own room in the basement, to an apartment in a former mansion on Washington Street. The apartment had only one bedroom which his mother used. (His sister, by then, was living in Seattle.) Oliver slept on the davenport in the living room and kept all his *stuff* in boxes in a closet. This was difficult, especially in his Junior year when he got the mumps, which he was afraid would go down on him. That meant that his testicles would become infected and swell up.

It's interesting that the phrase *go down on him*, today means something different. Even when Oliver was in the army the phrase meant getting the mumps in the wrong place. Of course, by the time he was a Junior in high school Oliver had heard men in town talking about the ladies in the hotels on lower Main Street who did something called *whole French,* and a variation called *around the world,* which cost more, and *Pabst Blue Ribbon* which was entirely different. He wasn't quite certain what those were, and it didn't occur to him that *going down* could mean something else.

Oliver was miserable and scared that his mumps were going down, and that his balls would inflate like grape fruit. Mumps can do that and it is very painful. He lay on the couch worrying and feeling all kinds of twinges down there, wishing that he had a room of his own. Fortunately only his neck glands swelled.

Oliver was changing, or more accurately Oliver's body was changing. He had reached puberty, but puberty hadn't quite reached him. His weenie, his dick, alternately embarrassed and gave him pleasure. It popped up at the wrong times; but when Oliver was alone he found it very consoling.

His balls, as he was beginning to think of them, had until then simply been there. Oliver didn't want them to get kicked, it hurt! But there had been no connection in Oliver's mind between those sleeping twins and what happened when he got a *heart on.* Now a new trio announced itself. Not the Father, the Son, and "that bird up there," which Oliver had dismissed some time before. It was much easier to accept eternal damnation deferred than to defer immediate pleasure.

The new triumvirate was persuasive and pervasive. Not only was there pleasure involved, sometimes Oliver's balls would ache. It was called *hot rocks* and was supposed to happen only if you had been necking with a girl. Oliver had never necked with a girl, but he still got hot rocks. The simplest way to get over hot rocks was to *beat off.* There was another way if you weren't alone. An older guy who had been necking, after saying good night to his date, would stoop and grab the bumper of his car -- which in those days was a heavy piece of metal that stuck out in front of the car and really protected it -- and pull up real hard like he was trying to lift the front end. The strain of lifting would make the pressure and pain go away.

Guys would get together after they had taken their dates home and complain about hot rocks, and pull up on the bumpers of their cars. The more they complained, the more Oliver envied them, because hot rocks proved something even if he didn't know quite what. He would sometimes pull up on the bumper of the Hudson Terraplane and imagine that he had been on a hot date.

His life now became crowded with references to balls. Like the doggerel that began, "'Balls, cried the queen, 'If I had two, I'd be king!'" Or the joke about the man who went around singing, "Give me land, lots of land, ..." to everybody's distraction, until they kicked him in the nuts and gave him a couple of *achers*. And the initiation into the Big Y Club at the YMCA. That was for athletes and never happened to Oliver with his bad eyes, but he'd heard about how they rubbed liniment on the initiates' balls, and how it burned something awful. Oliver didn't know whether to believe that or not. Balls were certainly on the mind of every high school male. At that point balls seemed even more important than girls.

The trio between Oliver's legs was always there, through good times and bad, sometimes causing him grief, sometimes consoling him, but never deserting him. They were his secret friends, part of his private life, never discussed. Oliver was well on his way to growing up Walla Walla.

II

The apartment was one block from the high school. Oliver could go back and forth easily, and came home to cook lunch. Lunch was Franco American spaghetti which came out of the can like a smooth, slippery column. It stood in the pot quivering gelatinously, until he broke it up with a fork. He would sit in the kitchenette looking out the window and imagining he was traveling to far places. Oliver was good at preparing lunch, for he had been doing it since the Fifth grade.

Oliver's Freshman year in Wa-Hi is a blur. Maybe more will come back, but he doubts it. During his Sophomore year, life for Oliver changed in an entirely new way. There were two reasons for this. He started working on the stage in the auditorium, and met new friends. Before that Oliver had playmates like Howard and Ronald, and there had been bullies like Bobby, but playmates weren't friends to whom he could tell things that he couldn't tell his mother or anyone else. Friends were people whom he could depend on, and later would enlist with him in the army.

III

Walla Walla was a small town insulated by its distance from other cities. It had two movie theaters as well as one that was forced to close. There was very little to do. Most of the kids didn't go to the library like Oliver did. On weekends they would get in their cars and drive up and down Main Street. Grown ups considered that anti-social behavior, and the town fathers decided to correct the situation. The firemen from the Fire Department and the members of the Chamber of Commerce got together and rented a small vacant store next door to the Roxy Theater.

The Roxy Theater on lower Main Street showed cowboy movies for a nickel on Saturday morning along with three cartoons and an episode of a serial like *Flash Gordon meets Ming the Merciless*, and a Three Stooges comedy, a News Reel, and maybe John Nesbitt's *Passing Parade* which discussed things like Nostradamus and his predictions. If you had a dime you could spend the extra nickel for popcorn or a big paper cup of Coke. Even really little kids went there.

The store which the city rented was made into a Youth Club for high school kids who didn't have anything to do on Friday and Saturday nights. Even a sophomore like Oliver found his way there. He stood around and watched the Seniors dancing in the back room where there was a juke box. In the front room was a soda fountain that the firemen took turns tending. There were also some tables in the front where you could play checkers or chess. The firemen kept the boards and pieces under the counter and would give them out if the borrower left his driver's license for security.

There was also a big refrigerator near the front window, a regular refrigerator like those found in nice homes. It was white and had a flat top six feet off the floor.

One evening Oliver was watching the Senior girls clustered at the fountain when unexpectedly, as if out of nowhere, a voice said to him, " Do you play chess?" Oliver looked up, and there sitting cross legged on the top of the refrigerator was a small blonde guy with a crew cut. He was smaller than Oliver, which was small. Oliver at that time weighed about ninety pounds -- like the Ninety Pound Weakling that the bully at the beach kicked sand in the face of until he found out about Charles Atlas. Oliver thinks his own small size was emotional dwarfism, the result of feeling so crumby about himself. After he met his friends, he sprouted six inches and gained fifty pounds.

Oliver said he didn't know how to play chess, and Jack, that was his name, Jack jumped off the refrigerator and said, "Come on, I'll teach you," and went and got a chess set from the fireman behind the soda fountain. He and Oliver sat down at a table and Jack taught Oliver the rules of the game. It was very funny because every time Oliver made a bad move Jack corrected him. Oliver won the first two games they played that night, but not because he knew anything about chess. Jack got frustrated and furious and kept rubbing his head and going "ooooh!" not at Oliver for being dumb, but at himself for losing, which really didn't make any sense.

Eleven o'clock came and it was time for the Youth Club to close and Jack returned the chess set. Oliver was about to leave by himself, when Jack said, "Aren't you coming with us?"

Us? Who were us? Oliver didn't know, but he followed Jack outside. It turned out that Jack, who was a Junior, had a bunch of friends who were Juniors. For some reason that Oliver still does not understand, from that moment on he had a bunch of friends who were a year ahead of him in school.

Perhaps it was because all of them were considered "brains" by the other students. There was Bill, now a famous medical Doctor, specializing in sleep disorders, and Everett, whom Oliver has lost track of, and Walter, the trumpet player, and Jack, who was very serious and interested in math. They went to Bill's house that first night and ate pancakes and stayed up all night. It is odd now that Oliver thinks about it, but it seems that he seldom let his mother know where he was, and she seldom asked.

IV

Oliver and his new friends played chess. Bill was the best. In addition to chess, they made up complicated games with intricate rules which now would be considered homemade *Dungeons and Dragons*. Bill drove them around in his new Buick sedan which his parents gave him. He was richer than Oliver and the others, but was always broke and borrowed money from his friends. Walter, who played trumpet, and Bill, who played the double bass, were the core of a group of aspiring jazz musicians. All of them were hip, knew about bop when it was in its infancy, and listened to Dizzy Gillespie so long ago that Walter owned a 78 rpm record of Dizzy playing on the *Fruit Salad* label under the name Izzy Eisenberg. Dizzy used that name because he had a contract with another company but wanted to record with his friends on *Fruit Salad* records. Oliver wonders how many jazz buffs know about that?

Another member of the group was Teddy, who didn't play an instrument but knew a lot about jazz, and hung out with them part of the time. He was head usher at the Liberty Theater, and had actually "gone all the way" with one of the usherettes. Oliver and his friends eagerly asked Teddy how it felt. He replied, "It feels like that's the place it really should be." Which is the best answer Oliver has ever heard. Teddy was a good person and the usherettes liked him.

Teddy had his misadventures, too. One time he ordered a book at the Book Nook, its title was *Duke Ellington*. When the book came, the clerk had made a mistake and it was the life of the Duke of Wellington which shows you most people in Walla Walla didn't know about jazz. Another time, Teddy wanted to learn to cook, and bought a book with a Chinese recipe for bird's nest soup. He used a robin's nest, an old one, which didn't taste at all like he and Oliver expected.

During the summer of Oliver's Junior year, that is his last year in high school, Teddy and Jack and Oliver took a Greyhound bus to San Francisco and slept in a cheap hotel even less expensive than the YMCA. They went out to Flyshacker's on the ocean, and to a restaurant above Seal Rocks. They met some girls there and Teddy had a date, but Jack and Oliver didn't. After San Francisco they took a bus back up the

Oregon coast. Oliver persuaded them to hike along the coast. They got off the bus at Florence and walked as far as Yachats. They then decide to hitch hike, but got only one ride on the back of a flat bed truck. In Newport they agreed it was time to go home and took another bus back to Walla Walla. That was Oliver's first adventure away from home and family. Friends are to share adventures with.

V

Oliver's friends held jam sessions. Oliver wanted to enter in and tried to learn to play the guitar. He knew it wasn't possible to learn quickly enough to play melodies, but if he could learn chords, he could at least provide some background to the others. The man who sold guitars sold Oliver one with a neck so thick that Oliver couldn't get his thumb around it to reach the G string. At least that's what Oliver says, but probably he hadn't much talent.

His mother had sent Oliver to a piano teacher when he was eight. He learned to play "Up the hill, down the hill, sliding," and that was all. His eyes jiggled and he was unable to read chords. Recitals, even baby recitals, were agony for Oliver. After one or two musical disasters Oliver's distress was so apparent that his mother let him stop.

Nevertheless, Oliver liked music, and later when he was a Freshman in high school and had his own money, he went to the Bendix Music Store on East Main Street on the same side as Vitart's Photo Studio but up a block. The store was one long room with console radios on display in the front, and on the left in back, a counter behind which were shelves with hundreds of 78 rpm records – the only kind there were. Across from the record counter were glass booths where customers could sit and listen to records and decide which ones they liked well enough to buy. Oliver asked for "A Night on Bald Mountain" which he had heard on the radio. The clerk handed a big disc to Oliver saying, "Here's a recording I think you'll like. It's by the Philadelphia Symphony Orchestra." Oliver took it and holding it very carefully by the edges went into one of the booths and put the disc on the turntable and lowered the stylus arm onto the record where its hair thin grooves began. He listened to it twice all the way through and then bought it. Another day when he had more money, his second purchase was Ferdi Grofe's "Grand Canyon Suite."

Because he couldn't learn to play an instrument, Oliver thought it over and asked his mother to teach him to sing. She went to her little blonde upright piano -- Oliver is certain now that it was a present from Steve -- and started to play and sing the "Habañera" from "Carmen." (Remember, she had two MFA's.) She turned to Oliver and said, "Sing after me."

What fifteen year old can start singing the "Habañera?" After that, when he was alone, Oliver would sing along with the Sons of the Pioneers on the radio. He learned some of their songs like "I'm Riding Old Paint." which he loves, and sang to his daughter when she was a baby. Anyway, that's the story of Oliver's love for music, and how his friends helped him learn about jazz and be-bop at a time when very few people knew what it was.

VI

Oliver did all kinds of crazy things so that his friends would notice him. One evening he climbed up the wall of the Montgomery Ward building on the corner of the block where the Roxy Theater and the Youth Club were located. He was shouting, "Unk! Unk!" That was the name of the ape man in a comic strip in the Sunday newspaper. The name of the strip was "Flying Jenny," and the heroine was marooned on a tropical island. She found the ape man living there. He had been lost on the island as a child and grew up without anyone to talk to. That's why he was only able to say "Unk, unk."

The strip was patterned after the exploits of Amelia Earhart. Oliver didn't know that; he was just showing off, climbing up, hanging on to narrow brick ridges that stuck out of the building. A police car came by and the cops made him climb down. All his friends were across the street draped over each other's shoulders helpless with laughter, but the police were very nice and just warned Oliver not to do it again.

Another time Oliver figured out how to disgust people. On the corner of Second and Main Streets, kitty corner from the Baker Boyer Bank, was a restaurant with window seats next to the outside sidewalk. Oliver chewed some gum and rolled it in the palms of his hands until it formed a string. He then stuck one end of the string up his nose and stood outside those windows acting like he was trying to snuff up a long bugger. The people inside were disgusted, and the manager started to come out. Once more, Oliver's friends were across the street having a laughing fit. It's plain that Oliver was desperate.

VII

Other friends came and went in Oliver's life. There was David whom he really liked. Oliver and David drove around town in David's souped up coupe. David wasn't the kind of person you'd think would soup up a car, but behind his placid face and inside his round body lurked a hot rodder.

David and Oliver went camping at Wallula Gap thirty miles west of town where the Columbia River flows into its famous gorge. That's where the two tall rocks called the Twin Sisters are located. The boys camped for two nights in one of the canyons that run back behind them. They were hunting for gold that an old timer had told Oliver had been hidden there by two stage coach robbers. The bandits were fleeing with saddle bags full of gold coins when the pursuing posse caught them. In their enthusiasm, their captors took the robbers down to the river and hung them from an old willow tree. It wasn't until after the two were swinging that the posse remembered the saddle bags. No matter where they hunted, the gold was never found. The treasure is still out there, because Oliver and David didn't find it either. No matter, friends are to go exploring with.

VIII

Sometimes Oliver's friends made mistakes or booboos that lightened his own ineptness. Oliver had a friend Tom, who was a Senior when Oliver was a Junior. Tom was going on a special date and wanted to buy some whiskey, because everyone knew that girls were easier when they had something to drink. The bootlegger wouldn't' sell Tom anything except Rock and Rye, a vile concoction. A bottle of R & R has a string covered with rock sugar candy hanging inside it, and the rye is syrupy. Tom didn't know the devastating effect of sweet alcoholic drinks, and had lot more of the rye than his date. They parked in the countryside and Tom made his move and kissed her. At that moment the rock and rye caught up with him; nauseated, he leaped out of the car and threw up. The girl never spoke to him again.

When Tom told Oliver what had happened, Oliver commiserated with him, but was secretly consoled for his own dateless life. That episode was typical of how the high school students experimented with alcohol, although Oliver didn't drink until he was in the army. He simply didn't like the way it tasted. He does now.

Oliver was told when he returned from the army that his high school graduating class threw a big party at Lake Wallowa, in northeastern Oregon, and brought beer to the festivities. Their indiscretion was discovered by the high school principal, and the class was denied their Senior Prom, as well as suffering a mass grounding for the remainder of the school year. There was one Jewish student who hadn't participated and was told that he didn't have to be punished like the others. He said, "They are my class mates," and took the rap just like the rest. Oliver thought, "Good for him! That's sticking by your friends." Of course, this is all hearsay because Oliver was in Japan when it happened.

Oliver thinks it ironic that the good town fathers with their whore houses and card games, and sexual escapades, were so *holier than thou*. But again, he knows that is the way the world goes and the ball bounces. Whoever said life was fair?

IX

There are friends who may last a lifetime, but time abrades most relationships. Boulders turn to pebbles, pebbles to sand, sand to silt. As the river flows to the sea, childhood friends disappear, those of the teen years last a little longer. Maybe some persist, especially if one doesn't stray too far from home.

Oliver hasn't contacted his high school friends in many years, with the exception of Gordon who has amazingly reappeared as an true friend after sixty five years. Back in high school, Gordon, talked to Oliver with honesty, even when it hurt. Oliver was in awe of him. He had won a state-wide oratory contest, was intelligent and literate, and physically much bigger than Oliver. One time he showed Oliver a book he was reading. Its title was *The Quintessence of Ibsenism*.

He told Oliver to stop saying, "I'm sorry," which Oliver did endlessly, not about his stupid practical jokes, but about himself. Gordon told Oliver he had nothing to be sorry about, and that Oliver's acne made no difference to the people who really liked him. Oliver knows now that Gordon was right, although Gordon's advice at the time came as big news to him. Gordon now practices law in London, England.

X

With that exception, Oliver knows very little of whom among the others still survive. (He is ashamed to say that he was too busy to attend his own Fiftieth reunion. And besides, he should have attended his friends' Fiftieth the year before, rather than his own.) Oliver received a photo of his peers' Fiftieth, all of them grouped in the Elks' Club banquet hall. He could not recognize a single person. Nor, he supposes, would they recognize him.

Oliver knows that Bill has become a medical doctor famous for his research on sleep, and often sees his name in the newspaper, but he has no idea where Jack, and Everett, and Teddy, and Walter, and David are.

XI

There have been other friends, John N. from graduate school who is still dear if not close by. Another who shall remain nameless, who offered to launch a commando raid in the Middle East if it were necessary to rescue the child of a friend of Oliver's. Fortunately the situation resolved itself. And Tom, a true scholar and gentleman. And Ray, terrible Ray, the soldier of fortune, raconteur sans rival, dead now. And newer still, the younger friends for whom Oliver has become a very imperfect mentor.

Oliver once complained to his Aunt Mary that he was forty years old and had only two true friends. "I am almost seventy," she replied, "and I have two true friends. Count yourself lucky."

XII

So what's to make of all this? Our lives from beginning to end are bounded by our perceptions of the space-time continuum in which we exist. Imagine if you will, that each person follows a trajectory through time. This trajectory can be plotted as the abscissa of the self's perceptions. Each person's life trails out behind the *present,* that instant which separates the past from the future. Memories of earliest childhood fray and disappear; our views of the future are even more limited. We anticipate this evening's dinner, tomorrow's commute to work, summer vacation, old age, and even death. But the future is unpredictable. Oliver, when he was a professor, told his students that no matter how certain life seems, they never can know when they get up in the morning what might happen to them before going to bed at night. Thus, *self* with its perceptions occupies a position on the temporal axis much nearer the future than the past.

At right angles to the temporal trajectory is a second axis or ordinate representing the spatial dimensions of the perceived world. The fetus knows the womb; the baby knows its crib; the child knows its house and yard. Oliver has already talked about the changing spaces of each person's world. Plotted to the right and left of the temporal axis, memories of such limits begin microscopically in the womb, expanding steadily to the perceptual *now*. Intimations of the future are attenuated by uncertainty.

The resulting image resembles a comet, tear drop shaped: bluntly rounded at the front, the past tapering behind to nothing with perhaps a few bits of unconnected memory glowing like bright particles of ice lagging behind the tail, melting in the flux of time.

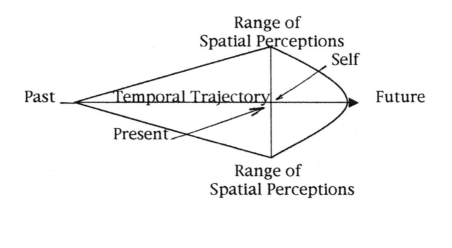

--- --- ---

Let's get on with it! There's more to tell about working back stage at the high school auditorium, and of Miss Little who saved his life, and to whom this book is dedicated, and about his going to the army, and in between, about the road apples and cow pies still to hit the fan.

CHAPTER TWENTY-ONE
NOTES ON THE DIGNITY OF LABOR

I

The political vortex forming over Europe and the Pacific sucked in the United States, Walla Walla, and Oliver. World War II, was an economic opportunity for sixteen year olds. It was a "good" war and everyone wanted to enlist, or almost every one except a few farmers' sons who suddenly became essential to wartime food production. Maybe they were. Oliver was too young to enlist and too small to fake his age. He bought a National Geographic map of Europe and plotted the day by day advances and retreats of the allied forces. He did the same on a map of the Pacific theater, but it seemed less real to him. The Battle of Midway came early in the war and those tiny dots of islands where so many died weren't the same as the steppes of Russia or the deserts of North Africa to someone who had never seen a tropical island but had seen steppe and desert right at home. Oliver remembers slogans like "Loose lips sink ships," "Lucky Strike Green has gone to war," (whatever nonsense that meant), and "Too little, too late, Tulagi," which was the name of an island near Guadalcanal where the Japanese suffered an early defeat. The "too little, too late" referred to our losses in the Philippines and Wake Island. The slaughters at Tarawa, Iwo Jima, and Okinawa were still to come.

Only later when Oliver talked to his brother-in-law who had fought through the southwest Pacific with the Pine Tree Division did he learn of the horror of the jungle campaigns.

Back home, people feared the threat of invasion. Residents along the coast of Oregon formed mounted posses to repel invaders; farmers around Walla Walla reassured themselves that, "We'll beat those little yellow monkeys if they come." A Japanese submarine fired one or two shells at an oil storage tank on the Oregon coast without success. The worst that happened were fire balloons. These were large balloons carrying incendiary bombs which the Japanese launched from their home islands with the hope that the jet stream would deliver them to Pacific Northwest where they would start devastating forest fires. Some of them actually arrived, and one killed a minister who found it on the ground in Oregon. To Oliver's knowledge, he was the only American casualty of war in the forty-eight states.

Oliver's fortunes were affected in a more positive way. The government announced that sixteen was old enough to hold a job. This meant that he could apply for summer work at the Libby, McNeil and Libby pea cannery beyond the railroad station on the north side of town. Oliver was eager and healthy and manpower was scarce. He was given a job on the night shift, 7:00 PM to 7:00 AM, seven days a week as long as the pea crop lasted. In order to understand what that meant, it's necessary to hear how a pea cannery works. Oliver worked at several stations in the cannery on different jobs. He started when he was sixteen and returned at seventeen. His eighteenth summer was spent in Japan. Upon his discharge he worked at the cannery for three more summers. It's easier to talk about that work and the cannery as though Oliver's jobs were continuous, so some of the details that follow are paced to peas moving through the cannery rather than to the exact times when Oliver was involved.

II

The peas are delivered from the fields in lug boxes piled high on trucks. They must reach the cannery in a very short time or they sour and can't be used. At the cannery they are dumped into tanks where they are washed and loose trash is floated away. Next they are mixed with clean water and lifted by pumps to a station called the Grader Room, high above the main floor of the cannery. Oliver worked there his last summer at the cannery. The Grader Room is a cavernous, dim loft with six great rotating drums which slope down and across the room from where pipes disgorge the peas from the receiving shed down below, to the other side where the peas fall into vats to be blanched. The grader room drums are perforated with small holes at the top and big holes at the bottom so that the peas are sorted into different sizes. The smallest are described on the labels as "young spring peas," but are from the same vines as the great big commercial peas which fall off the lower drums destined for gallon cans sent to prisons and the army. Oliver's job was to pour sand on the rollers under the drums which were made so slippery by crushed peas that the drums would come to a stop. If that happened, the endless supply of peas from down below would spill on the floor and go sour. That meant a big clean up job and money lost. Being Grader Room Operator was not stimulating, but required a responsible attendant, and was one of the better paying jobs in the cannery. The grader room operator worked entirely alone and unsupervised. It was up to him to see that the drums never stopped, for if they did, the entire cannery line would come to a halt. Not good!

The job was so boring and the room so dim and the noise of the drums so hypnotically lulling that it was easy to go to sleep, especially on the night shift. Oliver would read until his eyes tired in the poor light. He would exercise from time to time. He passed much of the time in sexual reveries. At times, strange creatures lurked in the steamy, darker corners of the room. Once a lovely woman spoke to him and vanished. Somehow, he stayed awake and seldom missed when a drum groaned to a halt. If one did, he had two or three minutes, at best, to restore the flow of peas. Cannery CPR.

Twice each shift, at midnight and six AM, the cannery line was brought to a halt. When that happened, Oliver's job was to wash down the drums and the floor and the walls, all splattered with crushed peas.

He used a Steller Machine to do this. At clean up time, Oliver would put on a slicker and gum boots which made him just as wet from sweat inside as he might have been from water on the outside. The Steller Machines were tanks on wheels with thick narrow hoses, each ending in a long steel nozzle with a pump handle grip. The machine heated the water almost to steam and mixed soap into it, and ejected it with terrific force. It was necessary to fight for control of the nozzle and to force the scalding jet into every crevice and cranny where peas might lodge and rot. It was exciting, exhausting, and dangerous work.

At the far end of the grader the peas fell off the drums into kettles on the main floor where they were blanched with steam and very hot water. This further prepared them for canning, and killed any grasshoppers and small snakes that might have slipped through.

After being blanched the peas poured out onto the Belt. The Belt was very grim. It was about three feet wide and brightly lighted by banks of overhead lights. The Belt, which moved at an inexorable pace, was lined on either side by rows of little old ladies who stood there picking pebbles and dead grasshoppers and other flotsam out of the peas. The peas steamed, the overhead lights were hot, and the movement of the belt was hypnotic. Often, one of the little old ladies, who had no other source of income and therefore worked at the cannery, would fall face first into the peas or backwards onto the cement floor. If the lady fell into the peas the Belt had to be stopped, which the foreman didn't like. On the other hand, the management tried to be kind to the little old ladies and took them to the first aid station where they got a glass of water, while the nurse made certain that they were OK and could go back to work. Their pay wasn't docked for short interruptions, but if they had to go home they were checked out at the time clock. Even though you might get your face burned by falling forward into the peas, the little old ladies thought it was preferable to falling backwards and hitting your head on the cement. If that happened, they usually made you take the rest of the night off, which meant wages lost

Oliver was glad his grandmother never worked there, although when Percy died and she moved back to Walla Walla she worked in a laundry to add to her railroad pension, which wasn't that much. She did faint at the laundry because of the heat; it was summer. After that Oliver's mother made certain she had enough money so that she didn't work again until she died the summer after Oliver came back from the army.

III

From the Belt, the peas were lifted to hoppers over *the seamers* where Oliver worked for two of the three summers after he returned from the army. The seamers are powerful machines that consist of two elements. The first part is a revolving column to which empty tin cans are fed from a ceiling track leading in from the Can Department. The cans are engaged on a revolving disc and filled with a mixture of peas and a brine made of water, salt and a little sugar. Once filled, they spin to the next machine which is a press that sets a lid on each can, and then lowers a powerful clamp which crimps the lid onto the can. The seamer operator must make certain that there are always enough lids to go on the cans, and that the seamer doesn't jam or start coming down so hard on the cans that instead of crimping the lids it spews out messy, metal hockey pucks. The seamer operator must also ensure that a steady flow of peas and brine is filling the cans.

This is a VERY noisy job. So noisy that to get the attention of a seamer operator one has to touch him. Otherwise, someone standing beside the operator could shout and not be heard.

There is a tangle of steam pipes surrounding the seamer, and the job can be dangerous. If an operator is careless and puts a finger near the crimper, his finger could be crimped off. A terrible accident happened on the seamer line while Oliver was in the army. That summer a steam pipe burst in the face of a student working a seamer. He was permanently blinded. He is a real hero, for he went on to school and earned a law degree.

After the full and sealed cans leave the seamer they ride out on a long belt and fall into huge metal baskets perched on trolleys. If the cans fall unattended into the basket they will dent each other. This is prevented by having someone stand by the basket with a big, flat board which he uses to deflect the cans so they land more easily. This is a very low level job usually assigned to transient workers, though Oliver saw teachers from Whitman College, with Ph.D.s, deflecting cans in order to supplement their salaries.

Oliver and the other members of the crew at clean up time would wash down all the seamers, and the floors, and the Belt, to get rid of the mashed peas. Once an entire load of peas went sour and was dumped from the hoppers hip deep onto the floor. Everyone was there pushing sour peas into the gutters. The peas fell inside their boots, worked under the collars of their slickers and up their sleeves. It got worse and worse, until with shouts of disgust and rebellion the clean up crew shed their water proofs and finished the job naked from the waist up, oblivious to the scalding splatters of soapy water!

Oliver still remembers the permeating stench. He thought, "No way will I ever eat canned peas again!" But in the army, when northern Japan was isolated by a typhoon and the railroad was washed out, that was all the regiment had to eat for three days. That is another story.

There were stories enough in the cannery: the time Red the seamer foreman -- why did all the foremen have nick-names that were colors? -- was escorting food inspectors and paused at Oliver's seamer. He told Oliver to stop the machine so that the inspectors could examine the contents of the cans that were coming through. There, right in front of Red and Oliver was an open can with a grasshopper, cooked, floating in it!

Red was very resourceful. "Oh, I can't resist these peas," he said, and grabbed a handful, including the grasshopper, from the can, and ate it all, including the grasshopper. The inspectors didn't see it. Red became a legend after that.

IV

Before following the cans to their next stop, let Oliver describe where the empty cans came from. They came from the can department where he worked the first two summers before he went in the army.

194

One word describes the weird, endless labor of the can department, Kafkaesque. Tin cans were shipped to the cannery on the railroad in regular box cars. When a car of cans was opened, the first job was to take out a series of two by four wooden braces and cardboard sheets to make room to get in. The subsequent open space was the width of the open box car door. Inside, on either side, were walls of open, empty tin cans. This wall was thirty-two cans wide and thirty cans tall. The worker's job -- they were called *can forkers* -- was to remove the cans and place them in a metal tray that was put up inside, along one wall of the box car. This tray sloped down to a vertical chute made of four pieces of metal that had a half twist which opened into another sloping metal tray that went to another twist, which dropped the cans onto a moving belt that took them into the cannery and up to the overhead track leading to the seamers. Each seamer had its own half box-car of cans to draw from.

The cans were placed in the track by means of a fork which consisted of a bar from which sprouted sixteen short rubber tipped prongs. The can forker held this fork by two handles thirty inches apart, on the side opposite the tines. Oliver was a can forker; he stood on a portable platform resting on metal saw horses from which he could reach the top of the wall of cans. He then stuck the sixteen prongs into sixteen empty cans and lifted them with a little jerk which freed them from the rest. Then, with the cans hanging from the fork, he took a step and a half turn to the metal tray along the wall, hooked the dangling cans over the edge of the tray and jerked the fork back very carefully so that the cans fell into the tray and rolled down it into the twist and off to the seamer.

This was not easy to do and especially difficult if the seamer on the other end of the line was running fast, without stopping for two hours or more. Moreover, the forker had to lift off cans as far back as he could reach before going down to the next layer. This meant that much of the time forkers, like Oliver, were not only going back and forth across the platform, but also stretching forward to the extent of their reach in order to hook the rows of cans at the back. When the upper layers were removed, the platforms and the saw horses were pulled down and the lower tiers forked out. There followed a mad scramble to reset the platform and extend the trays in order to start at the top of the next tiered segment of cans. This went on, over and over until the forker reached the back of the box car.

Can forkers like Oliver developed a mad dance:

Reach up, thrust, lift, sidestep, turn, drop your hands, catch the cans on the lip of the tray, jerk, turn back to the can wall. Reach, thrust, lift, step, turn, drop, catch, jerk, turn; reach, thrust, lift, step, turn, drop, catch, jerk, turn; reach, thrust, lift, step, turn, drop, catch, jerk, turn; reach thrust lift step turn drop catch turn; reachthrustliftsteptur. . . . . forever.

As the dance continued hour after hour, Oliver hovered between despair and madness. 'Oh please, please let the line stop!" Or, "I will fork more cans in one shift than anyone else ever has!!!! I will be the John Henry of cans!"

A good can forker could empty half a box car before lunch and a full car during his shift. About 80,000 tin cans. That is 8,000 cans per hour, allowing 10 working hours in a 12 hour shift after set up time, cleaning time, seamer down time, etc. Or 133 cans per minute, which is eight forkfuls, or one fork every eight seconds. The dance had its own music, the clattering din of metal on metal. Oliver's ears rang for weeks from that tin can tarantella.

--- --- ---

Gallon cans were different, so big that they were forked by hand, two in the right, two in the left. A skilled gallon can man could handle six at a time, three and three. Sometimes the gallon cans arrived in box cars of their own, but there was also a mountain of paper bags, each holding 64 open cans -- 4 x 4 x 4 -- piled in the yard next to the railroad tracks and the horizontal belts that moved cans to the seamers. These bags were constantly being shifted around as more arrived by train or as cans were needed on the gallon line. In their off time, the forkers extra job was to help move the bags. Oliver, while shifting a stack three bags high, worked his hands in between the stacks on either side of the one he was inching out of the pile.

He felt a sharp, slicing pain on the back of his right hand, he wasn't wearing gloves. When he pulled his arm out of the pile, he saw that an open gallon flange had sliced him from knuckle to wrist. The nurse pulled the wound together with butterfly bandages and he went back to work. After all these years, he still sports a four inch scar for a souvenir.

V

Beyond the seamer lines, the metal tubs full of cans, were lowered six to a tank into cooking retorts by electric hoists. There they were steamed eighteen minutes, pulled back out and sent on their way thorough a long water trough which cooled them enough to be handled by men at the other end, who ran them through labeling machines and packed them in cases for shipping. That part of the cannery was *terra incognita* for Oliver and his co-workers. Someplace, farther on, the cases were loaded onto railroad cars for shipment.

The war seemed far away except at the far end of the cannery. There, a dozen German prisoners of war worked nights loading the cases. A single guard watched them. Where could a prisoner go if he escaped? One actually did walk away as the guard slept. The escapee was found, wandering and thirsty, in a gigantic wheat field down near Pendleton. He seemed very happy to be captured and returned to work with his fellow prisoners.

VI

The cannery was where Oliver learned about the dignity of labor, working for strangers, working for money.

Of course, it wasn't always endless sweat; only on nights when the peas came in too fast. But work they did, twelve hours a night, and if they were lucky, thirteen, the extra hour on special clean-up, which meant double time, seven days a week, five or six weeks without a break. Oliver and his friends were young and eager, and had the energy to do it.

Not at all bad for a sixteen year old who one week made $100.80 after taxes, take home. That was a lot back then. Not to mention the good times and the crazy times.

197

CHAPTER TWENTY-TWO
CANNERY KNIGHTS AND DAZE

I

Speaking of the good times and the crazy times, the most astounding sight Oliver ever saw at the cannery happened one night when he was working a seamer. Bored as usual, he amused himself by tracking an odd colored empty tin can as it came along the ceiling track down to the seamer, watched it as it was filled and crimped, and then followed it out to the end of the belt as it was deflected into a tub. Oliver looked at the man deflecting the cans, gasped, looked again.

Seamer operators often became hypnotized by the noise and endless movement of the seamers, and would stare blankly at their machines. Sometimes Red, the foreman, had to come along and wake them up. Therefore, it wasn't unusual that Oliver hadn't looked out to the end of the line until that moment. The man deflecting the cans was a black man with wild fuzzy hair, a bone through his nose, and weird, dangling ear rings. He was a Fiji Island cannibal, or was meant to fool people into thinking he was. To the right of the cannibal at the next belt and tub was a second deflector at least seven feet tall who weighed all of one hundred pounds soaking wet, a classic thin man. On the cannibal's left was another deflector, totally tattooed from his sandaled feet to the top of his head! Dragons danced across his chest. A sunburst crowned his shaved skull. His arms were entwined with vines and roses. Snakes crept up his legs and under his shorts.

A carnival had come to town and its manager had run off with the gate receipts. The people from the side show were stranded with no money for food, or tickets to get back to Florida or wherever home was for them. Their only choice was to work at the cannery. As Oliver said, the deflecting job was one given to transients.

II

Among the regular crew on the seamers one summer was Bill Edmond, a student at Whitman College. Bill was very athletic. He designed and packed his own parachutes and was an avid jumper. One midnight at clean up, the crew, in gum boots and slickers, was waiting for their next task. Bill said he could do a standing back jump. Someone said he couldn't. He said he could do it right there, dressed as he was. Bets were made. Bill flexed his knees, and gum boots and all went up and over and down with ease.

Bill rode a vellocette (motor bike) which had a pillion seat. Oliver thought the pillion was very romantic because you could give girls rides. Oliver still hears the phrase echo in his head: *Edmond's vellocette has a pillion.*

At a party, one time, a drunk started picking on Bill because he was small. Edmond leaped high in the air and hit the bully just once on top of his head with his balled up fist. The bully left the party without saying another word.

It is not Oliver's custom to anticipate events far beyond the time frame of this story, but he feels he should mention something illustrative of life's changes. Years later, Oliver ran into Bill in the office of a major publishing company in New York City. Bill was a junior executive there. Oliver was very excited and started recalling all the things that have just been described. Bill became very quiet. It was obvious he wanted Oliver to change the subject. Bill was wearing a very conservative suit and a power necktie, and there were senior executives nearby. Oliver stopped talking and Bill hustled him out of the office and bought him lunch. They didn't talk about old times.

Oliver hopes Bill has escaped and is working in the cannery again, but he doubts it.

III

One night at lunch break, Oliver and a friend, Frank, lingered by the refreshment stand over glasses of Hawaiian Punch and returned to the can department somewhat later than the other workers. It was customary for empty box cars to be switched out at midnight and new, full ones, to be brought in. When Frank and Oliver entered the can department they found the entire crew and Blacky, the foreman, assembled in an empty box car which was about to be switched out. The crew had discovered that the empty space of the car made a great reverberation chamber and were massed inside singing *Meadowlands*, the Russian cavalry song. "Onward to arms comrades, through the grassy plains and meadows !!!!!" What an echo!

Frank and Oliver looked at each other and as the poet said, "without a word spoke," Frank slipped under the car and Oliver sneaked up to the door on the cannery side and BANG!! They slid the doors shut and dropped the hooks in place and then walked as inconspicuously as possible back to the refreshment stand. There they engaged Red, the seamer foreman, in a long discussion about hiring them to work on the seamers the following summer. Actually, they were building an alibi.

The switch engine came in and switched the entire can department crew, minus two, out to west Walla Walla from where they were retrieved an angry hour later. Frank and Oliver were suspect but had a good alibi. Pranksters from the warehouse were blamed, but no one was ever caught. One of the unsolved mysteries of Libby, McNeil and Libby.

IV

Blacky -- another foreman with a color for a nick-name -- was a man of immense knowledge of sex and the world. He told Oliver and the other young men in his crew that the best way to keep a woman from getting pregnant when you screwed her was to shake up a bottle of Coke and give her a douche. That's when Oliver found out what a douche is. Blacky one time walked into an empty box car where they were pitching nickels, heads against tails. Oliver called "Heads," and someone else called "Tails," and Blacky called "Everything Else." The nickel rolled up against the wall of the box car and stood there on its edge. Blacky pocketed it and all the crew admired him for being so hip, which was the word they used.

And then there was Everett Allen Oaten. Dear, sweet, Everett Allen Oaten who told jokes everyone called Oatens. For example, "Did you ever hear about the man who said, 'Look every one, I'm superman!'?" Or, "Did you ever hear about the man who walked into a drug store and said, 'I want a bottle of Old Crow'?" These may not seem funny to you, but when you've worked twelve hours a night, seven nights a week, for four or five weeks, they are hilarious.

Ah Oaten! Near the season's end, the clean up crew was cutting the tops off dented cans which had gone bad and sour and swollen. The idea was to salvage the metal, but when the can was punctured by the opener a jet of foul liquid would spew out, soaking the poor can opener operator. It was AWFUL!

The crew tossed coins to see who would get the detail. Someone said to Oaten "Heads I win; tails you lose." Oatan lost, he always lost. When the joke had worn off, Oliver and the others tried to take their turns, but Oaten would say, "I lost fair and square and it's my turn to open those cans," and he would insist on doing it. Everyone felt guilty and determined to teach Oaten that "Heads I win; tails you lose" wasn't fair. They tried and tried but never succceded. Oater never could understand it.

Oaten was a good guy, really good. He worked hand forking the gallon cans from a separate box car, where he picked up two in each hand and put them on a special tray. It was straight forward work and a good job for him.

Everett really liked the beautiful young red head who was the only woman working in the can department. She worked the switches by the can elevator and if the cans got jammed going up into the cannery she would turn off the elevator and unjam the cans. She sat there all night long. Everyone loved her, and nobody bothered her. Blacky would have killed anyone who did. Blacky had his code, too. Everett would stand just around the corner and peek at her. She liked him and didn't mind his adulation.

There was a transient who came to work in the can department. He lived in the Arrow Rooms above a store on lower Main Street. He was grimy and rough, and tough, very tough, and had grown up in the migrant labor camps. He carried a knife. His work was all right, but he never mingled, probably because the Walla Walla bunch wouldn't let him. He made passes at the red headed girl until Blacky made him stop, and he teased Everett Allen Oaten cruelly.

One night he went into the separate gallon can box car and began teasing Everett about the red headed girl, said she was a whore and that he would screw her. Everett went over and picked him up and threw him against the wall of open gallon cans like he was a sack of wheat. The open flanges of the cans were razor sharp -- Oliver had learned that the hard way -- and left great crescent moon cuts all over Oaten's tormentor's face and hands and arms. He went to the infirmary and then to emergency at the hospital to be stitched up. Blacky spoke to the night manager and the transient never returned. He must have some interesting scars. Oliver wonders how he explains them.

V

Nights at the cannery were punctuated by the days in-between. The year that Oliver returned from the army his group of friends expanded to include another outsider. (Oliver would soon discover Colin Wilson's book by that name, and decide that he, himself, was an "Outsider," as were his friends.) Frederick was gay. In those days people didn't use that term. To the world at large, he was either a queer or a fairy. To Oliver and his friends, Frederick was another footloose, returned veteran waiting out the summer in Walla Walla, planning to attend the University of Washington in the fall.

Why mention this at all? Because Frederick was a good friend. He was there, and never made an issue of his choice of life. Nor did he conceal it, like so many in Walla Walla did, as the scandals of the forties would reveal. In later years, Oliver realized that his good, gay friend taught him to understand how benign the complex world might be if left alone.

Frederick had been a navy medical corpsman and returned to Walla Walla with his mustering out pay, the GI Bill, and a quart bottle of Benzedrine tablets which he generously shared with his new friends.

Benzedrine was not entirely unknown to high school students. There were, for sinus conditions, Benzedrine Inhalers which could be bought across the counter at the drugstore. To experience a Benzedrine hit, the inhaler was cracked open and the strip either chewed, which tasted vile, or soaked in coke and taken that way. Shortly after the war the inhalers were replaced with benzedrex which was harmless and useless for thrill seekers.

The pills allowed Oliver and company to wander through hot summer mornings in a suspended haze. They went to a nine hole golf course in the hamlet of Dixie north of town. There, they fumbled through several rounds. The high point of the morning came when an older golfer's ball landed at their feet on the green and rolled into the cup. A hole in one! It was followed by a red faced and stammering executive type in a splendid Hawaiian shirt and shorts. Tears visible in his eyes, he asked them to come with him to the clubhouse and sign statements that IT had really happened. Bemused by the emotion that a hole-in-one could evoke, upon his insistence, they repeatedly shook his hand, until he let them escape. On the way to the cannery that evening they made a solemn vow to never play golf again.

VI

On other days, Oliver spent hours at the Natatorium hazily baking in the sun. He no longer dived for coins on the bottom of the pool.

He remembers how shocked he was one day by small town attitudes. The sun was pressing down on him as he lay on the cement border at the far end of the pool. Two young women, former classmates, were there as well. The three of them were talking idly, murmuring through the heat. Oliver had gained some status being a returned vet and conversations like this came to him more easily. One of the girls turned to him and asked, "Are you that way?"

"What way?" Oliver replied.

"You know." She licked her little finger and brushed back her eye brow. This was supposed to be how all men who were "that way" behaved.

"No. What makes you think so?"

"Well, you run around with Frederick. And that jacket you sometimes wear." It was a robin's egg blue sport jacket Oliver had brought back from his Junior summer's trip to San Francisco.

"Well, I'm not." That ended the conversation. Oliver felt detached from Walla Walla, detached from what the girls thought. He was on his way, away.

VII

A week passed with the group running essentially on pills and empty. The Benzedrine episode came to an end one late afternoon. Oliver went over to his friend's house to drive with him and the others to the cannery. No one answered the door so he pushed it open and went inside. Walter and another of Oliver's buddies were tumbled, asleep, in the center of the living room floor. Sleep suddenly seemed very appealing to Oliver who hadn't had much, if any, for seven or eight days. He lay down on the floor with the first two. They were soon joined by two others. The five of them slept, piled together like walruses on a beach, for the next sixteen hours. Somehow or other the cannery didn't fire them for missing a night's work.

They awoke hungry, sobered, hung over. Walter's parents, with a wisdom seldom found in parents, left them to sort it out for themselves, and said nothing. None of them ever touched Benzedrine again. There was alcohol, and later in Seattle, pot, at a time when no one except black musicians really knew what it was. Another story, another story. But life was simpler then, and somehow or other Oliver and his friends passed through the drug bit unscathed.

VIII

One of Oliver's friends bought a Cushman motor scooter. One afternoon before work, they took turns riding it around the block. The young sister of one of them sat on the porch steps watching. She was so Finnish fair that her skin seemed translucent. Her hair was a silvery casque. When Oliver's turn came on the scooter he asked if she would like a ride.

"Oh, Yes," she said, and climbed on behind him, and wrapped her arms around his waist. Off they went. He didn't go around the block; they went out East Alder Street, miles into the country. The speed -- yet how safe and unlike a motorcycle it was -- and the wind excited them. As they zoomed along, Oliver could feel her nipples harden and touch his back. She wore no bra; she was that young. He had never felt nipples before. They seemed like points of fire. And then they were back at her house. That was it. But Oliver still remembers that lovely scooter ride, and wishes her long life and hopes she found a true love. Oliver was well on his way to being a romantic.

IX

Frank and Oliver, one waiting-for-the-cannery afternoon, composed an *Ode to Angus McNeil*. It's dedicated to McNeil (Angus is a made up name) who was never mentioned by anyone: as in, "Where are you working this summer?" "Out at Libby's." Never, "Out at Libby and McNeil's."

ODE TO ANGUS MCNEIL

List oh ye workers at Libby's
Ye workers with peas and with cans
List the raw deal of Angus McNeil,
History's forgotten man.

It was early one warm summer evening
When Angus McNeil met his fate,
The shift started work at six-thirty,
Angus came one hour late.
In his haste to get into the cannery
He slipped and fell flat on the floor,
Slid into an open retort,
and the foreman, unaware, closed the door.

Oh Angus got full eighteen minutes
Just like the rest of the lots,
Till nothing was there, but some false teeth and some hair,
and a series of small greasy spots.

Oh Angus McNeil, oh Angus McNeil
Oh where have you gone poor dear Angus?
Oh nothing's been found
Out there on the ground
But a series of small greasy spots.
And now on the long winter evenings
When the goblins and ghosties all squeal,
You can hear through the halls
The dolorous calls
Of the ghost of Angus McNeil.

Bad Huh? But that was Libbys.

CHAPTER TWENTY-THREE
CARS!

When people think about teenagers in the Forties, one picture comes to mind -- it appeared in a major news magazine, *LOOK? LIFE?* The scene is all blurry with speed. Kids in a roadster, all standing up and grabbing for the steering wheel, but no one is steering. That game was called "chicken" and the first kid to grab the wheel was chicken. "Chicken" in those days meant cowardly, not "unreasonably mean" like it does now. (Back then, "unreasonably mean" was "chicken shit." The current usage probably has evolved because nowadays most kids have never stepped in chicken shit, which is really not nice stuff.) That picture was taken in California where movie stars live, and everyone in Walla Walla knew what that meant.

Walla Walla kids weren't that wild, but cars were important! Every high schooler wanted wheels, and the big sixteenth birthday meant he or she could get a driver's license.

There were no driving classes in school, you just learned. Farm kids learned much younger than city kids by driving tractors and trucks, part of the work they did. Town kids were taught by their fathers, or big brothers, or sometimes a friend. Oliver's mother took him out to an abandoned apron at the air base and let him lurch around and around the paved expanse until he learned to steer. (This puzzles Oliver for it indicates that the army air base was closed by 1946, or that at least part of it was abandoned by then. The tricks memory plays!) He still remembers his being taught to drive by his mother was embarrassing. The pangs of growing up.

I

Driving a car was a sign of being grown up. There were kids with their own jalopies like David, Oliver's friend who worked on his car, made repairs, changed the oil. Then there were kids like Bill who drove the big Buick, with fenders that swept back to the rear of the car and looked like it was going very fast even when it wasn't. Oliver and his friends drove around in Bill's car except when he went on dates, which the rest of them didn't. Then there were kids like Oliver who could sometimes borrow their parents' cars. And then there were farm kids who drove flat bed trucks which had cow manure on them and didn't count.

There was a special automobile game that high school students played in Walla Walla. It was called *chase*. Kids would pile into their own cars, or their parents' cars which they were allowed to use, although their parents certainly didn't know about the game of chase. Oliver's mother was among the uninformed and let him drive the Terraplane. The object of the game was for the car that was *it* to go ahead of all the other cars and to lose them by weaving through alleys, or by racing very fast down straight roads. Oliver played chase like everybody else. One time Oliver was with David in his coupe roaring along the road by the cemetery south of town. Just as the speedometer hit 100 miles an hour, the car began to shimmy and forced them to slow down. Somehow Oliver lived through that and all the other games of chase.

There were no shopping malls and no drive-in theaters, but on weekends the kids drove out to the Triple XXX Root Beer stand and parked and called to each other from car to car. By the end of the evening that calling back and forth erupted into a game of Chase. All the cars were parked, and then without warning, one would roar away. However, Oliver cannot recall that anyone ever "burned rubber" or did "wheelies," tricks which he read about in magazines that described life in California.

The first car usually was full of girls. The second car was full of guys like football players. After that there might be another car with girls in it, but those girls were definitely less, less . . . what? It had to do with vague feelings of desire and glandular urgings and cashmere sweaters and maybe the model of car that they drove. After them came people like Oliver in the big, awkward Hudson Terraplane which he felt was as bad as a farm truck and didn't count. Anyway, off everyone would go one after the other, turning corners, going down alleys, racing along straight stretches. The odd thing is no one ever caught anyone. They just drove faster and faster until it was time to go home.

II

Cars were also for necking, though that was only hearsay to Oliver. There seemed to be a lot of necking going on, but he never knew anyone who had actually *made out*, as it was called, in a car. Some of the older boys exchanged cryptic remarks about "four on the floor and two in the back seat," but If there were any automobile pregnancies they were kept secret. Some of the guys after they had taken their dates home would complain about hot rocks. Like Oliver has already said, they made a great show of pulling up on the bumpers of their cars to ease the pain they felt. Hot rocks proved something even if they didn't know quite what.

III

For Oliver, his mother's car was a terrible burden. The Hudson Terraplane was big and brown with sills on the doors that you had to step over and a funny little finger tip gear shift alongside the steering wheel. By the time he was in high school it looked a little worn, and he had convinced himself that this car was the reason he never could get up the courage to ask a girl for a date, that the Terraplane had some deep, hidden connection to his acne.

He loathed and drove the Hudson and longed for a new car, maybe a Buick like the one Bill drove. But the Hudson Terraplane was the family car and sometimes Oliver got to drive it and sometimes he played chase -- way back in the comet's tail of cars behind those laughing, impossibly remote, cashmere girls.

IV

Driving cars back then was different. No one Oliver knew drank and drove, no one played chicken, and he cannot remember anyone's being killed. Maybe it was because Walla Walla was remote and that it wasn't practical to drive to another high school in the evening and get in trouble. There were no gangs and no rivalries of that sort. All of that was for another generation. Everyone knew everyone else, and no one ever thought of driving to Milton and Freewater, or Touchet, or Waitsburg, which were nearby but tiny and beyond the pale. Cars had not yet become Drive-by Weapons Platforms.

Accidents did happen, though Oliver doesn't recall any serious injuries among his classmates. There was that frightening evening when Oliver was driving with two friends in his mother's car and almost died. He had just gotten his license and was still steering with stiff inexperience. They were on the road near the Triple XXX Root Beer stand heading west on the way to College Place. It was just after sunset, and Oliver was squinting into the glare. A car came towards them and as they passed each other suddenly there was a terrible, metallic ripping sound. They had sideswiped each other! Oliver jammed on the brakes and stopped; the other car raced on towards town. If they had been two inches nearer each other they would have crashed head on.

Oliver and his friends got out of the car and looked at the damage. There was a big gouge along the side of the car. Oliver didn't know which was worse, almost being killed or having to tell his mother what he'd done. Why hadn't the other car stopped? Oliver will never know. Were they responsible, or was Oliver? What was he to do?

He and his two friends talked and talked and then decided on a plan. They drove to his friend's house and carefully parked the car at the corner of the block with the gouged side facing out. It was just possible that a car coming around the corner might have scraped Oliver's car as it stood at the curb. He and his two friends went inside the house and waited for their courage to build – thank goodness no one else was home. Then Oliver called his mother and told her what had happened -- or actually what hadn't happened. Some how or other she believed him and reported the "accident" to the police, who believed him – or couldn't prove otherwise.

Oliver thinks that everyone suspected him, but he managed to escape the blame. Now he regrets his trickery, although no one suffered, except the insurance company that paid for the repairs. And yet, that dishonesty has been like a tiny rose thorn in his flesh, never quite healed. Oliver was learning about his two sides, just as he learned about the two Walla Wallas.

CHAPTER TWENTY-FOUR
HOW WORLD WAR II CAME AND WENT

Oliver doesn't remember VE Day. That means Victory in Europe over the Nazis. Maybe he was out to lunch, but he thinks it means that no one really thought the war was over until it was over. Sure, there were newspaper headlines and a quiet sigh of relief and then all eyes turned west.

I

VJ Day, which stands for Victory over Japan Day, may seem a little odd to all the people now driving Japanese Cars, and who can't afford to spend $5.00 for a Coca Cola if they visit Tokyo, or have been body blocked at the Grand Canyon Lodge gift store by some very aggressive Japanese souvenir hunters. In 1945 all of Walla Walla was waiting for the end of the war, even the kids who hadn't been in it.

It ended suddenly. Harry S Truman made a very difficult decision. He ordered atomic bombs dropped on Hiroshima and Nagasaki. Young apologists currently blame Truman for dropping the bombs. They are not looking at the world as it was then. If the bomb hadn't been dropped there, sooner or later someone else, maybe the Russians, would have dropped it somewhere else. We all needed a bad fright to get slightly rational. That is an apologist view.

On the other hand, let's not forget about the Bataan Death March, and the Rape of Nanking, and Asian women forced into prostitution for the Japanese military. That is an angry point of view.

Or let's take a horror for horror approach. The United States Air force methodically fire bombed the large Japanese cities. To do this, two flights of bombers, perhaps a mile apart, would ignite two lanes across Tokyo or Yokohama. Then, two more flights of planes the same distance apart would fly at right angles to the first flights. This would create a hollow square walled with fire. The updraft in the center created a fire storm and the entire square mile would be incinerated. More Japanese died in the two or three biggest fire raids than died at Hiroshima and Nagasaki. So how about demonstrations against napalm?

Oliver's own experience presents still another point of view. Eighteen months after the bombs were dropped, he was stationed in northern Honshu, Japan, at a place called Mitsu Ishikawa near Hachinohe. His regiment was restricted to its own area, but Oliver was not one to linger in the beer hall. He had a rather meaningless Class A pass, and to fill his leisure time he did a lot of walking in the forests and rice paddies stretching as far as the Japanese Alps to the west behind the camp. He found on those hikes that the hills there were honey combed for miles inland with caves and tunnel defense works. He also learned from the farmers he met that they had been armed with sharpened spears and told if the enemy came, that is the Americans, they were to die for the Emperor. This included young women known as "Bamboo Spear Fighters" and *Tokko* special attack units composed of young men. These young fighters were to take the brunt of our assault, disrupt out troops, and make follow-up attacks by mature Japanese troops easier.

When Japan surrendered, the emperor told his people to accept the occupying Americans, which they did. Easier for everyone than dying piecemeal on the beaches and in the hills.

That was the situation in a small back water place in northern Honshu. Can you imagine trying to take Kobe or Tokyo? Remember that a hundred thousand American soldiers were killed or wounded taking Okinawa. The Japanese defenders lost many times more men. That was just a taste of what was to come. So maybe death by radiation and heat is worse than death by flame throwers and sharpened spears, and Oliver realizes there is a MORAL ISSUE involved as well, but he thinks Harry S Truman did the right thing.

So maybe everybody should admit their guilt and never do it again. End of sermon.

II

So the bombs were dropped, and the Japanese surrendered, and it was over. Oliver doesn't know what the adults did to celebrate, although he saw soldiers and sailors who happened to be in town kissing any pretty woman or girl they met. The women and girls didn't seem to mind. The pre-kiss cohort of which Oliver was part, got in their cars or their parents' cars and drove up and down Main Street honking their horns until it got dark. Then everybody parked and double parked and milled around on Main Street.

The youth club next to the Roxy Theater was closed and a bunch of kids were outside wondering what to do. Oliver knew that the transom over the door was unlocked -- he had in his own way noticed it was never locked -- and somebody boosted him up there. Surprise! The Youth Club was open, and Oliver got behind the counter and gave out free ice cream because it was a special celebration. He reasoned that if everyone piled behind the counter wanting ice cream there would have been a mess. Oliver is inherently neat, and didn't want there to be a mess, just a good time because it was VJ Day. He also showed the kids how to trip the juke box by putting a wire hanger down inside the coin slot in order to have free music.

After a while one of the Firemen came and asked, "How did this place get opened?" Oliver didn't exactly tell him, he just said that he was there dishing out ice cream to keep the place orderly. The fireman was very understanding and helped dish out the rest of the ice cream. Not a single kid was hurt or killed in an automobile accident in Walla Walla on VJ Night. That is one part of his life of crime Oliver is proud of.

III

But what about when the war started? One Sunday Oliver went to the Scout Bluffs without his bike. His mother gave him a lift in the Hudson Terraplane to where the dirt road began. She agreed to pick him up at that place in four hours. He climbed around the bluffs and then walked back and waited under a tree until she came. It was a warm, early winter day, December 7, 1941. The sky was clear. An hour passed, and his mother raced up full of excitement. The Japanese had attacked Pearl Harbor in the Hawaiian Islands and President Roosevelt said America was at war.

The next day at school the principal brought all the Seventh and Eighth grade kids together in one of the big double rooms. They listened to the radio as the president declared war on the Japs and the Nazis. People predicted the Japs would be beaten in six weeks. They weren't. Meanwhile, back at Sharpstein School, the students pledged allegiance to the flag and to the republic for which it stands. They didn't say "under God," because in those days there was an active separation of church and state.

IV

There were real heroes like Jimmy Doolittle and the crews of his squadron of B-25 bombers that attacked Japan in April 1942. News about the attack was sparse, but civilians at home learned the bombers were launched from a carrier on one-way flights; the lucky crews crash landed in unoccupied China. (Amazingly, seventy-one of the eighty fliers survived, though this was made known only after the war.) Headlines like those generated by the Doolittle attack were scarce in the early days of the war and generated pride and raised civilian morale.

215

But Oliver became disillusioned by the war effort at home. One day, he was exploring the city dump on the far side of Mill Creek from his house. He didn't go there often; it was smelly. That day, he was wandering around the back of the dump looking for treasure when he found something which changed his view of the world still further. Part of the civilian war effort was to save tin cans. They were cleaned and flattened, and once a week the students brought their collected cans to school to be hauled away and made into guns and tanks for our soldiers.

Oliver couldn't believe what he found. At the far end of the dump where very few people ever went was a giant pile of flattened tin cans. Oliver realized that *they*, whoever they were, were making the students feel like they were doing something useful for the war effort, but that *they* didn't need or want the tin cans.

That made Oliver angry and sad. It also made him think about the black market gasoline that almost everybody bought during the war. Announcers on the radio and articles in the newspaper told how a bomber that was returning from a raid on Japan ran out of fuel and fell into the sea. Its crew drowned because of the black market gasoline users. So DON'T USE BLACK MARKET GAS!

Well, Oliver thought it over and knew that B-19 bombers didn't use automobile gas, and besides shouldn't the pilot or the navigator have been more careful? So why was it the fault of people in Walla Walla any more than the people who produced low octane gasoline instead of aviation fuel, or why wasn't it the fault of the supply people in the Air Force? Certainly, no one should allow the bomber to take off if it didn't have enough fuel to return home. Those weren't suicide missions.

You will notice that Oliver and the other teen-agers drove up and down Main Street celebrating VJ Day, before parking their cars and going into the youth club. Cars! Where did all the gas for all those cars come from? Farmers got special rations for their farm equipment, and if some leaked elsewhere who was to know?

It was the same with those little plastic bags full of white margarine with the pellets of orange dye inside. The pellets were broken by the consumer, who then massaged the bag until the ingredients looked something like butter. That was for the war effort, too.

Along with gasoline rationing and white margarine were ration stamps for sugar and other food. If, however, you needed more sugar for canning, you could always get the grocer to give you some extra. It was that way with almost everything. Remember the nylon stockings Oliver found for Molly whom he wanted to impress.

Civilians were urged to do their part by planting Victory Gardens in their yards. Oliver responded patriotically by attacking a large patch of Alfalfa behind his house on East Alder. Alfalfa has deep, tough roots. Oliver thought of those roots as enemy roots, Jap and Nazi roots, and fought them with shovel and hatchet. The roots slowly won. The garden tract he had laid out with rocks at its corners shrank from 100 X 50 feet, to 50 X 50 feet, to two rows of radishes ten feet long.

The *golden waves of grain* and rows of tall corn he had imagined were forgotten as the heat of summer washed across Walla Walla. Oliver was not alone in defeat. His abandoned plot was one among many little weed patches scattered around town, though in fairness there were some successful urban farmers whom he secretly admired.

V

Back to the War. There was the U.S. Army Air Base and the crews wandering around down town, and the cadets at Whitman college, and the wounded vets out at the hospital where they used to treat men with TB and where Oliver's father died from a different war, and ration stamps, and Oliver's wall maps with the colored pins stuck in them showing places like Iwo Jima and Bastogne. But that was all another world. And all the kids who hadn't ever heard of a place called Korea and were going to die there didn't know about it, and all the unborn kids who were going to Viet Nam didn't either, and all in all it was it was a good time

217

when sixteen year olds could get real jobs in the canneries, and Oliver and everyone else wanted their chance to kill Nazis and Japs and it was all either good guys or bad guys.

And then there were the few strangers who reappeared in high school trying to fit in, to finish their degrees after having seen too much, too often. Oliver remembers one returned vet who lit up a cigar in the hall at Wa-Hi and when the principal told him to put it out stared the principal down before grinding it out under his heel. It didn't happen again, but there was no mention of disciplinary action. Just aching silence. Post traumatic syndrome hadn't yet been invented as an explanation of what happens when old men send young men to war.

--- --- ---

It seems now to Oliver that the war was far away from Walla Walla. Gold Star Mothers moved like ghosts through the town. Wounded soldiers recuperating at the converted TB hospital sometimes found their way into Walla Walla homes. Oliver remembers meeting one soldier who came to dinner at his house who spoke with the voice of an eighty year old man. He had been bayoneted in the throat in hand-to-hand fighting at Anzio, but to Oliver these were strange, surreal encounters with a different world.

The closest Oliver came to realizing that the conflict was real was when his sister's new boy friend, a radio operator on a B-17, was shot down on a milk-run over Calais and captured by the Germans. For two agonizing years she lived with only two tiny Red Cross post cards from him. These terse messages came from a Stalag Luft camp somewhere in Prussia. His story was one of horror which ended only when he was found unconscious in a ditch by a British patrol, abandoned as dead by his German captors as they fled the advancing Russians. He survived, but revealed this little known death march only years later to Oliver's sister.

VI

Oliver belongs to that anonymous group too young to have fully suffered the Great Depression, too young to fight in WW II, too old or classified 4-A (having already served, thank God! He's a realist now.) to fight in Korea. His cohort scooted in on the coat tails of the genuine veterans. He was among the first non-combatants to occupy Japan, and came at the tail end of the GI Bill students who flooded the colleges. Oliver and his friends were *The Inbetweeners*, a misplaced generation.

"How innocent we were," he says.

CHAPTER TWENTY-FIVE
OLIVER IS ASKED TO LEAVE THE HOME OF THE BLUE DEVILS

I

It is time for Oliver to tell about Walla Walla High School, Home of the Blue Devils, and of his being kicked out at the end of Junior year. While that was the best thing that ever happened to him, for it took him to the army, gave him the GI Bill, and let him gracefully leave home, he realizes that being asked to leave confirmed the sense of abandonment that shaped his life to that point. On the other hand, the army gave him direction and purpose, so that today he is, in the words of William Butler Yeats, "a fifty year old public man," although Oliver is older and retired and not much of a "public man." Nevertheless, the high school kid inside him is at last free to tell the story as he knew it and felt it.

II

The high school, Wa-Hi as it was known, was a three story building -- two floors plus a half basement --that smelled of floor wax, chalk dust, and teen age glands. Built in 1920, it faced east on Palouse Street. Across from it was a seedy grocery store, forbidden during school hours, where students hung out. By an unwritten agreement, teachers never patrolled the store, and students were reasonably circumspect about being seen there.

Two broad stairs, divided by an arching bow of auditorium back windows, gave access to the main building from the street. The first floor halls were in the shape of an east-west H, with the auditorium filling the eastern embayment with doors opening onto either arm. Stairs to the second floor went up both eastern arms of the U to where doors on the landings opened to the back of the main floor auditorium. Another half flight led to doors opening onto the balcony, the Freshman peanut gallery, and the second floor class rooms. Behind the auditorium on the cross-bar of the H was a hall with stage doors on one side and study halls on the other. The western arms of the H were lined with class rooms and opened onto the yard at the back of the school and the next street.

Behind Wa-Hi on the south side was a second building which held the Music Department, some practice rooms, the marching band's equipment, and ROTC headquarters complete with rifle racks. (Wa-Hi as a land grant school was obligated to have a Junior Reserve Officer's Training Program.)

On the north side of the main building was a modern gym built around a basketball court where the Blue Devils played. On the south side of the gym were the girls' locker rooms, opposite them on the north were the boys'. Despite the fact there was no swimming pool, the signature odor of the place was chlorine. Football practice and games took place at a stadium on the north side of town.

III

Midway along the right hall on the main floor was the office of the Wa-Hi Daily, a student run, mimeographed sheet for announcements and items of interest or fun. Oliver managed to unwittingly get in trouble through the *Daily*. In his Sophomore year, the editors asked him to write a humorous column for the paper. They thought he was funny and knew a lot of jokes. He wrote his first column, which was about the cafeteria. In it he said "The server could get a job at a state institution for the feeble minded because he was good at serving everything from soup to nuts." Oliver also wrote "Fat people shouldn't be upset if others had a little fun at their expanse." Oliver knew nothing about the server and had never seen the cook.

The server turned out to have been a convict at the state penitentiary, and the cook was immensely fat. Both of them took offense and complained to the principal. They thought Oliver was teasing them. Oliver *never* teased people, well almost never, having been teased all his life about his eyes. The principal didn't believe him, and Oliver lost his job writing the column.

IV

Wa-Hi had the biggest auditorium in town. There was the Whitman College Conservatory auditorium, but it was small. When a special entertainment event came to town, like the Community Concert Series, the artists would perform at the high school auditorium.

Oliver's grade school playmate, Ronald, who lived up the block and around the corner from Oliver's apartment on Whitman Street was an amateur magician. He was talented and knew about theater, and even as a Freshman was appointed stage manager of the high school auditorium. He started working for the drama coach, Marshall Alexander -- yes, Wa-Hi actually had a speech and drama coach. Meanwhile, Oliver and Ronald had maintained their friendship after Oliver had moved to the house on East Alder. When Ronald became stage manager Oliver tagged along and became a stage hand.

The following year, Ronald and his parents moved to another town and Oliver inherited the position as student stage manager. It was a wonderful job for it allowed him to see all the performances held there. Marion Anderson came and gave a concert. Oliver remembers how the audience was so moved by her singing "Were you there when they crucified my Lord?" that they were totally silent, didn't clap, when she finished. Then a matron who was wearing a fox stole -- the kind with those little glass eyes -- clapped and everybody felt that if she did, they should too. Miss Anderson just stood there. Oliver, watching from back stage, could sense her disappointment.

She should have been disappointed. No hotel in Walla Walla would provide a Negro with a room. Finally, two rich spinsters, who were known as sisters but weren't really related, invited her to stay with them in their house. Oliver's mother was angry about the hotels' insult to Miss Anderson. Oliver supposes that in her own way his mother was as unprejudiced as anyone could be in Walla Walla, despite her Irish mother who couldn't stand anyone who wasn't Irish, especially the British.

There was only one Negro family in town that Oliver remembers, and maybe two Jewish families. Black people were called Negros by polite people; Oliver had no idea what a synagogue was or looked like. The town was white, Protestant, and insular, except for the Catholics who managed to fill St. Patrick's Church on Sundays with their own view of things.

He also saw General "Vinegar" Joe Stillwell ~~Jonathan M. Wainwright~~ get an honorary degree from Whitman College at the auditorium, and Marina Svetlova and Alexis Dolanov in a *pas de deux*. Oliver was working the stage curtain and missed his cue. That left Alexis holding Marina Svetlova above his head by one arm. He was looking over his shoulder and hissing, "Pull the curtain!!!!" When Alexis came off the stage he was very angry at Oliver.

It was also at the auditorium that Oliver learned that if you made a clown of yourself you can get attention. Oliver needed attention. When he was a stage hand the first year, there was a performance during which the MC stood outside the curtain to use the standing microphone. When he finished and came back stage, the drama coach told Oliver to bring in the mike. Oliver was very shy and felt he couldn't go out in front of the curtain and face the audience. Instead, he stood behind the velveteen drapes, opposite the mike, and pushed his arms out and around the mike stand. Holding it in a curtainy grip, he slowly worked it from hand to hand until he could maneuver it off stage. The audience was breaking up seeing the mike being moved across the stage with just billowy curtain hands doing it. When Oliver got the mike off stage he said into it, "Any moron could do it the other way." Everyone applauded. That was Oliver's first clue about being an extrovert even when he wanted to run and hide.

V

Oliver remembers one day very clearly. It was mid-afternoon and he was working back stage. There was a stage door that opened onto the hall opposite the room where the *Wa-Hi Daily* was produced. The door was open and he heard a shout go up from the Daily office. One of the Snobby Thirteen, who shall remain nameless came, running out, gleefully jumping up and down.

The Snobby Thirteen were a group of girls, the leading coeds, who wore cashmere sweaters and make up. They were Prom Queens and Cheer Leaders and held jobs like Editor of the Daily, and wouldn't speak to people like Oliver. He knew they were hopelessly desirable, and beyond his reach, although Bill, who played football and was rich and drove a Buick, dated them.

Oliver came from back stage into the hall. "What's happening," he asked. "What is it?"

The girl shouted, "Roosevelt is dead, he's dead! It was just on the radio!"

Her parents, were among the Republicans in town who had never reconciled themselves to Roosevelt and his Third Term, and she was elated that the President had died.

Roosevelt suffered a stroke while resting at Warm Springs, Georgia. Oliver was sad, but the country had Harry S Truman, who may have been an even better president.

You will notice that there is no period after the S. Harry had no given middle name. He figured he needed a middle initial to run for office and took the S even though it stood for nothing. Nowadays he would be accused of dishonesty, but back then the worst thing the Republicans could accuse him of was that his doctor and his doctor's wife accepted a refrigerator and a fur coat as gifts. The media had not yet lost self control, or perhaps it was because the nation was recovering from the Great Depression and corruption had crashed along with the Stock Market.

VI

Half way through his first year as a stage hand, the Drama Club produced "A Connecticut Yankee in King Arthur's Court," followed the next year by "George Washington Slept Here." Oliver talked a local company into loaning the production a Cushman Motor Scooter to be ridden on stage during "A Connecticut Yankee." One day, showing off at class break, he rode the scooter through the halls. Oliver thought it was a good joke, but the principal was very angry; the fumes went everywhere and the noise was disrupting.

Oliver's pranks didn't end there. He discovered a trap door in the ceiling of an upstairs closet. Not even the janitors knew about it. There was a ladder that led to it hidden behind some old loose wall board. Beyond the trap door was a small room into which all the ducts from the fresh air system in the school opened. A fan in this room pushed attic air into all the classrooms and offices. This meant that Oliver could listen down the ducts and hear what was going on in all the rooms. Sometimes he would sneak up to the secret room and play a portable radio into the ducts leading to the study halls.

Another time he was even more disruptive. Oliver, at that time, was working downtown at the Vitart Photo Studio. The man who developed film accidentally exposed a roll of sensitive paper an inch wide and twenty five feet long, rolled into a disc. Oliver salvaged the film, and by pushing out the center of the disc very carefully made a long cone shaped tube like a *shofer*, that sounded like a moose call, when you blew into the narrow end.

The Whitman College Choral Contest was held in the Wa-Hi auditorium. All the fraternities and sororities competed. The evening of the competition Oliver climbed into the secret room and blew the horn down the ducts to the auditorium. He then ran back down stairs and looked as upset as everyone else did. Oliver no longer thinks that prank was funny, but he did then.

The janitors began hunting for Oliver when he played the radio into the study halls. He could hear them going from room to room saying,

"He's not in here. He's not in here." They never caught him, and no one could prove it was Oliver, although by then people were aware that he was a nuisance.

VII

The stage was much improved during Oliver's Junior year. A special dressing room for the stars was built on stage left. It had rows of bright make up lights and a make up counter with a long mirror, and was very professional. It was there on a Sunday that a coed helped Oliver get in more trouble. A play was about to open and she had volunteered to sew costumes over the weekend. Oliver had keys to the school as well as the auditorium, and had let her in. He was working back stage building scenery. They were the only two people in the building. She was very beautiful and one of the Snobby Thirteen.

She was working in the star dressing room, and after a while Oliver took a break and went to visit with her. She was sitting on a folding chair with her feet up on the make-up counter. Her dress cut across her thighs above her knees. She seemed completely at ease as Oliver talked to her, and didn't move or bring her legs down. Oliver was becoming very confused and tongue-tied when she said, "Let's play hide and seek. Give me a minute."

She ran out of the dressing room. Oliver heard the back door of the stage open and close, and knew she was somewhere at large in the school. He hunted and hunted for her, and was about to give up when he heard her calling from one of the locked classrooms for which he didn't have a key. It was amazing! She had climbed through the transom above the door, a thing Oliver thought no girl could do. He crawled through after her, and there they stood in the classroom of a teacher who was the most absent minded person in the school.

Oliver and the girl suddenly became embarrassed, not for where they were but for their being alone together. Oliver said, "Let's pull a joke on her," and so the two of them turned all the students' desks around to face the windows instead of the teacher's desk, and put the globe upside down before climbing back out through the transom. Then the girl remembered she was supposed to be at home for Sunday dinner and left.

On Monday the teacher was in her classroom, but failed to notice how things were changed. She was very confused, and the students were giggling, not helping her figure out what was wrong. A janitor came by and saw the situation, and knew right away what had happened, and helped her straighten the room.

That day the principal called Oliver to his office and Oliver confessed to the trick, but never mentioned the girl who had helped him. The principal reprimanded him and took the keys to the school doors away from Oliver, although he let him keep those to the auditorium.. After that, Oliver had to break into the school on weekends in order to work on the stage. He always left a window or two unlocked on the second floor next to the drain pipes, and would shinny up the pipe and go in through a window. Teachers knew about this, and several times Oliver got a telephone call from a teacher who had locked her keys in the school and needed to retrieve them. Since Oliver lived only a block away, he would come and open the school door for her. It's interesting how the principal's punishment wasn't exactly a punishment since even the principal knew Oliver worked there on weekends without a key to the front door.

Oliver used to think about that Sunday and say to himself, "You idiot! That girl probably liked you and you never caught on." But nothing happened because she was very beautiful and beyond reach.

VIII

Oliver was becoming more Walla Walla, more a contradictory combination of respectable tree lined shady streets and secret excesses. His sense of responsibility as stage manager increased, but was matched by his desire for attention which expressed itself in the practical jokes he pulled on others. Those jokes were often undeserved. It was his need to be noticed that urged him on. It was also his secret desire to manipulate others, to control what at times seemed to him to be an unfair life. Only later did he learn the meaning of "Whoever said life was fair?" and got on with it and grew up. Along the way, Mr. Tack, the physics teacher, helped Oliver to understand.

Mr. Tack was unassuming and quiet but may have been more of a showman than many thought. His surface tension lecture was a case in point. Once a term he would illustrate the phenomenon of surface tension to his class. He would stand at his lecture table, which included a sink and water faucet, and fill a drinking glass brimful. He then carefully placed a small sheet of paper on the full glass. Ideally, surface tension would ensure that when Mr. Tack carefully upended the glass and took his hand away the sheet would hold the water intact within the upside down glass.

It seldom did.

The water would splash down onto the table, and Mr. Tack would ruefully mumble something, shrug his shoulders at the class, refill the glass, place another sheet of paper on it and up end the tumbler, only to achieve the same results.

Try, try again! By the end of the hour Mr. tack was soaking wet. The class loved it. The experiment failed famously, but somehow or other the idea of surface tension stuck in everybody's mind.

How could anyone want to play a joke on Mr. Tack, the ultimate jokester?

But Oliver did. He had observed that every day at exactly the same time – a quiet period when almost no one in the halls -- Mr. Tack would leave his class room office and go to a certain stall in a certain boys' lavatory and closet himself for a short time.

Oliver anticipated this very private ritual and shortly before Mr. Tack's scheduled visit went to that stall and carefully polished the toilet seat with a liberal coat of lamp blacking. Lamp black is unheard of today, but back then could still be bought in hardware stores and was used to shine up metal fixtures. It was extremely black and soot-like, extremely easy to get on one's hands, and extremely hard to wash off.

Oliver has no idea what actually happened that day. At the time it seemed funny to Oliver. Now it doesn't. Did Mr. Tack sit down and come up with a black bum? Or did he discover the trick in time? Or did he only learn about it later that evening at home? Mr. Tack never said a thing and the joke fizzled.

But the story doesn't end there. When Oliver returned to Walla Walla on his way to Japan, he visited the high school and wandered through the empty halls while all the students were in class. It was a strange and lonely moment of triumph, if it could be called in any way triumphant.

As he walked by Mr. Tack's office he saw the teacher at his desk, sitting there grading papers. On impulse, Oliver knocked and went in. Mr. Tack stood and smiled, and warmly shook Oliver's hand.

"Congratulations," he said. "You look splendid in your uniform; you're a real soldier. Sit down. These papers can wait." He gestured to the stack on his desk. For the rest of the hour Oliver and he had a warm, serious conversation.

Mr. Tack talked about the episodes in a person's life, and how one had to accept the role in which one found one's self at a given time. He indicated that sometimes grading papers wasn't his favorite activity but that it went with his job, just as KP might be part of Oliver's new life, that you had to learn to accept people as they were and learn to get along with them.

"Oliver," he said. "People are like vending machines. Only with people, words are the coins we use to get the results we want. Just as you must put in the right combination of coins to get the bottle of coke you're after, with people you must use the right combination of words and the right amount to achieve what you desire."

That simple truth came to Oliver as an apotheosis, a bit of insight, unnoticed, that had been there all along. Oliver was ready to hear it at that moment, and Mr. Tack used the right combination of words to achieve what he wanted Oliver to hear. Oliver was contrite about the lamp black trick although he never confessed it to Mr. Tack. Mr. Tack, on his part, must have thought Oliver was the culprit, but said nothing.

Oliver said good by to Mr. Tack, never to see him again. But the lesson was in place. Mr. Tack was a true teacher.

IX

Little by little Oliver was making a nuisance of himself, no matter how useful he was. Though he was careful and many of his pranks couldn't be traced to him, everybody eventually blamed him for every odd thing that happened. The end came in three ways.

The Christmas of his Junior year the music teacher put on a choral concert. Oliver worked very hard making stained glass windows out of oiled paper. They were back lighted and everybody said they were beautiful, and the audience thought they were real glass. He finished getting the stage ready the evening of the performance and went home for a half hour to eat. Meanwhile, the music teacher had asked one of her students who lived in the country to bring in some evergreen branches with which to decorate the front of the stage. Oliver was not told that this was taking place.

The student whom the teacher asked was very enthusiastic. He went to his place and cut down a fifteen foot fir tree which was covered with snow, and deposited it in front of the stage while Oliver was away. Oliver returned a half hour before the audience was to arrive and found the music teacher crying and hacking feebly with scissors at this great dripping tree which was blocking everything. She immediately thought it was one of Oliver's jokes. By then he was taking the stage manager job very seriously, and while he played jokes elsewhere in school, he never joked inside the auditorium, with the exception of the moose call, which was when he was a sophomore.

Oliver pulled the tree out of the auditorium and cleaned up the melted snow, but there wasn't time to decorate with evergreen branches. The teacher thought it was all Oliver's fault. He was never able to convince her or anyone else that he was innocent.

In the spring, there was another concert where a choral group sang "Stormy Weather." The male chorus director told Oliver to pull the master switch on the stage lights while one of his students rattled a thunder sheet, a big flimsy, metal sheet which when rattled sounds something like thunder. "Well," Oliver said, "lightning is an intensification of light, and pulling the switch turns everything dark. It's a contradiction, and I won't do it."

Oliver stood firm with his opinion, and the drama coach had to override him and pull the master switch himself. Oliver thought it was stupid, and said so, which wasn't very wise.

By then everyone was mad at Oliver. That was when he made a big mistake. There was a girls' style show being given in the auditorium and boys were forbidden to watch. Their attendance was strictly forbidden because some of the girls modeled men's dress shirts as night gowns, where the lower hem hit them across the hips. As Oliver learned, they all wore sensible panties, and it wasn't much of a show.

Oliver recruited his friend Gordon and they discussed the matter. They agreed that their rights were being abused, and sneaked into the projection booth on the second floor of the auditorium. They watched the style show from there; that's how Oliver knows it was really harmless. But the two of them were spotted in their hiding place and someone told the principal. They were caught.

Gordon wasn't blamed overmuch and shouldn't have been, but Oliver was in a different situation. That was it. He was removed from being stage manager and all his keys were taken away. He was forbidden to be on the school grounds except during classes. In fact, when a class ended, he had to immediately cross the street and wait on the far side until the bell sounded for the next class. When it did, he had to hurry not to be late reaching his next class room. That's how his Junior year ended.

X

Oliver was still in Coventry when school started the following fall. A faculty committee recommended to him that he would be happier if he left school and went in the army. He did and was. While in the army, he took the GED tests and the next year when his class graduated the faculty announced, as if it were something for which they were responsible, that he had scored 99, 99, 99, 98, 99 in the percentiles of all five categories, and that they were very proud of him. At least that was what his mother wrote him when he was in Japan.

XI

The deadline for earning the GI Bill through enlistment was October 5, 1946. Technically, that was the last day of World War II. The Bill was a good opportunity for people like Oliver; it paid college tuition, furnished books and supplies, and gave the veteran $75.00 a month to live on, which back then, was enough. Oliver needed the GI Bill because he knew that otherwise he could not afford college. His mother and father, when he was born, had bought him an insurance policy to pay for his college education. It was worth $500, and twenty years later, $500 wasn't enough for even one year of college. That decided Oliver to enlist in the army along with his friends who were a year older, and who also wanted the GI Bill. Oliver points out, too, that all of his age group felt left out of the war, and this was a chance to prove their willingness to serve, although the fighting was over. He enlisted at the age of seventeen, on October 5, 1946.

When Oliver was in high school Junior ROTC the cadets received old Springfield rifles everyone called "Splinterfields," with plugged muzzles. The students would drill and march to Pioneer Park and back. Oliver became a corporal and wore an olive drab uniform. There is a photograph of him in uniform beside his bicycle. He looks very serious. He felt he was ready if the Japs came, and practiced writing in the dark so he could receive messages during air raids, which everyone felt were coming because Walla Walla had the pea cannery, and the penitentiary, and the US Air Base, and was a prime target.

When Oliver arrived at basic training he told the Sergeant that he had been in ROTC and knew a lot of army stuff. The Sergeant just laughed.

CHAPTER TWENTY-SIX
MY TEACHER

Oliver has told me that he wants this chapter to be as he tells it, with no amanuensis to clean it up. So here it is, mistakes and all.

--- --- ---

Before telling you about going in the army I must tell you about Agnes Verne Little that is her real name because she was a fine teacher and a good and kind lady and she saved my life and this book is dedicated to her.

--- --- ---

Miss Little was my teacher long before I met her.

--- --- ---

The Walla Walla Public Library was located at the foot of East Alder Street on a triangle of grass and trees. There was a sort of ledge that went right around the library that you could go all the way around on if you were careful and not too big which I did. The children's library was downstairs on the right with an outside entrance. Miss Bustruck worked there. I liked her name a lot. I started reading in the back room where the A's began and read Altsheler about the Iroquois and about Buffalo Callers who weren't Nez Pierce but out on the plains wherever the plains were Back East. Anything east of the Blue Mountains that slumbered east of town was Back East. I exhausted the alphabet and the children's books before I can remember, so some way I got a grown up's card in the fourth grade and could go right up the front steps into the real library. Off to the right a room with books about people. To the left was the reference room where I spent time looking for information about sex in the encyclopedias but that was later. Center left, the check out desk. Straight ahead were stairs to the second floor all glass floors, frosted and strong enough to walk on, but it gave me a thrill to be walking on glass just the same! Stories fiction adventure all kinds of good stuff was there.

All kinds of books. Stumbled on *The Royal Road to Romance* by Richard Halliburton immediately decided to become another Richard Halliburton and "drink a thousand mugs of ale and kiss a thousand lips." I figured that meant 500 girls. Later on maybe 250. He swam in the reflecting pool of the Taj Mahal (which is only four inches deep but I didn't know that), sneaked up on the Rock of Gibraltar and was arrested as a spy. Sure! Came back from around the world two years later with the same fifteen dollars in his pocket with which he'd left. Talked about some guy a poet named Rupert Brook and visiting his grave in Greece, "If I should die think only this of me, there is some corner of a foreign field that is forever England." I became instantly English. Years later Halliburton disappeared somewhere in the Pacific in a Typhoon while trying to sail a junk from China to the U.S. Last radio message, "Having a wonderful time, wish you were here instead of me." Maybe he and Amelia Earhart ?? Not too bad a guy at that.

--- --- ---

Anyway that's how I discovered books and stories and writing if you are stuck in a life in a small town. I can't remember a thing about Freshman English except "Under the spreading chestnut tree the village smithy stands, the smith a mighty man is he with broad and sinewy hands." My friend Jack pointed out to me that if you took away the adjectives all that was left was "Under the tree the smithy stands, the smith a man is he with hands." I really liked that and told my teacher, like it was my own thought. The observation was unappreciated. Hung on to books kept right on reading but was bored right through Sophomore English. Boring. *Silas Marner*. I cut a thumb shape out of a carrot and tucked it into my right hand with the real thumb tucked under. Had help bandaging my hand and then went to Miss Draper (was it Draper?), "I can't take the test today, Miss Draper. I hurt my thumb." "Oh you poor boy how did it happen?" "I was so worried about the test that I was biting my nails and bit my thumb just like this." Stuck the bandaged carrot in my mouth and bit it into two pieces Crunch! Big joke on Miss Draper. I took the test.

--- --- ---

Then came Junior English. There was Miss Little, Agnes V. Little, I later learned what the V stood for. Knew her very well, friends by then. Asked her, What does V stand for? I don't like to tell, she said. Well then I will think it stands for Vomit. She actually laughed, All right it stands for Verne. Agnes Verne Little. But she was Miss Little to us all.

Us all? Her misfits and fits. Gordon who was/is fiercely bright, a small dark girl who was lonely and alone even at home, and me and a big returned veteran who had gone to the Navy on what was it the Oklahoma? I can't remember but the ship took torpedoes had to be towed half a world to the Brooklyn Navy Yard. It had a fifteen degree list the hold full of water and drowned sailors. The big guy was a cook a noncombatant, can you believe it, a non-combatant on something that a shell or torpedo can go right through! Anyway being noncombatant he was left in Brooklyn to muck out the hold too many body parts and swollen sodden buddies he got battle fatigue that's what it was called then in the hold of a ship in the Brooklyn Navy Yard, was discharged, came home to finish high school a real mess He found Miss Little's class and like all of us her understanding.

--- --- ---

I knew I would be all right with Miss Little because after about a week in her class she let me sit in the back of the room. We had an agreement, I was to write an essay or a story every day in class and she would correct it and that was my Junior year of English except that after a while I could go over to her house she had a grand piano and a library and all of us could visit and just read or talk to her. It wasn't exclusive and I really don't think anybody else ever got jealous they could visit too but the fact was we had a haven there, that there were books and more books, and she would put a piano concerto on the phonograph and play along with it and we all felt safe.

It saved my life I was pretty ragged by the time I got into her class and I think the lives of a lot of other kids too. She never demanded from us what we couldn't give but she found what we could and nurtured it out of us. I learned to write poetry from her and she got me to memorize some Rupert Brook which led to memorizing other poems and learning to love poetry which I still do if you hadn't noticed.

I carried a photograph of her in my wallet for years until it just wore out and disappeared into the creases in the leather. She sat there at the piano half turned towards the camera, smiling, gray hair though she was too young I thought to have gray hair. She never married I have no idea why. Her sister lived across the street and down the block with her husband. Later when he died the two sisters lived together. That is where I brought my ten year old daughter to meet her and later where I brought my second wife.

When Miss Little was living in the Odd Fellows Home on Boyer Street my wife and I went there to visit her and she held my wife's hand

and they looked at each other and very little was said but I think Miss Little was passing a trust - me - along and she cried and Judy cried and Miss Little died the next year and I am sitting here crying as I write this.

When I was in her class and when I got kicked out of high school and when I went in the army and when I came back it was always the same with her, I was me. This book is for her.

CHAPTER TWENTY-SEVEN
GOOD-BY WALLA WALLA

I

September 1946 was a difficult month for Oliver. He was more or less attending high school, but between classes he had to wait on the curb across the street. He had become both Walla Wallas: the clever, conscientious stage manager, and the devious, ostracized jokester. It would take him years to sort out the two Olivers and the anger underneath it all.

Persona non-grata wasn't an easy role for him. He also felt the approach of October 5th, the last day to enlist and receive the GI Bill. Later in life he would tell his students that "Nothing is worth undertaking unless it's scary." Well, Oliver was scared and uncertain. Leaving home for the army without finishing high school seemed a big step. He had heard about the GED (General Education Development) tests, however, it wasn't until he took them months later that he realized how easy they were. But sleeping on the davenport at home and being something of an outcast at school decided him. It also helped that his buddies who had graduated in June were ready to enlist. He went to the post office and picked up the enlistment form which, his being only seventeen, his mother had to sign.

Oliver's mother was recovering from surgery at Saint Mary's Hospital. He believes that she had had a hysterectomy -- but such things weren't discussed back then. It was there Oliver encountered his First Grade nemesis for the last time. Sitting beside her bed was Sammy, who had teased him in the first grade, whom in the sixth grade Oliver had beaten up for teasing him. Sammy was dressed like a Catholic priest, or more precisely like a novitiate. He was talking earnestly to Oliver's mother who, obviously trapped, was looking, wild eyed, out the window and at the ceiling, anywhere but at Sammy. Sammy was doing good Catholic deeds, and Oliver waited discretely outside the door until he finished. They were a bit stand offish when they met in the hall. Sammy said he was studying to be a priest and had put teasing behind him, and Oliver, by then, would not have hit a priest unless he deserved it. They parted with a handshake, one firm, the other saintly.

After Sammy departed, Oliver went in and told his mother that he wanted to enlist in the army. He explained that his being seventeen and under age, he needed her permission, and that he had to have her signature. He said he must leave in two days if he was to get the GI Bill. Getting her to sign was much easier than Oliver thought it would be; she signed the form without hesitation.

The next two days passed in a blur. Oliver can't remember how long his mother was in the hospital, but after she signed he went directly to the recruiting office. It was packed with young men enlisting, and the recruiting officers were pushing them through at a great rate. The government wanted to bring all the combat veterans home as quickly as possible, and were replacing them with recruits like Oliver. They scarcely questioned the people they were accepting. Oliver was very lucky because the recruiters were so busy that they forgot to check his eyes. If they had, they would have seen his nystagmus and would not have accepted him. This was made clear two years later when he was discharged from the army. At that time, the doctor giving him his discharge physical thought Oliver had been injured in the army because no one could enlist with eyes like his. When Oliver told him that they had accepted him, the doctor shrugged and said "Well you're a veteran now!" Oliver was classified IV-A, which meant he was completely healthy, had served his country, and couldn't be drafted. When the Korean War started Oliver was in college and exempt.

After taking the oath to serve his country, Oliver was given a bus voucher and told to report to the enlistment station in Seattle. He was to go from there to Fort Lewis, near Tacoma, for processing. However, before leaving for Seattle Oliver wanted to say good-by to Walla Walla High School, Home of the Blue Devils.

II

The Wa-Hi Blue Devil Basketball team was playing Waitsburg that Friday night. Oliver knew the cheer leaders and suggested to them an idea for the pre-game pep rally. They knew he was going in the army and were impressed. Oliver proposed a special going away stunt. They could put a big tank of mud in the basketball gym, and then he would let them lower him, upside down, into it from the steel girders high above the gym floor. There would be a rope around his ankles (and another around his waist for safety) and the cheer leaders could tell the crowd that the louder they cheered, the sooner Oliver would land in the mud.

That's what happened. Oliver's friend Lowell, who lived on a ranch, brought in a stock tank and a load of dirt on his father's flat bed truck. They spread a piece of canvass on the gym floor and on it put the tank, an extended, metal oval four feet wide, eight feet long, and three feet deep. Then the cheer leaders and Oliver filled it with water and dumped in the dirt until it was two-thirds full of gooey, sticky mud made from the rich Palouse loess Oliver had grown up with.

Game time came and the cheer leaders exhorted the crowd. They announced over the PA system that the big event was to lower Oliver into the mud. There he was on the girders high above them, and when everyone began shouting, "Do it! Do it!" he slid cautiously off the steel beam -- at that time he was very afraid of high places, but was determined to complete the stunt -- and as the crowd cheered louder and louder, he was slowly lowered until he landed in the tank with a satisfying splash.

Oliver was completely covered with mud. He waved at the crowd and then untied the ropes and climbed out of the tank and dripped his way across the gym floor to the entrance to the boys' shower room. Inside the shower, all by himself, he took off his clothes and threw them in a corner. Then he showered and put on the dry, going-to-Seattle Levis and shirt that he had brought with him. He left the muddy, soaked clothes where they fell. On a bench by the dressing room door was a paper bag of underwear and socks and soap and a tooth brush, the stuff the recruiting sergeant had told him that he should bring to Seattle.

Oliver picked up the bag and walked to the door leading to the basketball floor and looked out at his classmates. The cheer leaders were standing in a circle around the big tank full of mud. They had on blue and white sweaters with a devil's head on the back and "Wa-Hi" on the front. The girls wore short, blue skirts, and the boys had on blue sweat pants. It was five minutes to game time, and nobody had anticipated how were they going to remove the tank so that the game could begin.

Oliver stood there for a minute, and then went out the back door of the gym and down the street past the library where he had read Richard Halliburton and learned about travel and Rupert Brook and poetry. Then he turned left down another street and walked by the house of the girl named Phyllis, who was very beautiful. He sometimes would say her name to himself. She was OK and talked to Oliver, unlike some of the Snobby Thirteen. Her father ran the Liberty Theater which was the best theater in town. But Phyllis was back at the gym, and Oliver wouldn't have knocked at her door her even if she had been home. So he walked past her house to the stage depot. The sky was dark, and Oliver remembers how the space where the busses parked was a brightly lighted diagonal cutting across the corner of the depot building. The bus for Seattle was in, and there was Bill standing by its door waiting for him. They climbed on and gave the driver their government vouchers, and he said, "Recruits, huh?"

241

The bus pulled out and went over to Main Street and turned left, and went down Main Street one block to the Baker Boyer Bank and turned right, and went on past the Marcus Whitman and turned left, and headed west along the highway where they had cut asparagus, and beyond there, past the Whitman Monument where Alan and Bobby and Oliver had hunted for artifacts, and then by Wallula Gap where Oliver and Dave had searched for gold but didn't find any, and then to Pasco, Richland and Kennewick, with Hanford in the distance, but no one knew then that the tumble weeds piling up along the fences were radio-active, or that the winds that blew from west to east carried radioactive iodine put there by scientists just to see what would happen, and after a while the bus went through Yakima and past the turn off to Selah, on up the Ellensburg Canyon echoing with the ghosts of big freight engines, and over the Cascades to Seattle and Fort Lewis, taking Oliver to another life.

AFTER WORDS

The Walla Walla High School, Home of the Blue Devils, that Oliver attended is gone now. When he went to Walla Walla with his ten year old daughter whom he wanted to show the school building, Wa-Hi was just a hole in the ground. The gym was there next to the hole, but the grand old high school building had vanished. Oliver thinks it was vanished for the same reason that the lovely old Victorian brick buildings on lower Main Street were vanished and morphed into macadam parking lots. The wrong memories were clinging to them. By just standing there, they reminded people of too much. The good burghers cleansed the town, got rid of those souvenirs of things past and forgotten. But those stories are all hearsay to Oliver. When he returned from Japan people whispered to him what had happened; someone else will have to write about all that.

Though Oliver visited Walla Walla after the army, he never went home again.

POST SCRIPT

So Oliver grew up and so did Walla Walla. Just minutes ago, he finished reading rave reviews about Walla Walla on his computer. The *London Trip Advisor* says of Walla Walla: a fine place to live, to visit, to retire. I agree.

Oliver has changed some, too, he hopes for the better. There are still two sides to him, but perhaps time has smoothed some of the rough edges

Oliver's life led him to Japan in the first cohort of the non-combat Army of Occupation. College followed along with five summers as a lookout-fireman in Oregon. A lot happened there! More college and field work in Africa and the Middle East. Strange times in Sardinia. Hexed in Tanganyika by a witch doctor; exploring the Serengeti fifty years ago; Turkey as a second home; trekking with nomads; a brief experience as one of the living dead; a professorship at the University of Michigan; the U.S.A.F. Academy; second-track Middle East water mediation with my wife Judy. Yeah, it sounds crazy but it all happened. It's in a second volume, nearing completion, *Oliver's Travels*. He'll let you know when it's published.

Complaints, hellos, and news all welcome:
kolarsjf@earthlink.net

About the Author

"John Kolars, born in Walla Walla in 1929, grew up there during the Great Depression and World War II. During those decades the town was transforming itself from a frontier settlement to the cultural center it is today. At seventeen, he enlisted in the army, and with the help of a G.E.D. diploma and the G.I. Bill, became Professor of Geography and Middle Eastern Studies at the University of Michigan. He is recognized as an authority on water in the Middle East, and has received the title of Distinguished Visiting Lecturer at the United States Foreign Service Institute."

9 781425 934231